Cornish Hotel
by the Sea

Karen King

Published by Accent Press Ltd 2017

www.accentpress.co.uk

Copyright © **Karen King** 2017

ISBN 9781786150714
eISBN 9781786150950

Printed in the UK by Clays Ltd, St. Ives

To my Dave. And second chances.

Acknowledgments

It takes a long time to write a book, to flesh out that kernel of an idea into a plot, to create characters that breathe and to find the words to describe the scenes in your head. Along the way an author draws on many things, places they have been to, things they've overheard, people they knew, family, friends, past memories all help gild the original idea and craft it into the book it becomes. During this time, the real world and family can often take second place. I'd like to thank my husband, Dave, for his support and understanding when I'm off in my writing world, for the constant cups of coffee, delicious meals and for answering questions such as 'how do you plaster a ceiling'. And to my four grown up daughters, Julie, Michelle, Lucie and Naomi for, once again, being a source of inspiration and chick lit knowledge.

I lived in Cornwall for many years and it was a pleasure to revisit it again in my mind while writing this book, to recall the glorious golden beaches, the cobbled streets and quaint fishermen's cottages, the invigorating smell of the sea air and the continuous squawk of the seagulls. It will always hold a special place in my heart.

Finally, many thanks to the wonderful team at Accent Press, in particular, my editors Caroline Kirkpatrick, Kate Ellis and Rebecca Lloyd, for their very helpful suggestions and support.

Chapter One

Ellie jumped as a horn blasted out behind her. Drat, the lights had turned green. As she took off the handbrake and slid into gear the horn blared again. Talk about impatient.

She pulled away, shooting a quick glance in the mirror at the car behind. A sleek silver Mercedes with a dark haired suited guy at the wheel. That figured. Some arrogant, aggressive businessman off to an important meeting no doubt, annoyed at losing a nanosecond because Ellie had been so busy worrying about her mum she hadn't noticed the lights change.

Mum would be okay. She had to be. Ellie couldn't

lose her as well. The pain of her dad's death two years ago was still pretty raw.

Ellie bit her lip as she recalled the phone call from Mandy just as she was about to leave for work that morning. She'd known as soon as she'd seen Mandy's number flash up that something was wrong. Mandy was the receptionist at Gwel Teg, the small family hotel that had been Ellie's home until she'd moved to the Midlands a few years ago, wanting more than the sleepy seaside town of Port Medden offered.

And to get away from Lee and Zoe's betrayal.

"Mandy, is Mum okay?" she'd stammered anxiously.

"Now I don't want you to worry dear ..."

Ellie felt the colour drain from her face as she listened to Mandy tell her that her mum had been rushed into Truro hospital early that morning with a bad bout of pleurisy.

"Is she very ill? I'll drive down straight away." Ellie threw back the duvet and was out of bed in a shot.

"You mustn't worry, she'll be fine. You know how tough your mum is," Mandy sounded reassuring. "Don't get rushing, lovey. I don't want you haring down the motorway and having an accident."

"Do you have the phone number of the hospital? What ward is Mum in?"

Ellie grabbed a pen and scribbled the number

down on the back of her hand, said goodbye to Mandy then telephoned the hospital.

"Mrs Truman is as comfortable as can be expected," the nurse on the other end of the phone told her.

Which could mean just about anything. So Ellie had immediately packed a case, phoned up work and explained she needed to take a couple of days off – luckily, she was due to take her two weeks holiday on Monday - then set off for the long drive to Cornwall.

She should have visited more often, she reprimanded herself. Mum had sounded so tired the last few times she'd spoken to her, although she insisted she was fine. That's why Ellie had planned to drive down to Cornwall tomorrow evening, straight after work, to spend her holiday helping out at Gwel Teg.

I should have realised it was too much for Mum. I should have gone back to live with her when Dad died.

She was here at last. Turning into the hospital car park, she looked for an empty space. Damn, there was only one place left and it was going to take some very careful reversing to get in to it. She gritted her teeth and manoeuvred very slowly.

It took three attempts but she finally squeezed into the narrow parking bay. She glanced over her shoulder half expecting to see Merc Guy watching in amusement but thankfully no one was around.

A few minutes later she was rushing into the hospital ward.

"Mrs Truman's very poorly at the moment so don't be too shocked how she looks," the nurse on duty said when Ellie introduced herself. "She should pick up in a day or two though. We're lucky we caught her in time."

Ellie *was* shocked to see how pale and thin her mum was. She barely recognised the drained, gaunt face with dark shadows under sunken eyes, framed by short wispy dark hair streaked with grey – very unusual for her mum who reached for the bottle of hair colour at any sign of grey. Her cotton pyjamas hung loosely on her, emphasising her slender frame. She seemed so frail and fragile. And much weaker and older than she'd looked at Christmas, when Ellie had last seen her. That was six months ago, she scolded herself. She should have made the effort to come down more. After all, she was an only child and all the family Mum had left now.

"Hello, love." Sue Truman smiled weakly. "You shouldn't have rushed down to see me. You were coming down tomorrow evening, anyway."

"I wanted to make sure you were all right," Ellie said softly, sitting down besides the bed and gently squeezing her mum's hand. "Mandy's call gave me quite a scare."

"I told her not to bother you," Sue said. A harsh bout

of coughing overcome her and she struggled to sit up. Ellie helped her, reaching over to plump up the pillows behind her mum's back for support. "That's a bad cough, Mum."

Sue waved her hand dismissively. "I'm fine, dear," she croaked, between coughs." I'll be out of here in no time."

She didn't look fine, Ellie thought worriedly. "You stay as long as you need, Mum. Just concentrate on getting better. I'll look after the hotel," she promised.

"Nonsense, dear. It's your holiday…" Sue protested feebly.

"I've come down to look after you," Ellie told her firmly. "And that's what I'm going to do."

She should never have left Mum to cope alone, Ellie thought as she headed off for Port Medden. She should have moved back in and helped.

The sun was out in force now so she was glad of her sunglasses to dull the glare. She wound down her window, loving the feel of the soft wind blowing through her hair as she drove along the winding country lanes, her foot hovering over the brake, ready to stop if something shot around the corner. The hedges were a riot of tiny purple and blue flowers, the air filled with birdsong. She felt her heart lift as the narrow lanes gave way to open fields scattered with grazing cows and frolicking sheep until finally she could see the sun dancing on the ocean in the distance.

You offered to move back in, Mum didn't want you to, she reminded herself.

When Dad had died, Ellie had tried to persuade Mum to sell up and move to the Midlands, where she could keep an eye on her. But Sue had steadfastly refused. She loved Gwel Teg, it was her life, and kept her busy. "I don't want to sit in a little bungalow twiddling my thumbs all day," she said firmly. "Your dad and I spent some happy years here and I intend to keep the place up and running."

Ellie's offer to move in with her had also been stubbornly refused. "I'm not that old and doddering that I need my daughter to look after me!" Sue had retorted.

So, knowing that her mum loved the hotel, and thinking that maybe it was good for her to have a purpose in life – and to be honest not really wanting to live in the remote Cornish town again - Ellie had returned to her flat in the Midlands. She'd phoned her mum regularly and visited as much as she could - but not often enough by the look of things.

The insistent honking of a horn jolted her to the present. Drat, she'd been so preoccupied with her worries about Mum that she'd turned into Gwel Teg's car park without noticing the car coming out. She frowned. It was that silver Merc again. The guy behind the wheel was impatiently gesturing her to move back, she held up her hand in apology and reversed to let him out. He threw her a cutting glance as he passed then shot off. *Charming! I hope he isn't staying at the hotel.* An awkward customer was the last thing she needed.

"Ellie, lovey!" Mandy came around the front of the desk and gave Ellie a warm hug wrapped in her trademark *Sexy Lady* perfume. "Have you been to see your mum? How is she?"

Mandy had worked at the hotel so long she was more of a friend than an employee. With her bleached blonde hair, red lipstick and flamboyant clothes she was often taken for a bit of an airhead but she was a big-hearted woman who would help anyone.

"Recovering well the nurse said. But Mandy, she looks so weak, so tired."

"Oh lovey. The hotel's too much for her. I've been trying to get her to rest up a bit, but you know your mum, stubborn as a mule." Mandy's heavily mascaraed eyes were full of concern. "I help her a much as I can but…"

Ellie nodded. "I know. I should have come down more often. I could have helped at weekends."

Mandy wagged a finger at her. "Now don't you start guilt-tripping yourself. You've got work and your own life, you can't make a trip from the Midlands every weekend." She stepped back and cast her eyes over Ellie's face. "You look tired. It's been a long journey for you. Why don't you go and freshen up and have something to eat? I can hold the fort here a bit longer."

A freshen up and cup of coffee was exactly what she needed. "Thanks, Mandy. When's Susie due to take over?"

"Susie left a couple of months ago, lovey. Me and your mum manage the reception between us now."

That surprised her. Mum had always hired two receptionists and helped out herself when necessary. Why hadn't she replaced Susie?

And that meant Mandy had been looking after reception since she'd phoned this morning so must have already completed her shift. "Then it's time you went home. Give me half an hour and I'll take over from you," she promised.

"Take your time, there's no rush," Mandy replied but Ellie was already wheeling her suitcase over to the door that led to the private quarters.

The previous owners had converted the left wing of the hotel into an apartment for their personal use, so that's where Ellie and her parents lived. It was bright, airy and spacious. There was a dining kitchen, lounge and two bedrooms, one of them an ensuite, a bathroom and an attic room with an ensuite - which Ellie had fallen in love with as soon as she'd seen it and immediately claimed as hers. She'd adored the sloping roof, the white shutters on the window, and best of all the view over the rooftops to the beach.

The name Gwel Teg – Cornish for 'beautiful view' - suited the hotel. The view from the back was breath-taking, stretching over the cobbled streets of the quaint former fishing town right down to the beach and harbour. Situated about halfway up the hill, with a side-view over to the shops and main beach, on a clear day like today the hotel had far-reaching views over the ocean. How Ellie used to love to sit on the seat her dad had made her under the window and watch the big ships on the horizon, trying to guess what country they were heading for, and dreaming of sailing off to see the world herself one day. Ellie's room was just as she left it when she'd moved out six years ago. Mum cleaned it, of course, and put fresh bedding on every time Ellie came to stay but the contents remained untouched. The soft toys from Ellie's childhood sat on a shelf across the far wall, her shell collection still cluttered the windowsill and her dreamcatcher fluttered at the window. The only things she'd taken with her were her clothes and laptop.

Gradually she'd started to leave a basic collection of clothes, jeans, tee shirts, summer dresses, jumpers and underwear in the wardrobe for emergency supplies if she came down and stayed longer than she intended.

She walked over to the window and looked out over the rooftops at the harbour, flanked on one side by huge cliffs where a smattering of whitewashed houses nestled. A couple of colourful boats were moored next to the jetty, swaying slightly on the rippling sea. Alongside it was the soft golden sands of the town beach, popular with holidaymakers and tourists who just wanted a quick paddle, or half hour in the sun. Opening the window, she leaned out and inhaled the salty sea air. It was good to be home. She loved Cornwall. Always had from the moment they had moved down here when she was six years old. She probably would never have left if it hadn't been for Lee. Lee and Zoe. The two people she had been closest to, trusted. Her two best friends. So she'd thought.

She shrugged. That was years ago. History. She'd moved on since then made a new life for herself. One that she enjoyed.

She showered, changed into a cool lemon cotton dress, tied her long, chestnut brown hair off her face, replaced her prescription sunglasses with contact lenses then went down to the kitchen to make herself a much needed coffee and sandwich. Exactly half an hour later she joined Mandy at the reception desk, taking her unfinished coffee with her. "Thanks for holding the fort, Mandy. I owe you one. Come in a bit later in the morning to make up for the extra time you've worked."

The older woman shook her head. "I will not. You need all the help you can get while Sue's ill. I'll be in for the first shift." She pointed to the notebook. "I've left you a couple of messages and the bookings are all up to date but phone me if you need me. Anytime."

"Thank you. I will. Now go home!" Ellie told her firmly.

Mandy grabbed her bag. "I'm out of here. It's all yours."

Ellie placed her coffee on the shelf, away from the computer, and sat on the comfy red swivel chair. She selected the admin file and entered the password - knowing that Mum always kept to the same one because she was scared of forgetting it - anxious to check the books and find out how the hotel was doing. She'd already clocked that the curtains and cushion covers in the foyer looked faded and the windows needed a clean. Not at all like her mum who always prided herself on keeping Gwel Teg immaculate. That, and the reduction in staff was triggering alarm bells in Ellie's mind.

"Excuse me."

The man's voice made her jolt. Ellie tore her eyes away from the figures on the computer screen and looked up, straight into a pair of deep grey eyes set in a ruggedly handsome face topped by chocolate-brown hair. *Very nice*. It took her a few seconds to realise that it was Merc Guy, now wearing a black tee shirt and jeans, and to notice the angry set of his jaw and the frown lines in the middle of his thick eyebrows. He was staying here then. Great. An unhappy customer was all she needed. She just hoped he didn't recognise her from this afternoon when he was blasting his horn at her. Thank goodness she'd been wearing sunglasses.

She fixed a pleasant smile on her face. "Can I help you?"

"The shower isn't working in my room and I have an important business meeting in less than an hour," he informed her curtly. "So will you either arrange for it to be fixed immediately or provide me with the use of a shower in another room?"

Great. Problems already.

"Did you hear what I said? I haven't time to waste. I have an important meeting to go to."

The man's abrupt tone annoyed her but she kept calm. "Of course, Mr...er..." she glanced at the hotel register for the man's name.

"Mitchell." He supplied. "Reece Mitchell. I arrived

12

earlier today. And I'm in a hurry."

Yes, I got that. A quick glance at the register told her that Reece Mitchell was in Room 12. Luckily the room next to him was empty and there was a connecting door between the rooms. Problem solved.

"I do apologise, Mr Mitchell. I'll get it sorted for you today. Meanwhile, please use the shower in the room next to you. It's vacant at the moment and you can access it through a connecting door." She reached for the key and handed it to him. "I'm very sorry for the inconvenience. Would you mind popping the key back on your way out?"

He didn't look too pleased. "Well, I guess it will have to do. I must say this hotel isn't what I'd expected. I'm surprised you do any business at all." He almost snatched the key out of her hand.

She swallowed the angry retort that sprung to her mouth reminding herself of Mum's mantra that the customer was always right. And if they weren't you didn't tell them so. She watched, fuming, as Reece Mitchell stormed off.

What an arrogant man!

Chapter Two

Reece Mitchell was right though, Ellie acknowledged. Gwel Teg was in a state and there were hardly any staff. Her mother seemed to have cut things right down to the bone, which wasn't surprising as even though Ellie had only had time to glance at the figures she could see that the hotel was hardly making any profit at all. Mum was obviously struggling to manage since Dad had died two years ago.

She bit her lip as memories of the night she'd received the late night phone call informing her that her Dad had died flooded back.

"Ellie, I am so sorry lovey. It's your Dad." Mandy's

voice was breaking and Ellie's stomach clenched as she instinctively knew what was coming next. The tears spilled out of her eyes as she listened to Mandy's words. 'They did everything they could, love.'

Mandy had assured Ellie that his death was instant and he wouldn't have suffered at all. She was trying her best to comfort her but Ellie was devastated to think she would never see her lovely, kind, dependable dad again. He'd always been there to turn to and offer advice – sometimes advice she didn't ask for, Ellie remembered with a smile. She had immediately packed a bag and driven down to Cornwall, knowing how heartbroken her mum would be. Her parents had been together for forty years, they were childhood sweethearts. They loved running Gwel Teg together. Mum dealt with all the admin and looked after the guests while Dad did all the maintenance, made sure everything was in working order – and entertained the guests at the bar in the evening with jokes and anecdotes. How would Mum manage without him?

Ellie had taken compassionate leave from work and spent a few weeks helping out until Sue had shooed her back home insisting she could cope just fine. And continued insisting that she was managing perfectly well, in their twice weekly chats.

I shouldn't have taken Mum's word for it. I should

have visited more often. Then she wouldn't have ended up making herself ill.

Guilt flooded through her. She was an only child, all the close family her mother had, yet had been too too wrapped up in her own life to spare any time for her mum.

A key flung down on the counter in front of her startled her back to the present.

"Well, I've managed but that bloody shower's leaking! I'm not impressed with the standard here at all."

It was Reece Mitchell again. And what a transformation. The tee shirt and jeans had been replaced by a snazzy black suit that fitted so well it just had to be designer. Teamed with a navy and white pin-striped shirt and a navy tie he really looked something. And far too important to be staying in a sleepy little seaside town like Port Medden.

Stop gawping every time you see him!

She pulled herself together. "I'm so sorry. I'll arrange for both showers to be fixed…" she started to say but he was already walking briskly away. *God he was so rude!* She hoped none of the other guests were as unpleasant.

She reached for the phone, dialled Harry's number and asked him to come and take a look at the showers in Room 12 and 13. "Can you do it asap, please?" she asked. "The guest is a real grouch."

16

"Of course, Miss Truman."

Ellie smiled, the old man had worked at the hotel for years but still insisted on calling Ellie Miss Truman and her mother Mrs Truman, despite them constantly telling him to drop these formalities. He was one of the old school and nothing would ever change him.

"Thank you, Harry. I'm going to have a look around in the morning and make a list of any repairs that need doing. Could you see to them all before my mother comes out of hospital? I'd like to get the place as straight as possible for her."

"Of course. I did tell your mother about a few jobs that needed doing but..." he paused, as if he feared he might be overstepping the mark.

"Go on, please," she urged him.

"Well, between me and you I think things are a bit difficult for Mrs Truman right now, money-wise I mean."

Ellie had suspected as much. "I see. Well if you let me know what the jobs are and the approximate cost I'll see what I can do."

"Certainly, Miss Truman. And how is your mother?"

"Recovering well, thank you, but she'll be in hospital a few more days." *And she'll be back in again if she doesn't take it easy. I've got to find a way to help her.*

Ellie spent the rest of the evening trying to sort out

the figures. She was shocked to discover that the hotel was running at a loss and had been for the past few months. Why hadn't Mum mentioned it to her? Probably because she didn't want to worry her. Well now Ellie knew and she *was* worried.

The day had started off wrong and carried on that way, Reece thought as he walked into the foyer of Gwel Teg later that evening. He'd been stuck in traffic on the way down from London, the quaint hotel his secretary had booked him into at very short notice had turned out to be a small shabby family one run on a skeleton staff. The shower in his room wasn't working and to top it all the deal he'd been hoping to complete today had fallen through. All in all a wasted trip. Steve, his business partner, had warned him that Adam Hobson was having second thoughts though but Reece had been hoping to talk him round.

He and Steve both agreed that they wanted another business in the South West though which meant Reece would have to remain in Cornwall for a few more days and find a replacement. Not at this hotel though. Tomorrow he'd find somewhere a bit more upmarket.

He glanced over and saw that the receptionist was still hard at work on the computer. He watched her for a minute, biting her lip and frowning as she stared at the

18

screen. She was pretty – beautiful, actually – with hazel almond shaped eyes, a tumbling cascade of rich brown hair which she'd now released from the band that constrained it, high cheekbones and perfect cupid bow lips. She looked tired, he noticed. And worried. He shouldn't have been so hard on her this afternoon. It wasn't her fault the shower wasn't working. Although her holding him up at the traffic lights earlier and then nearly driving into him as he came out of the car park to go to his pre-meeting brief with Steve hadn't helped his mood when he was already late. Still, he wasn't normally so bad-tempered, he should make amends. He paused, then walked over to the desk.

"Still working then?" He smiled, to show her that he wasn't always so cranky.

She looked up, startled. "Mr Mitchell. Is everything all right? I believe that your shower's been fixed now, although I haven't had time to check yet." She obviously thought he'd come to complain again.

"That's good. Thank you." He flashed her what he knew was a devastating smile. It never failed to win anyone over. "Look, sorry if I was a bit of a grouch this afternoon – and for blasting my horn at you earlier. Twice," he added ruefully. "I had an important meeting to go to."

She blinked and stared at him as if momentarily

19

stunned. Damn, had he been that much of a grouch? Then her cheeks bunched endearingly as she smiled back. "And you could do without the shower not working? I guess that me holding you up earlier and cutting you up in the car park, didn't help either. I was a bit…distracted. Sorry."

"Apology accepted." For a moment their eyes locked and he felt an irresistible tug. He drew in his breath. She was pretty hot but making out with the receptionist wasn't his style. "Well, I'm off to bed now. Night."

"Night."

He walked away then glanced back but she'd already returned her attention to the computer screen. It was almost midnight now, surely she wasn't on duty all night? Was the hotel really so short staffed? No wonder it looked so in need of repair.

As he stepped into the lift it suddenly occurred to him that this hotel might be just he was looking for. It was in a great position with fantastic views, there was plenty of potential for improvement, and it was obvious that the owner was struggling with its upkeep so might be happy to sell for a knockdown price. Maybe he wouldn't check out tomorrow as he'd planned.

Chapter Three

The high-pitched squawk of the seagulls jerked Ellie out of a deep sleep. It took her a couple of seconds to realise where she was then she bounded out of bed and over to the window, pulling open the curtains. What a glorious day. She gazed out in delight at the sun sparkling on the cobalt ocean just a few minutes away, positively begging her to walk barefoot over the golden sand and paddle in the cool sea.

What was stopping her? Mandy had insisted on covering the morning shift so she could spare half an hour to walk down to the beach, surely? The fresh sea air would do her good.

Ellie remembered her dad always telling her, 'make time to enjoy life.' It was a mantra she often repeated to herself. She enjoyed her work as a PR officer helping firms improve their image by 'giving back to society' but spending her childhood in Cornwall had taught her that taking time out, relaxing with family and friends, doing things you enjoyed were just as important. Whenever she visited her parents her first stop, often before catching up on their news, was the beach.

She showered and pulled on a pair of electric blue shorts and a white vest top over lacy white underwear. Ever since the total mortification of being examined by a very dishy doctor while attired in greying underwear after she'd slipped over in Ben's Bistro two years ago, hurting her bum and ending up in A&E, Ellie always wore pretty, matching underwear. She grabbed a bottle of sun lotion from her dressing table and rubbed some sun cream onto her exposed limbs and neck.

"Did you sleep well, lovey?" Mandy asked as Ellie walked into the foyer.

"I flaked out as soon as my head hit the pillow. I think I must have been shattered. Are you okay to look after thing here while I have a walk along the beach? I'll only be half an hour or so."

"No problem. Take as much time as you want. I doubt if we'll be very busy." Mandy switched to the booking screen. "We've got a couple of guests leaving today. Mr Mitchell from Room 12 and Mr and Mrs Wilson from Room 4."

So Merc Guy was leaving. Good, she didn't want another run in with him. Mind you, he'd been nice last night. She'd been surprised when he'd apologised. He'd actually seemed rather charming. She guessed his meeting had gone well so he'd been in a better mood. In her experience, many business men were like that, they switched on the charm when it suited them and switched it off just as easily.

"Have we got any other guests booked in?" she asked. When she checked the register last night there were only seven and if three were leaving...

"There's a Mr and Mrs Smythe booking in tomorrow but that's all for the foreseeable."

June and the hotel wasn't even half full. Ellie remembered when Gwel Teg was teeming in the summer months, her parents often had to turn people away.

"How long are the Smythes staying for?" she asked.

Mandy glanced at the computer screen. "Two nights. They've asked for the Honeymoon suite. Apparently they spent their honeymoon here and now it's their Silver Wedding Anniversary so they want the same room."

"How romantic." Ellie paused." Maybe I should

check out the room before I go for a walk. Mr Mitchell's shower was out of order yesterday and the one in the connecting room was leaking, he got in a real strop about it. I don't want any other guests upset."

"Don't worry, I checked the room yesterday afternoon and it's all fine." Mandy glanced at her. "So you've met Mr Mitchell yet? Quite a hunk isn't he?"

Ellie shrugged. "Is he? I hadn't noticed."

"Course you haven't, lovey." Mandy gave her a knowing wink.

Ellie ignored her and continued. "I was looking through the books last night. Things aren't going well, are they?"

"They'll pick up again. The hotel needs a bit of TLC and your mum hasn't been up to it but she'll get her mojo back, you'll see. Now be off with you. Go take that walk!" Mandy shooed her away.

I hope Mandy's right and things do pick up again, Ellie thought as she set off down the hill towards the beach. Mum wasn't getting any younger. She was in her sixties now and should be thinking about retiring and taking it easy, not struggling to run a small hotel. It was a lot of work for her. Perhaps Ellie could persuade her to think about selling up and buying a little bungalow instead.

Property was expensive in Port Medden, as in any

part of Cornwall. Would there be enough left from the proceeds of the hotel to allow Mum to purchase a bungalow, and have enough to live on until she received her pension? Ellie bit her lip. She doubted it. Not unless she moved away, perhaps up to the Midlands nearer to Ellie.

No, that wouldn't work. Mum loved Cornwall. She would hate to live somewhere else.

Reaching the wall that overlooked the beach, Ellie looked over at the golden sand and glistening, almost turquoise, ocean and saw that there were already a few holidaymakers taking advantage of the low tide to paddle. A family with two children were building a sandcastle near the shore and a pair of teenage lovers were walking along the water's edge, holding hands and laughing as the sea lapped over their bare feet.

Just like she and Lee had done.

The memories were still there but six years had passed and the pain had long since gone. At first, it was all so raw that Ellie had avoided coming down to visit her parents. Soon though she had made a new life, new friends and was so busy she hardly ever thought of Lee but it had taken her a year to bring herself to come down to Port Medden again. Her parents had been delighted to see her, although had never reproached her for staying away.

After a while, Lee and Zoe moved to Bristol so Ellie no longer had to worry about bumping into them. Her parents were careful not to mention them when Ellie visited but she heard that they got married, had a couple of children.

She was glad now that Lee had finished with her, even if it was because he had fallen in love with her best friend. If he hadn't cheated on her they would probably be married now and it would be Ellie who was tied down with a couple of kids, never having had chance to find out who she was and what she wanted. She'd seen it happen to so many people. They met someone, fell in love and before you could blink had forgotten all about the plans they'd made for their future, their dreams, friends, the things they liked doing. They became 'a couple' and it was as if they stopped existing as a single unit. Everything had to be done together.

Well that wasn't for her. Not that she had massive plans for the future, she was enjoying her job, taking each day as it came. No one to answer to or to have to think about. Yes, she had dates. Lots of them. Kate, her best friend, laughingly called Ellie a 'serial dater' because she didn't allow any relationship to get serious, never went out with anyone for longer than a couple of months. That way the relationship kept its freshness and they both parted with good memories.

And it made sure she never got hurt again.

She walked down the steps then slipped off her sandals, relishing the feel of the soft sand beneath her bare feet as she ran over to the sea. She paddled for a while, letting the cool water lap over her feet. She'd always found the sea soothing. Many a time as a troubled teenager she'd sat on this beach, staring out at the ocean, marvelling at the vastness and wildness of it all. Whatever had been bothering her had faded away into insignificance and she'd always walked back home feeling lighter, as if she'd got things into perspective.

She remembered how she'd sat here for hours that day before she left, wondering if she was making the right decision. Was she letting Zoe and Lee drive her away? By the time she'd walked off the beach Ellie had been confident that she was doing the right thing. She needed a fresh start. To make a new life for herself. And it had been a good decision. She loved her life in the city and her job but that didn't stop her feeling guilty about leaving her mum to manage on her own these past two years.

Her mobile pinged in her bag. She reached for it and glanced at the screen. Kate.

Hows ur mum, hun?

She'd answered Kate's advert for a flat share when she'd decided to move up to the Midlands, thinking it would do while she sorted herself out. They'd hit it off straight away and Ellie had remained there.

Weak but ok. She'll be in for a few days yet. How r u?

They exchanged messages for a while then Ellie set off back up the hill, past the pretty, quaint tea rooms, the bakery and souvenir shop, until the charming white hotel came into sight. She paused for a moment to look at it, as a potential guest would, taking in the slightly neglected but still colourful hanging baskets and plant tubs that adorned the outside. Okay, the outside could do with a coat of paint and it needed some repairs but it was full of character and the location was stunning. She was determined to get Gwel Teg back into shape before Mum came out of hospital. And first stop was to check all the rooms and see what repairs needed doing. She didn't want to give any of the other guests cause to complain. Bad reviews on TripAdvisor wouldn't help gain more bookings.

Mandy wasn't at the reception desk. Guessing she'd gone for a loo break, Ellie picked up a notebook and the set of master keys. As it was a sunny day she imagined that their guests would probably be out so she should be able to check all the rooms before the cleaners did their rounds.

She made her way around the first floor, most of the rooms were unoccupied. Before she entered the ones that were occupied, she checked that the 'Do Not Disturb' label wasn't on the door then knocked loudly and called out before entering. Careful not to touch anything personal, she noted any repairs that needed doing. There were quite a few but they were mostly minor things that Harry could tackle. She was dismayed to see how dated and shabby the rooms looked though.

It looks like the whole hotel needs refurbishing, she thought as she made her way to the second floor.

She hesitated outside Room 12. Had Reece Mitchell left yet? She really didn't want another run-in with him. He might have been pleasant last night but her first impressions of him weren't good and she definitely didn't want a repeat performance.

She glanced at her watch. 10.45. Guests had to vacate the rooms by ten so he should be long gone. Even so, she banged on the door and listened intently just to be sure. Nope, there was no sound coming from the room. She unlocked the door and stepped inside. Glancing around, she immediately spotted that a couple of drawer handles were missing on the bedside cabinet, a plug socket was loose and the carpet was threadbare in one corner. *Not good. It's a wonder he hadn't complained about that.*

She made a note of them and starred them as urgent. She'd ask Harry to do them this afternoon, at least they wouldn't cost anything. And perhaps she could find a small cupboard to put over the threadbare patch of carpet.

She looked over at the closed ensuite door. She'd better check the shower too, and the one in the connecting room. Best to make sure they'd both been fixed before she booked anyone else into the room.

As she walked over to the ensuite the door handle turned. She stared at it, horrified. *Oh heck - he wasn't?*

The door started to open.

She'd better get out of here. Fast.

But before she could move the door was thrust open and Reece Mitchell walked out, completely naked, rubbing his hair with a towel.

Chapter Four

Shit. She was staring at his man bits. *Look away! Now!*

Ellie dragged her eyes upwards, trying not to let them rest on Reece's superbly toned tanned torso and so broad shoulders. She felt herself flush as she met his astonished gaze. For a moment they stared at each other, both rooted to the spot. Then in one swift sweep Reece moved the towel from his hair and wrapped it around his dripping, naked hips. "Don't you believe in knocking?"

"I'm sorry," she stammered, struggling to regain her composure and desperately trying to shut out the image of those perfect hips and … "I did knock. Really hard. But obviously you didn't hear me and I thought you had already checked out. So…" she licked her lips, refused to let her eyes drift from his face to gaze at the expanse of very hot body still visible above the casually tied towel. "I was just checking that the shower had been fixed."

She couldn't seem to stop babbling and he was obviously enjoying her embarrassment judging by the stupid big grin on his face and the even bigger twinkle in his eyes. "Your handyman fixed it last night. Go look if you want." He stepped aside, one hand casually holding the white bath towel in place and the other gesturing towards the open bathroom door.

"No, no." She shook her head rather too vehemently then realised how naive she must look. Get yourself together! Anyone would think she'd never seen a naked man before. "I mean, there's no need. Glad it's been fixed. If there's any other jobs that need doing could you let Mandy on Reception know before you go. Thank you." She made a quick exit, hoping her cheeks weren't flaming as much as she feared.

How embarrassing! Goodness knows what Reece Mitchell thought, walking in on him like that. But then how was she to know he hadn't checked out yet? He must have asked for a late leave. She wished Mandy had warned her.

A picture of his naked body sprung enticingly into her

mind. God, he was fit!

And he was a guest. She'd put them both in an embarrassing situation. One she wanted to avoid repeating. No more letting herself into the guests' rooms, she decided. She'd stick to the unoccupied rooms and have a thorough check over the others when the guests had gone. Much safer!

"Time for a break," she told Mandy, walking over to the reception desk. "Go and have a coffee and sandwich while I take over for a while."

"Thanks, lovey I could do with it." Mandy shuffled off the chair. "Is it okay if I pop and see Sue tonight?"

"That'd be great. Mum would love to see you." Ellie lifted up the hatch and stepped behind the desk. "I'll go at lunchtime before you finish your shift." She sighed as she put the notebook on the desk. "It's been a bit of a morning."

"Oh dear, found a long list of repairs that needed doing?"

"Quite a few yes, but I daren't check the occupied rooms on the second floor after the massive boob I made." Ellie told her about the shower incident with Reece Mitchell. "Honestly, Mandy. I didn't know where to look."

Mandy chuckled. "Lucky you. I think I'd know where

to look. Are you sure your eyes didn't stray just an itsy bit?"

Ellie felt a flush creep up her neck.

"I take it that's a yes then?"

"I couldn't help it," Ellie protested. "I was gob-smacked to see him standing there totally starkers. I thought he'd be long gone. Thank goodness he's checking out today so I don't have to see him again."

"He's not."

"What?"

"Mr Mitchell isn't leaving today. He's booked the room for another week."

"You're kidding me, right?" She looked at Mandy's face expecting it to break into her trademark wide grin but the receptionist shook her head. "Nope. He phoned to extend his stay this morning when you were having a walk along the beach."

Great. That's all she needed.

"Look, it's no big deal. I'm sure he's been naked in front of a woman before. He'll have forgotten about it by now," Mandy told her as she grabbed her bag. "See you in a bit."

Ellie remembered the twinkle in Reece Mitchell's eyes. She doubted if he'd forgotten it. He'd seemed to enjoy her embarrassment. Although he had been very gracious about it, she had to acknowledge. Mandy was

34

right, best to act as if nothing had happened when she bumped into him again. And she definitely wouldn't mention it to Mum when she visited later. Or talk about the state of the hotel and the repairs that needed doing. Cheerful, calm and competent - that's how Mum needed her to be.

"Good afternoon, Miss Truman," the nurse said as Ellie entered the ward "Your mother seems much better today. If she carries on making this progress she should be home early next week. Mind you, she'll have to take it easy for a while."

"I'll make sure she does," Ellie told her. She was pleased that her mother was getting better, but knew that when she came home the problems were only just beginning. If Mum carried on working the way she had been she'd soon be back in hospital again.

Sue Truman was sitting on the side of the bed, clutching a pillow to her chest for support, as her body wracked with a coughing fit. Ellie sat down on the chair besides the bed and watched her anxiously. When the coughing finally stopped she passed her mum the glass of water standing on the bedside cabinet.

"Thank you, dear." Sue swallowed the water then put the pillow down on the bed. "Don't look so worried, it's getting better. I don't cough as often or for as long and

35

holding the pillow against my chest helps ease the pain. The doctor suggested doing that."

Just how bad had Mum been before she was taken into hospital? Ellie wondered. Thank goodness Mandy had been around when she collapsed or it could have been a lot worse. Still, the doctor had said Mum's lungs weren't badly damaged. Luckily, she'd given up smoking years ago when Dad had had his first heart attack. It had shocked both her parents into quitting, and probably given her dad a few extra years, so they been told.

She leaned over and kissed her mum on the cheek. "You need to take it easy, Mum. You've been very ill."

Sue reached out and patted Ellie's hand. "I'm fine, dear. Don't worry. Another couple of days and I'll be back home again."

She did look a bit better today although still thin and tired, Ellie thought. She'd brushed her hair, applied a bit of lipstick and was wearing the apple green dressing gown Ellie had bought her for Christmas. If only that awful cough would stop.

Ellie opened her bag and took out the box of strawberry creams – Mum's favourites – and a couple of magazines she'd picked up from the corner shop on her way. "I thought these might cheer you up."

"Thank you, darling!" Her mother placed them on

the cabinet. "Now tell me what's happening at Gwel Teg. None of the guests are giving you any trouble are they?"

Ellie pushed the thought of Reece Mitchell to the back of her mind. "Everything's fine, Mum. Don't worry."

"Well I do worry. Are you and Mandy managing all right? I'll be home soon. Over the weekend hopefully."

"I don't think there's much chance of that, Mrs Truman. You've been really poorly and you're not out of the woods yet," the nurse reminded her. She picked up the progress chart at the end of the bed and scanned it. "Looking at this you're going to be in here for a few more days. Then you'll have to take it easy for a while, give yourself time to get your strength back."

"Don't worry, I'm going to stay and look after her until she's fully recovered," Ellie replied. "I'm here for two weeks so I can make sure she rests."

"You work hard enough. You need a holiday, not running the hotel while I lie around," Sue told her.

"I'm only too pleased to help out. So when you get home you're going to put your feet up and leave me to run things for a bit," Ellie told her gently.

"Now don't make a fuss dear. I like to be kept busy."

Ellie knew that when her mother compressed her lips like that there was no way she was going to change her mind. She could be very stubborn when she wanted to.

Well, Ellie could be stubborn too and she wasn't going to let her mum work herself into an early grave. She'd already lost her dad. She wasn't going to risk losing Mum too.

The evening shift was always a quiet one so Ellie decided to go through the accounts and the pile of paperwork and letters cluttering the in-tray. She wanted to see if the hotel was making enough profit to support extra staff. They need another receptionist at least, she thought.

"You must be dedicated to your job to work so late."

She recognised the voice instantly and an image of his knockout body zapped into her mind. She smacked it away. *Be professional.*

She looked up and smiled, determined not to show how awkward she felt. "I don't work here," she explained, "I'm helping my mother out for a couple of weeks. She owns the hotel."

A flicker of interest sparked in his eyes, then it was gone.

"I see," he said. "Well, that explains your devotion to duty. I don't believe I've met your mother. Perhaps you could introduce me to her."

38

Why does he want to meet Mum? To complain? He was smiling though, and looked very pleasant. A totally different man to the arrogant grouch yesterday. "I'm afraid that isn't possible at the moment, she's in hospital recovering from a bad bout of pleurisy," Ellie told him.

She was surprised to see the concern on his face. "I'm sorry to hear that," he sounded like he really meant it. "I hope she recovers soon."

"Thank you. Actually, she looks much better today. The doctor said she should be home early next week." Ellie sighed. "The trouble is if she doesn't take it easy I'm afraid that she'll end up back in hospital again. I'm sure that running this hotel is too much for her but she won't admit it, or get extra staff. I think that keeping busy is the only way she could cope with her grief after Dad died." Heck, why had she offloaded all that onto him? She hadn't meant to. The words had just tumbled out of their own accord. He probably wished he hadn't asked now. He was just being polite, not asking for her life story.

To her surprise Reece was looking at her sympathetically. "Has your father been dead long?"

"Two years." She swallowed the lump that sprang to her throat. Dad's death had left a big hole in Ellie's life so she could only imagine how devastated Mum must be. No wonder she was struggling to manage the hotel without him.

"It must have been pretty tough for your mother. It's lucky she's got you to help her out with the hotel."

That made Ellie feel guilty. "That's the trouble. She hasn't got me to help her," she confessed. "I moved away a few years ago. Mandy, the receptionist, phoned me yesterday morning to say Mum was ill so I came down to look after her. She's been managing by herself."

"I see. And I'm sure the last thing you needed was me being so bad-tempered yesterday. Again I apologise. Can we put it down to me having a bad day and start again?" He held out his hand and smiled. "Reece Mitchell – as I'm sure you already know. Pleased to meet you …" He paused.

"Ellie Truman." She smiled back and shook his outstretched hand. "And I apologise for walking in on you when you were having a shower earlier. I did knock, but I'd been told you were checking out that day so presumed you'd gone." Best to get it out there instead of both awkwardly skirting around it, she decided.

"Forget it. I have." He grinned. "And just to prove there's no hard feelings how about joining me for a nightcap at the bar when you've finished here? You look as if you could do with a break."

It was tempting but should she? It was one of her mother's golden rules that the staff never got personally involved with the guests. Not that she was staff but was it wise?

"No strings attached," he assured her as if sensing her doubt. "Just a friendly drink."

Oh, what harm would it do? He seemed – surprisingly – a nice guy and it would be good to unwind a little. "Thank you, I'd like that," she said with a smile. "Give me half an hour to finish off here first."

"Sure. I'll go and freshen up and meet you in the bar in half an hour or so."

Chapter Five

It was just over half an hour later when Ellie walked into the bar, the toenails peeping out of her sandals painted the exact shade of turquoise as the cotton dress she was wearing. She looked drop-dead gorgeous.

Forget it, Reece. This isn't personal.

He stood up and walked over to her. "You look whacked. Why don't you take a seat while I order the drinks?" He reached in his pocket for his wallet. "What would you like?"

"A sweet white wine spritzer please," she told him. "Tell Danny, the barman, to put it onto the hotel tab."

"Absolutely not. I'm paying for these. I didn't invite

you for a drink so the hotel could pick up the bill."

"Thank you." She made her way over to a table by the window rather than the one he'd been sitting at.

Obviously independent, he acknowledged. And he had the impression she could be a bit feisty too. It was the way her eyes had flashed when he'd been so rude about the shower not working, she'd forced a smile on her face and been incredibly polite but he'd sensed she wasn't a pushover. He'd better make a mental note of that.

She was gazing dreamily out of the window when he returned with their drinks. He paused for a moment, watching her, wondering what was going through her mind. She turned as if sensing his presence and for a moment her hazel eyes gazed into his and he felt a stirring in his loins. Hell, she was pretty hot.

"Thank you," she said as he put the glass of wine down on the table in front of her. "I hope you don't mind sitting here. I love looking out onto the street, even though it's too dark to actually see anything right now."

"Me too. You learn a lot by observing," as he sat opposite her. "So where do you live, Ellie? I'm guessing it isn't local."

"The Midlands. So you see, it's a bit of a jaunt for me to come and visit." She picked up her glass and ran her finger around the edge.

She looked worried, he thought. He guessed her mum's collapse had given her quite a scare. "I'm sure you come down as much as he can," he said, gently, taking a sip of his gin and tonic. "What made you move away from such a lovely place? Most people would love to live near the sea."

She shrugged. "I guess I wanted to spread my wings a bit. When you're young a sleepy seaside town is a bit boring, especially in the winter months."

"Yes, I'm sure it is." He relaxed back into his chair. "And there's lots more work opportunities in the city. What do you do?"

"I work for a PR firm in the Midlands. I enjoy the job and I get to travel all over the country, and sometimes abroad. She raised her glass and took a sip. "But it's a long way from Port Medden and Mum could do with my support right now."

"If you feel the hotel is too much for your mother perhaps she should sell up?" suggested Reece. "A hotel in this location would fetch a tidy sum and she could retire, maybe even move to the Midlands nearer to you."

Ellie shook her head. "I've thought of that but Mum loves this place. She and Dad built it up together. It would break her heart to leave. Besides, she would never move out of Cornwall and I doubt if selling up would provide enough money to buy her something down here and live on until she retires."

He hadn't considered that. He wondered how far off pensionable age Ellie's mum was "I can see that it's a difficult situation for you but there must be some way out," he said sympathetically.

"I'm here for two weeks - I'm on holiday from Monday - so I'll do what I can to help." Ellie chewed her lip. "If things don't improve in a couple of months I might have to think about moving back here permanently."

That surprised him. "Would you really do that?"

"If I had to. I offered to when Dad died but Mum refused, she said she didn't want me to give up my independence for her." She took another sip of wine. "To be honest, I was pleased. Does that sound awful? It would drive me nuts living in Port Medden again. Although of course I would if Mum needed me," she quickly added.

"It seems a nice place to live, but yes I'm sure it's … a bit on the quiet side."

Ellie nodded. "Oh, it's not so bad in the summer when you've got all the tourists about but it's dead in the winter. Besides, I enjoy my work and city life."

"Couldn't your mother take on extra staff? A manager perhaps?" He didn't want to sound as if he was prying, but wanted to find out as much as he could about the financial situation.

"I'm going to try and persuade her to, if she can afford it. It would take some of the pressure off her." She smiled ruefully. "I'm sorry, I shouldn't be boring you with all my personal problems. I hardly know you and you're a guest too! Tell me about yourself. What do you do for a living?"

Okay, he'd better let it go now or she'd feel he was intruding. "I work for a hotel group," he said. "Just a boring desk job most of the time although it does involve a bit of travelling, and some amusing things happen." He leaned forward. 'Like the time I was staying in a hotel in Egypt. "I came back late one evening and saw a naked woman banging on one of the hotel room doors. She looked really upset so I went over to see if I could help – averting my eyes, of course…"

"Of course." Her hazel eyes twinkled in amusement.

"It turned out she'd got up in the middle of the night to go to the loo and hadn't wanted to switch the light on in case it disturbed her sleeping husband. But she couldn't see where she was going, and opened the door leading out into the hotel corridor instead of the one into the bedroom and found herself locked out. So I gave her my coat to cover her modesty and went down to ask the guy on reception to let her in. Just as he unlocked the door, the woman's husband came through to the lounge to see his wife walking in naked with my coat over her shoulders, flanked by me and another man. You should have seen the look on his face! It took some explaining, I can tell you.'

"I bet!" she was, doubled-up with laughter. He loved the way she laughed, almost guffawing without any inhibitions, her eyes crinkled at the corners, her body shaking with mirth. She seemed so natural, so unaffected, so unlike the sophisticated, calculated women he usually came into contact with.

God, she's gorgeous.

He could sit here all evening, talking to her, listening to her. He wondered what it was like to feel his hands run over her soft skin, to kiss those cherry red lips.

Don't get personally involved. This is business.

They chatted away over a couple more drinks then Ellie glanced at the clock. "Oh gosh, it's almost midnight!" She stood up. "Thank you for a lovely evening," she smiled. "But I must go now. I've got an early start tomorrow."

Reece stood up to. "At least let me escort you to your room."

She shook her head. "There's no need, really. Goodbye, Reece. I'll see you tomorrow."

He watched her walk out of the bar, the dress

sashaying around her hips and felt an almost overpowering urge to run after her, ask her to stay a little longer.

He was attracted to her. Not surprising, she was gorgeous. Well there was no need for that to make things awkward. He'd never been one to let his feelings come before business and he wasn't going to start now.

The persistent rings of the telephone woke Ellie from her sleep. She reached out and felt for it, knocking the receiver off and mumbled, "Hello."

"Miss Truman. I'm so sorry to disturb you but it's almost ten o'clock and the reception is unattended." It was Harry.

10 o'clock. Crap, she'd overslept. She sat bolt upright and tried to haul her brain out of the fog of sleep that still enclosed it. She'd had far too much to drink last night. What was she thinking of, getting tipsy with a guest and oversleeping like this when she should be helping her mum?

"I'm so sorry, Harry. I'll be down in ten minutes, I promise. Thank you for calling me."

"I'll look after the desk until then," he told her.

She thanked him again, grabbed her glasses off the bedside cabinet, flung back the duvet and sprinted to the bathroom. Why hadn't she put her alarm on? What if one the guests had needed help, or new guests wanted to book in?

Her stomach growled hungrily reminding her that she'd hardly eaten yesterday. Well she didn't have time for breakfast now, she'd grab something later.

She showered, pulled a long white, cotton skirt and sleeveless red cropped top that finished just above her navel out of the wardrobe, put on a touch of powder and lip gloss then went into the ensuite to get her contact lenses. As she slipped one lens into her left eye her mobile rang. She grabbed it, saw Kate's picture flash up and left it. She'd call her back later, she was late enough.

Ellie had a struggle with the other lens and it was still irritating her as she made her way downstairs. She blinked furiously hoping it would settle down and hurried over to the reception desk where Harry was standing, looking very out of place in his blue overalls.

"Thank you so much Harry. I'm so sorry I was late. Have there been any calls?" She asked.

"Someone wants to book a double room for a week next month – I've written their names and telephone number on the notepad - I told them we had one free and you'd phone back to confirm. And the guests for Room 24 phoned to say they'd be a bit late," he told her.

Another booking, things were picking up. "That's great." She smiled at him as she stepped behind the desk.

She thanked him again, knowing how he hated answering the phone and dealing with customers, it was out of his comfort zone. Harry was only at ease when he was working with his hands, doing odd jobs such as painting or repairing things.

Ellie glanced at the address Harry had written down. It looked a bit fuzzy. Her left eye was itching like mad and the right one seemed out of focus. It was as if she wasn't wearing a contact at all in her right eye.

Then it dawned on her what had happened. She'd put the two contacts in her left eye - she must have got distracted by Kate's phone call!

She reached for her bag and searched for her contact solution. Damn she'd left it upstairs. There was only one thing for it. She slipped the contact out of her left eye – she was right there were two of them! With no liquid on her there was only one way she could moisten them, she popped them in her mouth and ran her tongue over them.

"Morning!"

Reece! She didn't dare answer him or she'd swallow her contacts. She turned around and nodded at him, pointing to her mouth, then turned back.

"Are you all right, Ellie?" He sounded concerned.

Oh please go away! She nodded, keeping her back to him as she took the contacts out of her mouth, placing them on the back of her hands, then slipping one into each eye. That was better.

"Well that's the first time I've seen anyone do that!" Reece's voice was laced with amusement. "Dare I ask why you had your contact lenses in your mouth?"

Because I'm a twat.

Ellie quickly explained, trying to make it sound like perfectly normal behaviour.

Reece roared with laughter. "That's priceless. And very innovative of you to come up with that solution. But is it safe?"

"Not on a regular basis, but it was an emergency. I was late up this morning and was in too much of a rush to remember put the contact lens case and solution in my bag."

"Then let me look after the reception while you go and sort them out properly," he said. "I'd hate you to get an eye infection."

She hesitated. She knew her mum wouldn't approve of her leaving a guest in charge of the reception desk. But her eyes were so irritated, and she'd be real quick. Besides, Reece seemed completely trustworthy. "If you're sure? I'll only be a few minutes."

"No problem."

She dashed back upstairs to sort her eyes out, popping both her lenses case with solution and prescription sunglasses in her bag, just in case. When she returned

Reece was finishing a phone call. "Thank you for your enquiry," he was saying. "Someone will get back to you shortly."

"Thanks," she said, stepping behind the desk. "What did they want?"

"It was a lady enquiring about staying for a week in August. She has a few questions about the rooms. I've jotted them down on the pad for you."

"Great. I'll get straight back to her."

"Are your eyes okay now?"

"They're fine. Thank you for stepping in. I appreciate it."

"Don't mention it. As it was my fault you went to bed so late it's the least I can do." He paused. "Fancy joining me for lunch later? Your receptionist will take over then, won't she?"

Well he was keen, first a drink last night then a lunch invite. She was tempted, she'd enjoyed his company last night but she really shouldn't get too involved with a guest. It was only lunch, she told herself, what harm could it do?

"I'd love to," she smiled. "I'm on duty until two though so it'll be a late lunch."

"That's perfect. I've got some business to attend to myself. I'll meet you here at five past two then," he said. He picked up a black briefcase from under the counter

52

and she realised for the first time that he was wearing a suit again. Another business meeting then.

He's nice, Ellie thought as she watched him walk out. Friendly, considerate – and so hot he was scorching. Talk about the full package. Not that she was interested, her life was too busy for complications, and anyway, he'd be checking out as soon as his business here was finished.

Chapter Six

Ellie dialled the number Reece had left on the notepad to arrange the booking for the week and was delighted to hear that the couple wanted breakfast and an evening meal, as well as a room with a sea view. All extra cost. She allocated a pretty room at the back and turned her attention to the computer. The reason she'd overslept this morning wasn't really Reece's fault, she hadn't gone straight to bed when she'd returned to her room last night. Instead she'd started thinking of ways she could boost the hotel's profile and attract more guests. She needed to increase business fast, it was already June so only two more months of summer were left. She'd created a webpage for the hotel a couple of years ago, and showed her mother how to use it. So first thing on the list was to check that out and see when it was last updated.

She clicked onto the website and frowned when she saw that it hadn't been attended to for over two years. Just before Dad had died. She guessed her mum hadn't even thought of it. A lump formed in her throat.

She'd take some new pictures later and upload them onto the Home Page to make it look more appealing. It would be good if she could get some reviews up from former guests too. She ticked 'check website' at the top of her list, wrote UPDATE beside it then moved onto the next item. Create a Facebook page.

Mum didn't like Facebook, as far as she was concerned it was too time-consuming and people posted too much trivia about their lives. Which might be right but most businesses had a Facebook page now, it attracted a lot of customers and was a good way for the customers to interact, ask questions and give feedback. She'd get one up and running now; she doubted if she'd be disturbed much.

Ellie logged onto her personal Facebook account and created a business page, adding her mother and Mandy as administrators so they could post and reply to comments. She would deal with it herself for the next couple of weeks then pass it onto Mandy once she'd returned home. Mandy wouldn't mind, she was a Facebook addict and constantly checking her smartphone for notifications and updates.

Ellie flicked through the photos on the computer, searching for a suitable cover picture for the opening page. Should she use a picture of the hotel itself or of the sea view from the back? A sea view was always appealing she decided. She wrote a new welcome message, uploaded a picture of the hotel and pinned it to the top of the page. That looked good. Now she needed some positive feedback comments. She searched through the visitor's book for a few glowing ones and posted them. Then she linked the Facebook page to the Hotel website and posted a couple more comments from the visitor's book there too.

By the time Mandy arrived to take over she'd started a Pinterest page for the hotel too. Which showed just how bad things were. A whole morning and there had been only the one phone enquiry. Hopefully her work this morning would soon rectify that.

"You look busy, lovey?" Mandy said. "What are you up to?"

"Updating Gwel Teg's social profile," Elle told her brightly. "We're going to get this hotel back on its feet again. I'm determined."

"Atta girl, you never were one to be defeated by anything. Such a stubborn child, like your mother." She edged behind the desk and glanced at the screen. "I like Pinterest. I've just started a page myself to show off my cake creations. I've got a load of repins." Mandy's hobby was to make cakes for special occasions, birthdays, christenings, weddings. She made some fabulous designs and there was quite a demand locally for them. Ellie remembered the cake Mandy had made for Dad's birthday, the year before he died. It was a replica of his garden shed, where he loved to spend his spare time, complete with an assortment of tools. Dad had been delighted.

"I've done more than Pinterest." Ellie switched screen to the Gwel Teg Facebook page she'd just created. "What do you think?"

"It's brilliant! Just what we need," Mandy said in approval. "That should bring the customers in."

"I hope so. I've added you as admin for all this, Mandy, because I know Mum won't want to be bothered with it. Is that okay? It'll be mainly keeping an eye on the Facebook page and replying to any comments. Perhaps you could take the occasional photo too, of a special meal, a lovely sunset, new cushions, that sort of thing."

"Leave it to me, lovey. It'll be no problem," Mandy

told her. She nodded towards the entrance where Reece was walking in, a smile forming on her lips. "Here comes our hot guest. Savour the view."

"Actually, we're having lunch together," Ellie told her sheepishly. No need to tell her that they had a drink together last night too, or about Reece looking after the reception for a little while this morning while Ellie sorted out her contacts.

"Really?" Mandy said the word very slowly, giving it a lot of meaning, her eyes fixed on Reece as he strode over to them.

"Bang on time," Ellie said, looking at her watch.

"I was guided by my stomach. I'm starving," Reece conceded. "Just give me ten minutes to change out of this suit and I'll be with you."

"Sure," Ellie nodded.

"Well, you two have got *friendly*," Mandy said as soon as Reece was out of earshot. "When did this happen? Yesterday you thought he was a right grouch."

She guessed she'd have to 'fess. "He apologised to me when he came in last night. Said he's been stressed because he was late for a meeting. Then he asked me to join him for a drink . . . So I did."

"And enjoyed his company enough to see him again today." Mandy whistled. "Lucky beggar!"

"I know he's a guest but I'm not staff. And he's only

58

here for a few days so what harm will it do?" Ellie told her.

"None at all. If I wasn't so happily married I'd be after him myself. "

"It's not like that," Ellie said defensively." He's really friendly, and a good listener. I could do with a friend right now."

"I know, lovey. I'm jesting you." Mandy wrapped her arm around Ellie's shoulders and gave her a squeeze. "You have a bit of fun, you deserve it."

"Thank you." Ellie thought back to how Mandy had comforted her when she'd found out about Lee and Zoe, and then again when her dad had died. She was like an older sister to her, with her soothing hugs and advice.

"I've updated the website too, Mandy. Let me run through the admin with you," she said. "I've altered it a little to make it easier.

They were both huddled over the computer when Reece returned, having changed into denim cut-offs and a black vest. "Ready to go?" he asked. "I'm starving."

"Me too," Ellie turned to Mandy. "I won't be long. Call me on my mobile if you need me."

"I'll manage, lovey. You go and have a break."

"Where were you thinking of going for lunch?" Ellie asked as they stepped outside into the basking sunshine. "Did you want a pub lunch? A sandwich?"

"Actually, I fancy a bag of fish and chips and a stroll along the beach. How about you?"

That surprised Ellie. She wouldn't have put him down as a 'fish shop man'. She guessed it was the sea air. Being by the sea always made her feel like fish and chips. "Sounds good to me. There's an excellent fish and chip shop just around the corner."

As they walked along the street teeming with holiday-makers, Ellie felt ridiculously happy and carefree. She actually had to fight down the urge to reach out and hold Reece's hand. *Get a grip, Ellie.* Anyone would think she was a love struck teenager.

When they turned the corner Reece raised his nose to the air and sniffed. "What is it about fish and chips that smells so tantalising?"

"Believe me, these taste as good as they smell," she told him. "They've been voted best chip shop in Cornwall for the past three years."

Luckily, there wasn't much of a queue and a few minutes later they were sitting on a bench, overlooking the beach, tucking heartily into their tasty lunch. The low wall in front of them blocked the view of the beach itself but they had a clear view of cotton wool clouds in a clear blue sky over the shimmering azure ocean - A couple of seagulls squawked overhead then soared down to perch on the wall, waiting to pounce on any scraps they dropped.

"Don't feed them or they'll never leave you alone," Ellie warned.

"Don't worry, I don't intend to. It's too delicious." Reece muttered, biting into a chunk of battered cod. He chewed silently for a moment. "It's been ages since I've eaten fish and chips out of a packet like this. Years, actually. I must do it more often!"

"The only time I have fish and chips is when I come back to Port Medden." Elllie picked up another chip and bit off the end. "It's a good job I don't live here anymore or else I'd be spotty and fat!"

Reece's eyes flitted over her appreciatively. "I bet you've never been spotty and fat. Not even as a teenager," he said. Finished eating now, he screwed up the chip paper. "I bet you were the gorgeous one in the class everyone envied."

They were both silent for a moment as their eyes met awkwardly and she felt her cheeks flush at this unexpected compliment..."I wish! But thanks," she said lightly, thinking nothing was further from the truth. She'd been the dippy, accident-prone one that everyone laughed at. Zoe was the beautiful, popular one with her long honey blonde hair, elfin face, big blue eyes and shapely legs that went right up to her waist. No wonder Lee had gone off with her.

"Feel free to tell me how fit I am too," he teased.

She shook her head knowingly. "Oh no, I never bolster a man's ego. In my experience most men have a high enough opinion of themselves without me adding to it."

"That's very cynical of you." Reece aimed the screwed-up paper ball at the litter bin hanging on the wall. "Yes!" He cried triumphantly as it landed inside.

"See what I mean?" Ellie chuckled.

Reece grinned back at her, then stood up and looked over the wall at the beach below. "The beach looks a bit crowded. I guess it gets really busy in the summer holidays."

Ellie watched him, her pulse playing table tennis. *Did he really think she was gorgeous?*

Calm down, Ellie, she told herself, it was a throw-away comment so don't make too much of it. He's probably forgot he even said it now.

She let her eyes linger on him for a while; sun-tanned, muscular legs, nice bum, tight black vest...and she already knew that it concealed a toned body. The image of him stepping out of the bathroom stark naked flashed across her mind and she felt a wash of heat flood through her. This guy certainly had some effect on her!

Knowing how bad her aim was she decided not to risk copying Reece, especially as the waiting seagulls would pounce on the wrapper at the first opportunity and shred if for the scraps. So she walked over to the bin and dropped her fish and chip wrapper in it, then joined him at the wall. The beach below was bustling with holiday-makers, sprawled out on the vast expanse of caramel and, sunbathing, paddling in the sea, playing ball. There was hardly room to walk between the mass of bodies.

"Maybe a stroll on the beach wasn't a good idea," Reece said. "It looks like the rest of the world has beaten us to it."

"This beach is always crowded but there's a little cove not far away that hardly anyone uses because you have to walk across a pebbly beach to get to it. Do you fancy going there?" asked Ellie. "It's a beautiful cove and the sand is really soft." She'd spent many an afternoon there in her teenage years. It was one of her favourite spots. "Mind, the steps down are pretty steep."

Reece grinned. "I'm game if you are."

They walked side by side down the cobbled street, so close that Reece's hand grazed hers at one point, sending goosebumpy shivers up her arm. *And chill!*

A couple more streets, a short walk downhill and they were standing at the top of a narrow set of steep stone steps, leading down to a pebbly and not very inviting beach.

"It looks a bit harsh on the feet," Reece remarked as

he stared down at it.

"That's why no one comes here, the pebbles put them off," she grabbed the metal rail and started to walk down the steps, leaving Reece to follow. "Be careful, the steps are a bit uneven," she warned him. If he slipped they'd both go crashing down.

"Best not to take off your sandals yet," she said when they reached the bottom.

"Don't worry, I don't intend to!"

Side by side they walked across the stony beach.

"How far is this cove?" Reece asked.

"Just past those rocks." Ellie pointed in front of them to where the beach was divided by a mound of black, mussel-covered rocks jutting out from the cliffs and sprawling into the sea. A few people were gathered around the rocks, peering into the rock pools to see what they could find. Just like she used to do when she was a child. She remembered collecting mussels and taking them home as a treat for her dad. He'd loved them cooked French style with white wine and onions.

"You can only walk to the cove when the tide's out," she said. "It's covered completely when the tide comes in."

"And when does the tide come in?" asked Reece. "I don't want to be left stranded!"

"About five thirty." She carefully stepped onto the

rocks, avoiding the slippery green seaweed and slime that covered them. "Don't worry, we've plenty of time. Anyway, I bet you're a good swimmer."

"I am. But I don't fancy swimming home."

They climbed over the rocks and stepped down into an oasis of golden sand, almost entirely surrounded by majestic granite cliffs. It was, as she'd expected, deserted apart from a few seagulls rummaging for food. Ellie gazed around at the almost untouched sand, the gently lapping Artic rolling to the shore in tiny waves of white foam, the ancient, high cliffs that had sheltered the secluded cove for centuries. As always she was taken aback by the beauty of it. "This is my very favourite place."

"I can see why." Reece nodded approvingly.

Ellie kicked off her sandals and ran barefoot over the sand, placing the sandals down by on a rock. "Coming for a paddle?"

Coming for a paddle? Reece hadn't paddled in the sea since he was a teenager. He watched as Ellie practically skipped over to the sea. There was something infectious about her joy of life, she was so refreshingly carefree and uninhibited. He guessed her upbringing was far more loving than his and for a brief moment he wanted a slice of that carefreeness. So he took off his sandals and crossed the beach in a few long strides.

When he reached the water's edge, Ellie was already paddling, a look of sheer enjoyment on her face as the waves lapped gently over her feet. Reece was watching her in amusement.

"Too old and boring to paddle?" Her eyes sparked a challenge.

He accepted it and joined her in the shallow water. It was cool and surprisingly refreshing. His thoughts jerked back to the last time he'd paddled in the sea. He was nine years old, his last summer holiday before his parents divorced but he hadn't known that then. He'd sensed that the atmosphere was even tenser than usual and had done his best to keep out of their way, paddling in the sea, building sandcastles and playing beach ball with a couple of kids he'd made friends with. His Mum had walked out a few months later, the day after his tenth birthday.

"Isn't it heavenly?" Ellie thrust her head back, arms outstretched, basking in the sun's rays.

Reece smiled as he watched her, marvelling and slightly envying her sheer delight in living.

She turned to him. "Have you had enough? Shall we sit down for a bit?"

She was out of the sea and across the sand in a flash, flopping down in the shelter of the cove. She folded her long skirt around her legs and hugged her knees. "When I come here I wonder what I'm doing living in a city," she confessed as Reece sat down beside her. "It's so beautiful here. I feel as if I'm in another world."

Reece felt something stir deep within him. He turned to her, gazed into her hazel eyes. "A world with just you and me in it," he said softly.

She gazed back, her eyes widening as he bent his head closer. She licked her lips. He hesitated, giving her chance to pull away if she wanted and saw her give a little shiver of anticipation, then, as he leaned even closer he heard a little gasp escape from her lips and she closed her eyes.

Chapter Seven

Wow! This guy could kiss!

It took all of Ellie's willpower to push Reece away instead of snog him like mad and run her hands over the toned body she remembered so well dripping wet from the shower, but somehow she did it. Sexy, as he undeniably was, it wasn't her style to get so 'friendly' with someone she barely knew. He could be married, living with someone, engaged. He wouldn't be the first guy to forget he had a wife or girlfriend when he was away from home.

"Woah!" she said breathlessly, sitting up and trying to compose herself. "Steady on!"

He lounged on his elbow, looking up at her. "Sorry, but you're so irresistible, I just couldn't help myself." He raised his hand and touched her face, running one finger softly, softly over her cheeks and down to her mouth. "I think you're a wonderful, beautiful girl, Ellie Truman, and I fancy you like mad. But if you don't feel the same way please say so and I'll back off." he said softly.

Ellie licked her lips, not sure what to say. She fancied him like mad too but he was a guest. She's only known him five minutes. And they'd both be going back home soon. Three very good reasons not to get involved.

Or maybe three very good reasons to have a bit of fun. At least things couldn't get too serious, could they?

"Let's say I'm interested but you being a guest complicates things." She paused, best to get it out there before things got any further. "And I don't know anything about you. Whether you're with someone . . . married." She looked him straight in the face as she waited for his answer. She had no intention of going out with a married man and if Reece was lying she was sure she'd be able to tell.

"Nope. Definitely no wife. I'm not the marrying kind. And no girlfriend at the moment. There's a vacancy in that department if you want to take it up?" He grinned.

She smiled back, relieved to hear that not only was he single, he wanted to remain that way. Just as she did. So

69

they could enjoy each other's company for the next week or so without worrying that anyone was getting in too deep and wanted more. No strings attached. Just how she liked it.

He raised a dark eyebrow questioningly. "What about you? Do you have a husband or boyfriend somewhere? A wedding dress in the loft you're dying to wear?"

A wedding dress in the loft you're dying to wear? What a strange thing to say. Perhaps one of his exes had tried to lead him down the bridal path. She'd known a couple of women who had their whole wedding planned even though they hadn't found the man they wanted to marry yet. Well he had no fears on that score with her.

She'd had a few boyfriends since Lee – make that several - but nothing serious, although a couple of them had wanted it to be. She'd long since got over Lee but had no intention of letting anyone close enough to break her heart again. Besides, she liked her freedom. She saw so many of her friends compromising their dreams to fit in with their partners and she didn't want to do that. She was going to live her life how she wanted to.

Mind you, she had no objection to having a holiday romance with Reece. He was charming and fun. Although a bit egoistic she reckoned, and she already knew about his grumpy side.

She shook her head. "Foot-loose and fancy-free, that's me. And that's the way I like it," she added just to make sure he got the message.

"It sounds like we're on the same wavelength," He bent forward and kissed her on the nose. "Pleased to hear the interest is mutual. Now, let's go for another paddle before I get too carried away."

He held her hand and pulled her up, and, with their fingers still entwined, walked across the sand to the sea. As they stepped into the cool water, Ellie scooped up a handful of water and splashed it over him, laughing as it sprayed over his face.

"You minx!" he said. "I'll get you for that!"

Lifting up her long skirt, Ellie turned and ran off, through the rippling sea, but with two long steps Reece was beside her and splashed Ellie with a shower of seawater that showered over her shoulders.

"Hey, be careful," she laughed. "I don't want my clothes to get soaked."

"Then you'd better jump!" Reece shouted.

Ellie looked over her shoulder to see a wave rolling towards her. Lifting her skirt even higher she jumped just in time. The wave crashed under her feet.

Another wave cascaded their way. Reece reached out for Ellie's hand, she held up her skirt with the other hand and they jumped the wave together, shrieking with laughter like a pair of kids. As soon as there was a lull in the waves, Ellie released Reece's hand and paddled towards the shore. "Race you!" she shouted over her shoulder.

She sprinted across the beach, Reece hot on her heels.

"Well, that cooled us down!" Reece grinned as they both flopped down on the sand.

"I ought to be getting back," Ellie told him. "I promised Mum that I'd visit her again today."

"Better let your skirt dry first." Reece's eyes danced. "You'll cause a traffic jam!"

"What?" Ellie glanced down at her skirt which was now drenched and clinging seductively to her legs. And completely see through. She hadn't realised she'd got it so wet. She couldn't walk back to the hotel like this.

"Hey, don't look so worried, it'll soon dry out if we sit here in the sun for a while. And just to keep my mind off how enticing you look, you can tell me a bit more about your job."

"A bit bossy, aren't you? Not an attractive trait in a man," she quipped, spreading her skirt out over her legs so that it would dry quicker.

"I really would like know more about it," he told her. "Exactly how do you help firms improve their image?"

Well, it wasn't often you found a guy interested in

your work. Sexy and considerate, Reece was turning out to be quite something. "My big passion is children's education," she told him. "I think every child has a right to an education so I encourage companies to sponsor education in third world countries, to donate towards the cost of building schools, sponsoring the children, providing books, etc. It improves their public image and helps children too. A win-win situation."

He seemed genuinely interested and asked a lot more questions. Ellie replied animatedly then realised that she'd been talking for ages. He must think she was all me, me, me!

"Sorry I tend to go on a bit. Tell me to shut up when you've had enough."

"Not at all. It's refreshing to hear someone talk about their work with such enthusiasm. You sound like you really enjoy it. "I do. What about you? What sort of work do you do?

* * *

"Nothing as altruistic as you," he said. "It's mainly boring meetings with clients."

She wanted to ask him more but a glance at her watch told her it was 4.30. "Oh gosh, I didn't realise it was that late. I have to get back to the hotel." She looked down at her skirt and was relieved to see that it was only slightly damp now.

"Me too." He stood up and held out his hand. "Need a hand up?"

"Thanks." She could manage but why turn down the offer of feeling his hand in hers? He pulled her up to join him, and enclosed his arms around her, kissing her once again. A kiss that was even more spine-tingling than the previous one had been.

"Now come on, I can't stay here all day, chatting to you," he teased. "I've got a couple of business calls to make."

Hand in hand they made their way back over the sand, the rocks and across the stony beach, only letting go when they reached the narrow stone steps. Reece went up first and reached for Ellie's hand again as soon as she got to the top. They walked to the hotel in companionable silence.

"Oh, Ellie, thank goodness you're back!" Mandy ran over as soon as Ellie stepped through the door. "A water pipe's burst and flooded out the Honeymoon Suite. Harry's called out a plumber and is trying to fix it temporarily himself, but Mr Smythe, the guest, is furious. The water's poured through the ceiling to the bed below, ruining the open suitcase full of clothes they'd left on the bed ready to unpack. He said he's going to sue us!"

"You bet your sweet life I am!" A stockily built man

with greying hair came striding over to them, followed by a slim, fair-haired woman who was trying to pacify him. "This is supposed to be our second honeymoon and now it's ruined. Someone's going to pay for this!"

Ellie caught her breath. She'd noticed when looking through her mother's papers yesterday that the hotel insurance had expired. She'd intended to talk to Mum about it today. *What the hell should she do now?*

"I'm so sorry…" she apologised, desperately trying to find the words to pacify him. If he sued for compensation it would bankrupt the hotel. *Think, Ellie, think!*

"Is that all you can say? You're sorry? Our clothes are ruined. Our room is a mess. The bed is soaked." Mr Smythe's face was bright red and Ellie was seriously worried that he was going to have a heart attack. *What would Mum do if she was here?*

Suddenly she was aware that Reece was talking. "I do apologise. What a dreadful thing to happen, but rest assured, sir, that we'll do our best to put it right. Can we offer you coffee and sandwiches in the lounge while Miss Truman sorts you out an alternative room?" He turned to Mandy, "Please escort Mr Smythe and his wife to the lounge, Mandy, and arrange for sandwiches of their choice to be made for them."

Ellie stared at him in astonishment. What the hell was he doing acting like he worked here, and in a position of authority at that? He had no right to deal with the guests and make these sort of decisions. She was about to tell him so when she noticed that Mr Smythe was no longer looking so angry.

"Ellie?" Mandy was looking questioningly at her.

Ellie fought down her anger. Okay so Reece shouldn't have taken over but he did seem to have calmed the guests down a bit. And she needed a bit of breathing space to think how to deal with the situation. The Smythes needed to be appeased and quickly. If they pushed for compensation….

She nodded at Mandy to indicate that she agreed with Reece then turned to the Smythes. "I'm so sorry this has happened, Mr and Mrs Smythe. I'll arrange for you to be moved to another room and for your clothes to be cleaned, of course."

"I should hope so too," huffed Mr Smythe. "I wanted this to be a special holiday for my wife. It's our Silver Wedding Anniversary."

Of course, she remembered Mandy telling her. No wonder the man was seething. How on earth was she going to put this right?

"I really can't apologise enough. I realise how distressing and inconvenient this is for you but we can assure you that we'll do our best to ensure your stay is just how wanted it to be." Reece said, once again taking control. "Miss Truman and I will assess the damage and call a plumber and then we'll join you in the lounge."

"Come on, dear," said Mrs Smythe, touching her husband's arm. "Accidents happen and they're trying to make amends."

"It shouldn't have happened. I've had that case years and it's ruined. So are our clothes," he muttered, but allowed his wife to take his arm and they followed Mandy into the restaurant.

"Sorry, I didn't mean to take over," Reece said as soon as the Smythes were out of earshot, "It's just that I know you have to deal with situations like this quickly and I just wanted to help. Shall we check out the damage? I'm sure it's nothing too drastic and your insurance will foot the bill."

It would if we were insured, Ellie thought in panic as they made their way over to the lift. Goodness knows how much the plumber would cost, and what other damage had been done. And what if the Smythes did push for compensation? What was she going to do?

"This is really worrying you, isn't it?" asked Reece as the lift doors closed on them. His grey eyes softened with concern as they rested on her face. "I know you feel responsible for the place while your mother is in hospital but I'm sure she'll understand. It shouldn't take long to put right."

She shook her head. "It isn't that." She swallowed. Might as well tell him. "We haven't got insurance cover," she confessed. "I was looking through the papers last night and discovered that it had lapsed. I was going to talk to Mum about renewing it today."

"I see." Reece looked thoughtful for a moment. "The way I see it," he said as the lift came to a halt and the doors slid open, "your only option is to appease the guests so that they don't sue. Do everything you can to make them happy."

He paused. "Look, would you like me to deal with this for you? I do have experience in this kind of thing but if you want to handle it yourself then I'll back off."

She wanted to tell him she would deal with it herself. That she wasn't a helpless little woman who needed a man to rescue her. She had a demanding job and was quite capable of dealing with things but to be honest she was out of her depth. Her mother's illness, seeing what a state the hotel was in and now this – it was all too much. If the Smythes sued them Mum would have to sell the hotel. She couldn't let that happen. She sensed that Reece had the charm and expertise to deal with awkward customers, he'd already soothed the situation, and she wasn't going to let pride get in the way of helping her mother. So she nodded. "Please. If you're sure you don't mind and think you can help. I'd be grateful. And so will

Mum. She's enough to worry about at the moment."

"No problem, but speak up if I'm doing something you don't agree with."

"Oh I will." She might be glad of his help but she still wanted him to know that she was calling the shots. "And please don't make any financial decisions before you okay them with me," she added. The last thing she wanted was for Mum to come out of hospital and be faced with bills that she couldn't afford to pay.

They'd reached the Honeymoon Suite now. The door was wide open. Ellie took a deep breath, braced herself and stepped inside.

Chapter Eight

The damage was far, far worse than she'd expected. There was a massive hole in the ceiling where the water had poured through, drenching the bed below, the open suitcase of clothes lying on it and the carpet. Ellie was horrified. She dreaded to think how much this would cost to put right.

Harry came into the room, looking agitated. "Oh, Miss Truman, thank goodness you're back. The leak's coming from the bathroom in Room 18. I've turned off the water supply to the room above and called the plumber." He ran his hand over his almost bald head. "Goodness knows how long it's been leaking. It's one of the rooms that's used regularly but no one's reported a leak or I would have seen to it immediately."

"Don't worry, Harry, it's not your fault," Ellie assured him. She thought about the shower leaking in the room next to Reece's. It sounded as if the hotel's plumbing system needed a complete overall. It probably hadn't had one since it was built.

"Is the room upstairs badly damaged?" Reece asked.

Harry looked surprised, as if only just noticing Reece was there.

"Mr Mitchell is kindly helping me sort things out a bit for when Mum comes home," she explained.

Harry didn't look too happy. Ellie guessed that in his book guests didn't interfere with the running of the hotel. He pointedly ignored Reece and addressed Ellie. "There's no obvious damage but the water's leaked through the floor tiles and seeped under the floorboards. I've no idea what state they're in. If they're soaked through they might need to be replaced."

This was getting worse and worse. Ellie gnawed her lip as she tried not to think of how much replacing floorboards would cost.

Reece gave her a reassuring look. "The floorboards should be okay if we leave them to dry out for a few days. The first thing to do is get the pipe fixed. Then I'm afraid you're going to need this ceiling taken down and replastered, Ellie."

And how was Mum going to afford that?

"We can't have this room out of use for long," Ellie said worriedly. "It's the best room in the hotel. How quickly can we fix it?"

She saw Reece and Harry exchange looks. "Two to three weeks, I'd say," Reece replied. "The floorboards need to dry out before the ceiling can be replastered, then that needs to dry before it can be repainted. That could take up to two weeks. Then you're going to need new carpet, new bed and maybe redecorating."

Ellie fought down the panic. She'd have to put it on her credit card and work overtime to pay it off. After all, it was partly her fault; she should have come to visit her mother more often, made sure that she was coping instead of selfishly getting on with her own life. She should have known that Mum would never tell her if she was struggling. She had merely told Ellie what Ellie wanted to hear and Ellie had been more than willing to believe it, too busy with her job, her friends and her dates to bother to go down and check.

"Are you all right, Ellie? You look very pale?" Reece's voice was edged with concern.

Ellie pulled herself together and flashed him an over-bright smile. "Yes, of course. Thank you so much for your help with this. You're obviously more used to this kind of crisis than I am."

"It's part of my job," he told her. "Now, if I needed to put a good PR spin on something like this, I wouldn't have the first clue where to start. Unlike you..."She smiled at his attempt to make her feel better. "What shall we do first?" she asked, looking around despairingly. She really had no idea where to start.

Harry's mobile rang. He answered it. "I'll be right down," he said, then ended the call. "That's the plumber's, Miss Truman. Do you want me to take him up to the room so he can sort out the leak?"

"Yes, thank you, Harry." She felt quite weak with the worry of it all.

"Look these things happen. It's not as bad as it looks," Reece reassured her when Harry had gone out.

She wanted to think that. She was a 'glass half full' person normally but she didn't see how it could be much worse. "The room is a complete mess," she replied, gazing around it. "And look at the state of their clothes and suitcase. How am I going to sort this out before Mum comes home?"

"I'm sure your mother won't expect you too. It's not your fault," Reece told her.

"Maybe not, but I'm all Mum's got and she's already ill. If she has to come home to this it will make her worse." She had to find a way to put it right.

"Okay, let's deal with it one step at a time. First, do you have another room free that the guests can use. One that's the same standard if possible?" asked Reece.

Ellie thought. "There's the Silver Room. It's our next best room but the Smythes especially wanted the Honeymoon Suite because they spent their honeymoon in it twenty five years ago."

"I know but if you fill the Silver Room with flowers and put a bottle of champagne on ice that should mollify them a little." Reece gave her a comforting hug. "We can sort it. In situations like this it's best to apologise and make amends quickly. Most people are satisfied with a heartfelt apology. Only a few will go on to officially complain if they can see that you're trying your best to put things right."

He was right. She could sort this. She had to pull herself together and stop panicking.

"Thank you. You've been a big help. I'll do what you suggest with the Silver Room and there's a one hour dry cleaning service in the town. I'll send their clothes to be cleaned. And offer to buy them a replacement suitcase." She dreaded to think what it would all cost but it had to be done. It's a good job she hadn't maxed out her credit card.

"Look, you're supposed to be going to the hospital to see your mum so let me sort it for you. If you don't turn up she'll worry that something's wrong."

He was right. Again. And worrying was the last thing she wanted Mum to do right now. "Are you sure?" she asked. "You've already done enough and you must have stuff of your own to do."

"Nothing that can't wait. I'd be happy to help."

She hesitated. It seemed wrong. He was a guest and she hardly knew him. You are sort of dating, she reminded herself. And she was glad of the help.

"Thank you, that's really kind of you," she said. "I'd better get you some money. How much will you need?"

"Leave it for now, you can settle with me later. I promise I won't bankrupt you and buy the most expensive champagne." He turned her to face him, tilted her chin up with his finger and kissed her on the nose. "It will be all right. I promise. Trust me."

She smiled and touched his cheek. "Thanks. I really appreciate it. I'll let Mandy know and ask her to give you the keys to the Silver Room."

They gazed at each other for a moment and she felt an incredible longing to sink into his arms, feel her body against his, drown herself into his kiss. *Did he feel it too?* She eased herself out of his arms while she still could. "I'll go and see Mandy now."

He hadn't meant to take control like that but Ellie had

looked so distressed that he'd jumped in to help without stopping to consider that it would be in his best interest if the guests did sue. Then Ellie's mother would probably have to sell and he'd get the hotel at a rock bottom price. That would please Steve.

Which was a first for him. He never acted on impulse. What had come over him? He'd only just met Ellie. How could he put business ahead of his personal feelings for her?

What personal feelings? Okay he liked her. So what? He'd liked plenty of women before her and was sure he would do so in the future.

Yet there was something different about Ellie. She was gorgeous, quirky – he smiled as he remembered the contact lenses episode – and fun – he thought of the way they'd splashed in the sea. But it was more than that. She had a freshness, a softness he hadn't come across in any of the women he'd dated before. She obviously cared deeply about her mother and would do anything to help her. They must have a very close relationship.

Unlike him and his mother, who he hadn't set eyes on for years. They didn't even exchange Christmas or Birthday cards. Not that it bothered him. He'd had little time for his mother since she'd walked out on him when he was ten, leaving his strict, workaholic father to bring him up. An only child, Reece had always felt in the way, a nuisance who prevented both his parents from living their life how they wanted. He'd been determined to make something of his life, to show them that he had some worth.

Ellie had obviously had a different childhood. The way her eyes had glistened over when she talked about her father's death showed him how close she was to him. And how she'd immediately come dashing down to look after her mother. And now she was trying to save the family hotel from bankruptcy.

That's why he'd stepped in to help. Okay, yes he was attracted to her. So what? She seemed to feel the same way. What harm would a holiday romance do?

It was mixing business with pleasure. Something he never did.

Just one of the things he never did and now found himself doing, like paddling in the sea, jumping the waves, taking over the reception desk. Even arranging for clothes to be cleaned and sourcing a replacement suitcase while Ellie visited her mother. And all to wipe that look of worry from her eyes and replace it with a smile.

By the time Ellie returned from visiting her mother the pipe was fixed, the Smythes had been moved to the Silver Room and their clothes cleaned and returned to them. Mandy also informed her that Reece had ordered a replacement suitcase and it would be with them by six that day.

"That man is a miracle-worker," Mandy told her. "You should see what he's done to the Silver Room. It's amazing." Reece had certainly won her over.

"Where is he now?" asked Ellie.

"I'm not sure, he was around a few minutes ago." Mandy turned as the phone rang. "I'd better answer that."

Ellie wandered off to find Reece. She found him having a cup of coffee with the Smythes in the lounge. He stood up as she came in. "Hello, Ellie. I see you're back from the hospital. How is your mother?"

"Much better, thank you. She's hoping to be home by Saturday." Ellie sat down in the empty chair beside Reece. She turned to the Smythes. "I am so sorry about the leak and the awful mess in your room..."

Mr Smythe waved his hand dismissively. "Please don't worry yourself. These things happen. Reece has had our clothes laundered and we are more than happy with our new room, and the generous offer of a free evening meal each for our anniversary tomorrow."

A free meal?

Ellie felt Reece's gaze on her. Was he waiting for her reaction? What could she say? She had given him permission to deal with the situation and two free meals was a lot cheaper than a compensation claim.

"The champagne, chocolates and flowers are lovely too," added Mrs Smythe. "You've gone out of your way to put things right."

Well Reece's idea seemed to have worked, the Smythes certainly looked happier.

Mrs Smythe leaned forward, perching her cup of coffee on her knee. "Reece told us about your mother being taken ill. It's so caring of you to help her out. We don't want to add to your problems. As far as we're concerned, it's a little accident that couldn't be helped. That's right, isn't it, Tony?"

"Yes, we'll not be making a fuss. Your man here has looked after us," Mr Smythe said pleasantly.

"That's very kind of you both." A wave of relief washed over Ellie. Thank God for Reece. "I hope you'll be comfortable in your new room. Do let me know if there's anything else we can do," she added.

"Oh Reece is looking after us fine, dear. You've got a good manager there," Mrs Smythe told her.

Startled at her words, Ellie swiftly glanced over at Reece. Had he told them he was the manager or had they simply assumed it? The fact that he wasn't contradicting them suggested that he'd told them this was his position here. He caught her eye and nodded slightly, as if telling her to go along with it. Well she guessed she'd have to. To be fair, it would have been really awkward if Reece had told them that he was a guest helping out. The most important thing was that he'd diffused the situation and somehow talked them around.

"Oh, I know, we're very lucky to have him on board." she said with a smile.

Leaving the Smythes in Reece's more-than-capable hands she decided to check out the Silver Room. After Mandy's comments and Mrs Smythe's obvious delight she was curious to see the room herself.

The scented aroma hit her as soon as she opened the door. Four cut-glass vases of expensive flowers were scattered about strategically. In the middle of the coffee table stood a bottle of champagne in a bucket of ice, besides that was a very expensive heart-shaped box of chocolates. Reece had pulled a masterstroke.

She turned as she heard footsteps behind her and saw Mandy grinning at her.

"It looks lovely, doesn't it? The Smythes are delighted with it."

"It's great. Really welcoming. I always find it amazing what a difference a few well-placed flowers make."

"Reece dealt with it all. He's charm itself that man." Mandy patted her hand. "How's your mum, lovey? You didn't tell her about the leak, I take it?"

Ellie shook her head. "No, not yet. I'll wait until she comes home. I'm hoping to have it all straight again by then."

"We'll all help. We'll get it done in no time. Have the doctors given you any idea when she will be home?"

"She's making good progress so it should be early next week." Ellie surveyed the room again. The flowers, champagne and chocolates were such a simple touch but they gave a hint of luxury to the room and made the guests feel special, cared for. Reece certainly knew how to handle people. She suspected he must be in a managerial position in the company he worked for because he'd taken charge so assuredly, as if he was used to doing just that. "Thanks for holding the fort, Mandy, but you should have gone home an hour okay. I'll take over Reception now."

"Take your time, lovey. I'm in no rush," Mandy told her. "I can stay an extra hour – no charge – if there's jobs you need to do."

It was tempting. She had such a lot to do but she couldn't keep Mandy any longer. It wasn't fair. The kindly woman had already worked a few hours unpaid overtime this week.

"Thank you but I can manage now. You get off and I'll see you Monday." She touched Mandy's arm. "I really appreciate your support. I don't know what I'd have done without you."

"Bless you, lovey, happy to help. Any time."

Just then the lift doors opened and the plumber stepped out. He walked over to the desk and handed Ellie a slip of paper.

"I've just finished repairing the pipe in room 12," He said. "Here's my bill. Can you pass it on to Mrs Truman for me?"

"Thank you. I'm her daughter, Ellie," she explained. "Is the pipe totally safe now?"

"It should be fine but to be honest your plumbing system is a bit dated, a cold spell and you'll have another pipe going. You mark my words."

"I'll let my mother know." Ellie hesitated. "She's in hospital at the moment. Is it okay if she deals with your bill when she comes out?" That would give them a little more time to get the money together.

"I'm sorry to hear that. Nothing serious I hope?" he asked.

"Pleurisy. She should be out early next week. Will that be okay?"

"I can give you a couple of weeks, in the circumstances. I've done a few jobs for your folk over the years. Don't take too long, mind. I have my bills to pay too."

"I won't," she promised.

She'd thought about how to pay for the repairs when she'd been driving back from the hospital and had come up with a solution. She'd had a letter from her credit card company last week offering an interest free balance transfer until next spring. At the time she'd shoved it to one side, ready to shred but now it seemed like a gift from the gods. She'd work out how much she needed for everything by borrowing that amount of money, and it would give Mum chance to get the hotel on its feet and pay her back, if she could. If not, Ellie could work some overtime. She had to repay Reece too, with what would probably be a couple of hundred looking at the flowers and champagne he'd ordered but she should have enough in her bank for that.

"I'll be off then, Miss. The floorboards will take a couple of days to dry out then you can get the ceiling plastered. Give my regards to your mother."

"I will. Thank you."

She'd have liked to get the ceiling sorted out before Mum came home but it seemed that was out of the question. Thank goodness her two week's holiday had coincided with Mum taking ill. Hopefully that would be long enough to get the Honeymoon Suite restored and the main repairs done before she went home.

A priority was to renew the insurance but she

wouldn't be able to do that until Monday, when the offices opened, so fingers crossed nothing else went wrong.

"How's your mother, Miss Truman?"

"Much better, thank you, Harry." Ellie looked up with a smile.

"That's excellent news, Miss Truman."

"It is, isn't it? I want to make sure that she rests when she comes home so I'm going to try and get all the odd jobs done. Could you make a start on them Monday? Of course, we'll pay you overtime if you can't finish them in your normal hours."

"That won't be necessary Miss Truman, I'm happy to help," Harry told her. "I can come in tomorrow if you want."

She thought about this. Sunday was usually Harry's day off, but Mum could be home by Tuesday and Ellie was desperate to get the hotel straight. She'd have to pay him overtime of course, but it would be worth it.

"Thank you, Harry. That's really kind of you. We'll pay you time and a half, of course. I'll sort out the repair notes left by the guests and give you them too. Let me know if there are any jobs you can't tackle."

"I will, Miss. And normal rates will be just fine. We all need to pull together until Mrs Truman gets on her feet again."

"That's so kind of you, we really appreciate it."

"Don't mention it, Miss. Your mum – and your late dad too, bless him – is one of the kindest people I've ever come across. It's a privilege to work for her." Harry nodded solemnly.

Ellie fought back the tears as she watched the old man walk away. It was a measure of her mum's character that her staff were so loyal. Mandy and Harry were both determined not to let her down. Well she wasn't going to either. She wasn't going to let a stupid thing like a pipe leak defeat her. She'd redecorate the room and fit a new carpet herself, if necessary. Anything to help put things right.

Chapter Nine

"Okay Steve, see you on Tuesday then." Reece finished the call, shoved his mobile into his back pocket and walked over to the window. Steve was interested in his idea of buying Gwel Teg and wanted him to draft up a report about the condition of the hotel, the likely expenditure it would take to get it up to scratch, and a rough idea of how the business was doing. The usual stuff. They were both going to discuss it on Tuesday. The worse state the hotel was in the less they had to fork out, so why had he helped Ellie sort out that business with the leak?

A compensation claim would have bankrupted the hotel and meant he and Steve would get if for a song.

That's the way business worked, always had. R.S. Incorporated – the R standing for Reece and the S for Steve – sought out hotels that were struggling, assessed their potential and then, if they were sure they could turn them around successfully, they would make them an offer. Okay, the offer was usually below market value but the hotel owners needed the money and it was R.S who were taking the risk. If they didn't offer to buy them out the hotels would go under, then have to sell up and come out of with little if any profit. Which would mean Steve and Reece could lose their investment. It was a business deal, pure and simple, and one that had seen them make a tidy profit over the last few years.

Gwel Teg was just another hotel they were thinking of taking under their wing. So why was Reece letting himself get personally involved?

Because of Ellie, that's why. She was so determined to get Gwel Teg back on its feet, and to help her Mum, that he'd found himself wanting to help *her*. Last night, when she'd opened her purse and anxiously asked her how much she owed him, he couldn't bring himself to tell her the correct amount, and instead had halved it. The look of relief in her eyes was worth it.

Well, that had come out of his own pocket, but he had to make sure that he didn't short charge the business. They needed to make a profit, to keep expanding.

He'd do the figures later, he decided. Right now he could do with some fresh air.

As Reece walked along the corridor he saw that the door to the Honeymoon Suite was open. He peered inside, surprised to see Ellie, a bright yellow scrunchie holding her hair back, her tongue sticking out between her teeth and a look of sheer concentration on her face, measuring the length of the room with a retractable tape measure. She looked heart-meltingly endearing.

"You look busy," he finally remarked.

She jumped and spun around, releasing the steel tape which immediately zapped back onto her hand. "Oww!" She yelled, shaking her finger.

He was beside her in a heartbeat. "Let me look."

"It's fine, don't worry."

Reece ignored her and scrutinised her finger. A red patch had already formed where the end of the tape had hit it. He raised the finger to her lips and kissed it tenderly, resisting the urge to trail kisses up her arm, to her shoulder, her neck ... "I'm sorry. I didn't mean to startle you."

"It's okay," she assured him.

Her lips were enticingly close to his, he satisfied himself with a feather light kiss, conscious that the door was open and guests could walk by, then released her hand. "What are you doing?"

"Measuring for a new carpet. I thought I might be able to buy a remnant and fit it myself." She moved away from him and started measuring the width of the room.

"Have you ever fitted a carpet before?" He asked, watching her.

"No, but how hard can it be? And it's got to be a lot cheaper than getting someone in to fit it." She took a notebook and pen off the windowsill and scribbled in it. "I've got the measurements now. I'll visit some carpet places tomorrow and see what I can pick up."

Really? The Honeymoon Suite, the best suite in the hotel and she was intending to buy a remnant carpet – if she could get one that size - and fit it herself? Much as he hated to burst her 'can do' balloon he had to persuade her that this wasn't a good idea. "It's not as easy as it looks…" he ventured.

Her eyes flashed. "It seems easy to me. Providing I get the measurements correct – which I have, check if you like – then all I have to do is tack it down. Harry will help me."

"You'll be lucky to get a remnant this size, and there'll be some cutting and shaping - around that alcove for instance. You need underlay too. And if it isn't fitted tight enough and anyone trips over it you could be faced with a hefty compensation claim." He paused, what the hell, it wouldn't hurt to help her. "Look, you can use the company we deal with then I can get you a discount – a big one," he added seeing that flash in her eyes again. "I can organise it for you, they'll fit the carpet too. And you'll have thirty days to pay."

He could see that she was considering it. "That's really kind of you but even so it will probably be too expensive."

"I think you'll be pleasantly surprised. You could order the bed from there too."

"I guess it wouldn't hurt to take a look, maybe it might be do-able. Thank you." Ellie leaned forward and gave him a peck on the cheek. "You are really kind."

"You're welcome. There is one other thing you need to think about though."

Ellie cocked an eyebrow questioningly.

"A new carpet and newly painted ceiling will probably make the rest of the room look shabby. You might have to think about getting the whole room redecorated."

She titled her chin. "I can do that. I'm going to paint the ceiling once the plaster's dry and I'll come down one of the weekends to decorate."

"Really?" Reece tried not to sound amused but she bristled.

"Yes, really! I have decorated my flat, you know."

He'd never met anyone so determined. And she looked so adorable with her eyes flashing like that and her chin jutted out. He wrapped his arm around her waist and kissed her on the nose. "I'm just trying to help, Ellie. It's a big job."

"I can do it." She sounded determined. "I'm going to get this hotel back on its feet if I have to work day and night for the next two weeks and come down every weekend for a few months."

She had some backbone, he had to give her that. She was a fighter.

He liked it that she was willing to do so much to help her mother. Family love and loyalty wasn't something he had come across much – not with his self-obsessed parents and getting caught up in their bitter divorce. Maybe it was that which prompted him to say. "I'll help too."

She scrutinised him sharply, as if to check that he wasn't mocking her. Then her expression relaxed. "Thank you but you've already done enough. You're a guest. You're supposed to be resting, sight-seeing, sunbathing and all the other things guests do, not working as an unpaid handyman and manager."

"I'm not actually on holiday, I do have some business to attend to. But I'm happy to help when I can."

"You really mean that, don't you?" She looked at him sharply. "Why?"

The question threw him for a moment. Why was he

offering to help spruce up the hotel he was intending to buy when they'd be able to offer a lower price if it was in a state of disrepair? "As a favour for a friend," he replied, answering himself and Ellie.

She looked worried. "We can't afford to pay you, or let you stay here for free in return for work."

He cupped her face in his hands and tenderly kissed her on the nose. "I don't want a free room or payment. I'm merely helping out someone I've grown quite fond of."

She still looked suspicious. "It's a very big deal. You hardly know me. We're virtually strangers."

"I thought we agreed to date yesterday? And we've shared a few kisses. That makes us a bit more than strangers, don't you think?"

Now she looked flustered. "If you're sure?"

"Absolutely." He smiled and wrapped his arms around her, pulling her closer. "Anyway, I've been looking for you."

He saw the worried look cross her face. "Why? Has something else happened?

"No, stop worrying. I wondered if you wanted to do anything this afternoon? It is Sunday, after all."

"You know, that sounds good," she agreed, relaxing a little. "How do you feel about going surfing?"

"Surfing?" he repeated, glancing up at her to see

if she was serious.

"Yes." She cocked her head to one side. "You do surf don't you?"

He hesitated for a nano second. "Yeah sure, but I haven't done it for years, not since I was a teenager. I might not even be able to still get on a surfboard never mind ride the waves."

"It doesn't matter if you haven't, it's only a bit of fun," she told him. "You can just splash about on the surfboard if you want. I'm not exactly brilliant it but I enjoy it." She frowned. "Or do you *hate* the idea? We can do something else if you want."

If there was one thing Reece hated it was not being able to do something well. His need to impress, to be successful, stemmed, he knew, from wanting to prove to his parents that he was worthy of their time and attention. To make them proud of him, proud enough that they would want to spend time with him. He used to surf well at eighteen. Fourteen years later he wasn't so sure.

His instinct was to suggest doing something else but he could see that Ellie really wanted to go surfing. Oh what the heck, he was sure it would come back to him.

"Sure, let's go for it," he agreed. "Though I warn you, I'm pretty rusty. My teens were a few years ago."

"Just a few?" She raised an eyebrow and grinned cheekily.

He playfully tweaked her cheek. "Come on then, let's see if I can still stand up on the board. I'm presuming there's somewhere I can hire a wetsuit from?"

"There's a hut on the beach, hires out boards and wetsuits but we keep some here, for when family and friends come down. I'm pretty sure we've got one that will fit you. Come up to the flat and I'll sort them out."

He followed her to the private quarters. He was surprised at how spacious it was. A large lounge, with a kitchen off to the left and a hall leading to what he presumed where the bedrooms and bathroom off to the right.

"This is a nice flat," he said. "How many bedrooms do you have?"

"Three. Mine's the attic room, it overlooks the beach, as does this room and the kitchen. Do you want to have a look around? You'll have to excuse the mess, of course, I haven't had chance to tidy up yet."

"If you don't mind. I'm really surprised how light and roomy it is up here."

"It is, it's great. Me, Mum and Dad lived here happily for years and we never got under each other's feet." She bit her lip and he knew she was remembering the happy times when her father was alive. *Lucky her to have such good memories of her childhood.*

Reece wanted to wrap his arms around Ellie, to kiss

the grief away, but he sensed she wanted time to compose herself so walked over to the large window that almost covered the main hall. He looked out at the beach below. It was a beautiful, panoramic view of the harbour and town beach, where sun-bronzed bodies sprawled out on the soft sand, children paddled in the sun-kissed ocean, and, further out, colourful fishing boats bobbled on the rippling waves. The sort of scene you'd find on a holiday postcard.

"Spectacular isn't it." She was standing beside him now. "Wait until you see the view from the kitchen."

It was a surprisingly modern kitchen with light tiles walls, beech fitted cupboards and a beech table and chairs by French doors which opened up onto a balcony. Ellie opened the doors wide and they both stepped outside. This gave them a different view, one from the side of the hotel, over the town below, the cobbled streets, quaint little shops, down to the main beach – which is where Reece presumed they'd be surfing. He could see a few people already out there, riding the white foam waves.

Suddenly he was back to being a teenager holidaying with his father, uncle and cousins in Rock, Cornwall. They went every summer, and were all so competitive, determined to be the best surfer. They had surfing lessons, the best gear. It had been more of a competition than fun but he remembered the exhilaration of riding the waves, of pitching himself against the sea. He'd got so hooked on it he'd got up at the crack of dawn to go surfing early every morning, his thick wet suit protecting him against the icy chill of the Atlantic sea. He'd entered into the Surfing Championships, an event that attracted competitors from all over the world and had tried their hardest to win. He'd never put so much effort into anything in all his life. He'd been no match for the professional surfers though, and hadn't been placed. The disappointment on his father's face had been like a blow to his stomach and he'd vowed there and then never to enter anything unless he was sure he had a good chance of winning. That was the defining moment when he was determined that he was going to be a success, that he was going to achieve something that would make his dad proud of him. He never wanted to see that look of utter disappointment on his father's face again.

He'd never surfed again either, so he hoped he wasn't about to show himself up today. He couldn't believe that he felt so comfortable with Ellie that he was willing to take a chance on messing up.

Chapter Ten

"Wonderful isn't it?"

Reece slid his gaze from the beach to her face and nodded wordlessly.

"Come and see the rest of the flat."

Ellie led him through the lounge and indicated a bedroom on the right. "That's Mum's room. I don't think she'd like me to show you in. She's a very private person." She opened the next door along. "This is the bathroom, although it isn't used much as both bedrooms have an ensuite."

To her surprise, Reece seemed really interested. "It's very spacious," he said. "I didn't expect the private quarters to be this big."

"Yes, it's like a self-contained flat. I've got the attic room, I love it up there." She reached for the handle of the next door. "This is the spare room. You can get changed in here if you want," Ellie opened the door to reveal another large room prettily decorated with floral curtains and matching bedspread on the double bed. "You can get in touch with your feminine side," she said mischievously.

"It's nice," he nodded. "Did you ever sleep in here or have you always been in the attic?"

"I fell in love with the attic right away, wouldn't sleep anywhere else." She grinned. "I was only six when we moved in but very determined, even then."

"I can believe that." He replied. "Do I get to see your attic room if I promise to behave like a gentleman?"

"Sure. I warn you, though, it hasn't altered much since I was a teenager." She led the way to the end of the corridor, opened a door and mounted the stairs.

Reece followed her.

"Take a look at the view," she said, making her way over to the window.

Reece joined her. And whistled as he looked over the rooftops to the beach he and Ellie had frolicked on the other day. "It must be amazing to wake up to that sight every morning."

"It is. Mind you, it's the seagulls that wake you up first. They make such a noise, squawking and pattering over the roof."

Reece's gaze swept around the room. "You know, this place must be worth a tidy sum. If your mum did want to sell she'd do very well out of it. It depends what mortgage she has to pay, of course, but I'm sure she should get more than enough to buy herself a little bungalow."

"She doesn't want to sell. She's determined to stay here and get the hotel back on its feet again." Ellie shrugged. "Maybe in another five years she'll feel like putting her feet up." She turned away from the window. "Now, let's go and get the wetsuits," she said, leading the way downstairs again to the large storage cupboard in the hall. She rummaged through the assortment of wetsuits, booties, gloves and various other surfing apparel left by the many relatives who came to see them in the summer. There was bound to be one to fit Reece. She took out a black and grey wetsuit. "This looks about your size. Turn around."

Reece obliged, standing still as she placed the wetsuit against his shoulders. "Yes, that seems perfect. Do you want to pop into the spare bedroom and try it on? Hang on, take a rash vest too," she handed him a grey vest. "Take a couple of the suits to try if you want. I'll go up to my room and put mine on too. We might as well walk down to the beach in them, it saves trying to wriggle into them when we're there."

"Sounds like a plan to me," he said, taking the wet suit off her and grabbing another one from the pile in the cupboard. "Am I okay to leave my clothes in your spare room until we return?"

"Sure. See you in a few mins." She set off down the corridor to the attic stairs.

Ellie changed into a bikini, pulling on a rash vest then her wetsuit – a turquoise and grey one she'd had since her teens - and tied back her hair. Going into the bathroom she swapped her contacts for dailies then popped saline solution, sun cream and sunglasses, her surf boots and gloves into a beach bag. What else did she need?

"Ready!" Reece called.

"Coming!" Beach towel. She grabbed two out of her wardrobe and shoved them in the bag then headed for the stairs.

Reece was waiting in the hall for her. God, he looked fit in that wetsuit. It showed his muscular shoulders and taut abs off to perfection and as for . . . well she didn't dare look down there. She kept her eyes firmly on his face. "I knew it would fit you."

He made no secret of the fact that he was enjoying the

way the wet suit moulded to her figure.

"Very nice!"

"Thank you. Now let's see if any of the booties and gloves are your size then we'll get the boards out of the garden shed and we're ready to go."

She rummaged through the boots, selected two pairs and handed them to him. "Try these."

The first pair were tight but the second pair fitted just right

"Great." Ellie put both them in the beach bag with her own. "I've got towels in here too. Now let's get the surf boards and we can be off. Medden Beach is the best one for surfing. It's about a ten minute walk. Oh, hang on, water!"

She grabbed two bottles of water out of the fridge and popped them into her beach bag. Then she led the way out the back entrance and, taking a surfboard each from the shed and tucking them under their arms, they walked downhill to the beach and found a quiet spot to put their things.

"Right, let's go catch those waves!" Ellie said excitedly, grabbing her board.

She walked her board until she was waist deep in water then lay on it. Reece was already ahead, riding his. He'd quickly got to his feet on the board, his weight centred in the middle, ready to ride the wave. He jumped straight in, just as she thought he would, whereas she preferred to paddle the waves for a while, building up her awareness of the sea before standing and riding them.

Soon she was lost in the exhilaration of riding the breaking waves to the shore. She glanced at Reece now and again and could see that he was enjoying himself too.

After a while she saw him paddle out to beach, flop down on the sand and reach in the beach bag for a bottle of water. She remained in the sea for a little longer, riding a few more waves, then padded out to join him.

"Can't keep up the pace, eh?" she said, holding out her hand as he passed her the other bottle of water he'd taken out of the bag when he saw her walking towards him."I told you it's been a few years since I surfed. I'm a bit rusty." Reece glanced at Ellie and she could see the admiration in his eyes. "You're pretty good. Did you ever enter any of the surfing competitions?"

She gulped down the water then shook her head. "No, I like to do things for fun. I'm not interested in being competitive." She gazed out at the sea. "You know. I love it down here. Maybe it wouldn't be such a big sacrifice to move back after all."

Besides her, Reece gazed silently out to sea. "I know what you mean," he said slowly. "I could be tempted to join you."

Did he mean that? Ellie gazed out at the sea, thinking about Reece's words, imaging them both living in Cornwall, maybe helping Mum run Gwel Teg.

"Penny for them?"

Reece's voice startled Ellie out of her thoughts. What was the matter with her? Going all gooey over stuff like that? She flashed him a smile. "I was just remembering the hours I spent down here with my mates when I was a teenager."

"I bet you were the local beach babe." He leaned over and kissed her, making her heart skip a beat. "Come on then, my stomach's starting to growl."

"Mine too. Will you join me for dinner again, on the house, as a thank you for your help with the Smythes?"

He grinned. "I'd be delighted to."

Kate telephoned Ellie later to ask how things were going. She was really sympathetic when Ellie briefly related the events of yesterday.

"Sorry you're having such a tough time, hun. Reece sounds a keeper though.' Kate replied.

That surprised Ellie. Reece? *A keeper?* No way. She didn't do serious and Kate knew it. Besides, they'd only just met and would soon be saying goodbye.

"He's a hottie, but not for me," she retorted.

"Well he's certainly pulling out all the stops to help you. Sounds like he fancies you big time."

"Of course he doesn't. He's just being helpful."

"So he's not made any moves?"

"Well…"

"I knew it!" Kate squealed down the phone.

"We did kiss on the beach. And we went surfing together this afternoon. Actually, we're dating." She confessed. "But it's just a holiday romance."

"Then why is he being so helpful?"

That was the big question. And one that Ellie thought about a lot when she'd finally finished taking to Kate.

Why was Reece helping her so much?

"That was a delicious meal." Reece pushed back his plate and rubbed his stomach appreciatively. "Your chef is excellent. Has he worked for you for long?"

"Five years. Marcus only lives a few streets away and fortunately is happy to come over in the evening and cook meals for whatever guests are staying at the hotel." Ellie paused, remembering how her parents had once provided meals at lunchtime too but since her father had died this had been cut to evenings only. At first Mum had worried this would mean she'd lose Marcus all together, but he was more than happy with the new arrangements as this gave him all day to spend on his artwork. "He's an artist. He painted the *Ships in the Storm* picture in the lounge and a few of the local cafes have some of his paintings for sale. He's starting to get quite a reputation now."

"I noticed that painting, it's very impressive. I can almost feel the waves lashing against the ship when I look at it."

"Yes, lots of the guests admire it." Actually that might be something to add to the website. Guests liked to read about personal stuff too. Perhaps she could have a photo of Marcus standing by the picture? She could even give a link to his website. It would be nice to get him some more sales. She stood up. "Would you like a coffee to finish off the meal?"

"Thank you that would be lovely. A white Americano, please."

When she returned with coffee and cheese and biscuits, Reece was sitting, head bent, occupied with his mobile phone. "Sorry, I had to attend to an urgent email," he said as she joined him. He closed down the screen and slipped the phone into his pocket. "Now, I'm all yours."

"Hey, don't apologise for using your phone, you're a guest here. It's very kind of you to help us out as much as you have. I realise that you've got other things to do and certainly don't expect you to give me your undivided attention." She sat down. Look, we've taken advantage of you enough. I don't want you to feel that you have to help out all the time." She raised her eyes to his then wished she hadn't because as his grey eyes gazed at her, Ellie felt a shiver tingle through her. She couldn't move, couldn't even tear her eyes away, she was lost in the feelings his gaze aroused in her.

She dragged her eyes away and raised the coffee cup to her mouth, slowly sipping the hot liquid. She had to get a grip. She couldn't go all ga-ga over Reece like a love-struck teenager just because his kisses were – well, *so damn sexy.*

"I don't mind helping, I've told you." He picked up one of the cheese and biscuits and nibbled it. "Have you thought any more about what your mother will do when you have to go home? Is there no way she can afford extra help?"

"No. Not even for a couple of hours a day." She risked meeting his eyes again. "I'll see how she is. If she's still weak then I'll take a bit longer off work. If the worst comes to the worst I'll have to give up my job and flat and move back in with Mum until she's well enough to cope by herself." It wasn't something she wanted to do but her mum's health came first.

"Is that wise? You've a good job and you're independent. You said yourself that you couldn't wait to get out of this little town and live in the big city. It would probably be very difficult for you to adjust and what would you live on? If the hotel is struggling as much as you say would there be enough money to keep two of you."

She had thought of that already. "I'll be saving on rent and might be able to do some freelancing PR work, set myself up as a consultant. Once we've built up the hotel again so we can afford help I can go back to the Midlands if I want. I think Martin might even give me a sabbatical from work for six months or so." She knew a couple of other people in the company who had done this. She'd be dropping Kate in the lurch though if she moved out of the flat, she'd struggle to pay all the rent by herself.

"Surely there's no rush to make such a major decision. Your mother might not want you to live here. Why not go home as planned next week and wait a month or two to see how she copes before you give up your life."

He was right. It was a big decision and she shouldn't rush it.

"Have you thought that your Mum might want to take it easy for bit? Selling up might be the best solution if she does find the hotel too much for her. It's a nice location, you should get a good price for it. And I know you said that she wouldn't be able to afford somewhere in Cornwall but have you actually looked into that? Some of the apartments are very reasonable."

It might be the best solution but she couldn't see Mum agreeing to it. "I suggested it when Dad died. Mum refused point blank. She said this was her home and she was staying right here until she was carried out. I reckon she still feels the same way. She can't wait to get out of hospital." She grinned ruefully. "She can be quite stubborn."

His eyes twinkled. "I can see where you get it from."

She sighed. "You don't know what a relief it is to have someone to talk to about this. It's so kind of you to take the time. There must be other stuff you should be doing."

He reached for her hand and squeezed it gently. A light, barely there touch but it sent her blood pressure racing.

"Nothing else I want to do. I like you. And I admire the way you look out for your mum."

His unwavering gaze held a zillion unsaid words. She swallowed. Licked her lips. Fought to control her racing heart.

It was crazy. Why did he have such an effect on her? Did he feel the same?

Was Kate right, is that why he was being so helpful?

Chapter Eleven

What was it about Ellie that got under his skin so much? Reece pondered as he walked along the empty beach. When she'd left him saying she had to do some paperwork before going to bed, he'd wanted to go after her, ask her to come for a moonlight walk with him. But alcohol, moonlight and Ellie would have been too risky. So he'd gone for the walk alone.

He was returning to London at the end of the week, and Ellie was going home the following weekend. He'd thought that perhaps they could have a pleasant dalliance for a few days, maybe spend a couple of nights together. They were both adults, and it was obvious the attraction he felt for Ellie was mutual, so why not have a bit of fun before they said goodbye. But when he'd sat opposite her tonight he hadn't wanted to say goodbye. And all the time he was telling her not to give up her life and move down to Cornwall he'd been thinking how he didn't want her to go out of his life, to disappear without a trace.

It was crazy. The sooner he got this deal tied up and went back to London the better.

He stood and watched the moonlight shining on the sea for a while, casting shadows everywhere. It was so calm and still, soothing almost. He'd loved going to the seaside when he was a lad, when his mum had still been living with them. Before she'd walked out and left him, a distraught ten year old living with his strict, emotionally distant father, taking all the love and laughter with her.

"I guess we both had the same idea."

He turned at the sound of Ellie's voice, surprised to see her standing barefoot in front of him, looking almost ethereal, her sandals dangling by the straps from her left hand.

"Finished your paperwork then?"

"Yes, for tonight anyway." She turned to face the ocean, her face silhouetted in the moonlight. "I always used to come here before I went to bed. I loved the stillness of the sea at night, it's so peaceful. It helps get things in perspective, don't you think? Makes you realise that you're just a cog in the wheel of a huge universe which will carry on long after you've gone."

He whistled. "That's deep."

"Oh I can be sometimes." Her voice was soft, hushed and he wondered if she was thinking about her father. Like he'd being thinking about his mother. If she had, he guessed her thoughts were a lot happier than his had been. "Fancy going for a paddle?"

She put her sandals down onto the sand and almost skipped over to the sea.

"Watch you don't get your clothes wet again," he shouted as she stepped into the water. An image of her long, wet skirt clinging to her legs flashed across his mind. *Down boy.*

"I won't. I'm not going in far." She paddled along the edge, stopping now and again to let the water lap over her feet. Then she stood still and looked up at the full moon, beaming down onto the still, indigo water, making the surface shimmer and glow.

She glanced over her shoulder then smiled. "You coming in?"

"Can't leave you to paddle alone at night." He slipped off his sandals and rolled up the legs of his trousers, wondering what his business colleagues would think if they saw him now.

Suspecting that the water was cold he braced himself, then stepped in. It was cool but not unpleasant. He stood still as the sea lapped over his feet, feeling himself relax. Out here like this, on the deserted beach, with the ocean spreading for miles in front of them it seemed like there was just the two of them in the world. He felt all his cares and worries flitter away if only for that moment. He no longer felt driven by success, for the desire for his parents to look up to him, to be proud of him, that had almost consumed him since his childhood. None of that mattered. All that mattered was the here and now. Him and Ellie paddling in the sea at midnight. He had never felt so comfortable, so at one with someone in all his life.

"Isn't it wonderful?" As Ellie turned to him he noticed that they were standing directly under the moon, surrounded in its beam. Like two lovers alone in the universe.

Without even realising what he was going to do, he reached out and wound his arms around her waist, pulling her to him. "Not as wonderful as you," he whispered. Then he kissed her like he'd never kissed anyone else before. And she was returning the kiss with the same fervour. Their bodies melted into each other, entwining as their kiss got deeper and deeper until Reece was sure that he wouldn't be able to stop himself from lowering Ellie onto the sand and making love to her under the stars.

Almost in a dream, Ellie felt Reece's lips on hers, gently first then deeper, his hands were around her waist, pulling her towards him, then his right hand moved up her body and caressed the back of her neck, his fingers were running through her hair, gently pulling her head closer. She closed her eyes, losing herself in the passion of the moment, her heart thudding so loud that she was sure he could feel it against his chest.

She was lost in the feel of him, the potent smell of male mixed with tangy aftershave, the electrifying tingle of his touch, the taste of his lips on hers, the sound of him breathing deeply as he pulled her every bit closer until it seemed that they were not two bodies but one. She could feel the hardness of his body, knew that he was aroused and was filled with an overwhelming desire to free herself, and him, of the clothes that formed a barrier between them and let their passion take its course.

"Ellie." It was the way he said it, a deep, guttural, almost primeval groan that brought her to her senses. God, what was she thinking of? Making out on the beach like this? She quickly pulled herself away, her breath coming out in shallow gasps as she put a safe distance between them. He reached out to pull her back but she slipped out of his grasp. "Whoops…getting a bit carried away there," she said as lightly as she could.

For a moment Reece seemed stunned then he gave her a wry grin. "Sorry, I didn't mean to do that. You looked so damn sexy standing in the moonlight that I just couldn't resist you."

Nor me you. She didn't voice the words. She didn't need to. She'd already made it crystal clear that she desired him as much as he desired her. She might as well have written 'I want to go to bed with you' in ten foot tall letters.

They looked at each awkwardly for a moment, then Ellie mumbled "I'd better be going back." She forced herself to turn away, paddle over to the shore, stoop down and pick up her sandals without looking back at him, although every nerve in her body ached to.

"I'll see you in the morning."

She ran off like Cinderella at the Ball at midnight, leaving Reece on the beach, staring after her. He probably thought she was nuts. Well he'd be right. She was. She was nuts about him and she didn't like it one little bit.

She hadn't felt this way since Lee.

She'd been smitten as soon as Lee walked into the classroom when she was in year ten at Smireton High, all big blue eyes and tousled sandy hair. She'd followed him about doe-eyed for months, treasuring every word or scrap of a smile he'd cared to throw her way, cried herself to sleep for weeks when he'd started dating Lily Graham instead and then walked on air when he finally asked her out. They'd been inseparable for the next few years. Lee was the love of her life and she'd been sure she was the love of his too. She'd imagined them getting married, having kids someday, growing old together. Then she'd found out that the love of Lee's life was Ellie's best friend Zoe and they'd both been cheating on her for ages.

Although she'd never been short of a date if she wanted one, Ellie hadn't given her heart to anyone since Lee and she didn't intend to. That way she got all the fun and none of the heartache. Love was overrated.

That's why she'd agreed to date Reece. He fancied her and she fancied him so it made sense to hang out together, have a few laughs. He was only here for another week so therse was no way they would get too involved.

But now she wondered if it had been a wise decision. She had a feeling that if she spent too much time with Reece she was going to find it very difficult to walk away.

Reece was on Ellie's mind so much that night she found it difficult to sleep. Images of the way he'd kissed her filled her dreams. It was as if her body had been expecting it, waiting for it, and she'd returned the kiss with passion. She wanted him, she acknowledged, more than she'd ever wanted anyone in her life. Even Lee. And that scared her.

Ellie finally gave up trying to sleep at 6 am and decided to get up. There was so much to do. The first thing on her list was to spruce up the foyer. First impressions were important so she wanted to make it look clean, bright and welcoming as soon as guests stepped into the hotel. She had a shower, dressed in a pair of distressed denims and a yellow tee shirt and went into the kitchen to make herself a cup of coffee. She'd have breakfast later. She sat at the kitchen table, slowly sipping her coffee and thinking about Reece. Part of her – a big part – was eager to see him, but another part of her wanted to avoid it. She felt embarrassed at how she'd ran off yesterday. Anyone would think she'd never made out with a guy before.

Finishing her coffee, she went downstairs, collected the cleaning material she needed, popped them into a carry basket and walked through into the foyer, wanting to get as much done as she could before any of the guests came down. She started by taking down the curtains and putting them in the washing machine then took out a spray cleaner and cloth to do the inside of the windows. The outside didn't look too bad so it seemed as if Mum hadn't got rid of the window cleaner completely. She sprayed on the glass cleaner then started to wipe it off with the cloth.

"Need a hand with that?"

Reece. Already her skin was tinglingly aware of the nearness of him and she tried to shut out the image of their almost-arrestable embrace last night.

Keep calm.

She glanced over her shoulder. "Thank you but it won't take me long."

"You're up and about early. Didn't you sleep well?"

No I was thinking of you all night.

Ellie carefully finished wiping the window then turned around. Reece looked enticingly fit in black shorts and a tight white vest. "Not really. There's so much to do here before Mum comes home. I thought if I got up early I could make a start."

"Want any help?" He wrapped his arms around her waist and kissed her on the cheek. She forced herself not to melt against him and bury her head into his chest. *Play it cool!*

"I wouldn't say no if you're sure you've got time." She pulled herself out of his arms, bent down and took another cloth out of the box. "How about you do the doors and I'll do the windows."

"Sure." Reece picked up the glass cleaner spray and walked over to the double glass doors.

Ellie sneaked a glance over now and again to watch Reece stretching up to clean the top of the door, his muscles rippling. An image of his naked body walking out of the bathroom flashed across her mind. Yep, okay face it Ellie you really have the hots for him.

"Time for a break," she said when the windows and doors were gleaming. "Fancy a coffee?"

"Sure," he wiped his hand across his forehead. "Those doors were a bit grimy."

"I know. Mum did have a regular window cleaner but it seems like he's only cleaning the outside of the windows now. That must be another of her money saving cut backs." She put the cloths and glass cleaner back in the basket. "Come through in the staff kitchen."

She picked up the basket and led the way into the kitchen, indicating the small wooden table. "Take a seat. Do you want some toast too? I haven't had breakfast yet."

"Please, I haven't eaten either." Reece covered the kitchen in two strides, picked up the kettle and filled it up with water then switched it on. "I'll make the coffee, you make the toast."

Ellie took two mugs out of an overhead cupboard and handed them to him. "White, one sugar please."

Reece had already spotted the pots containing coffee and sugar, and picked up a spoon from the draining rack. "Got it."

"One slice of toast or two?" Ellie took a sliced loaf out of the bread bin.

"Two please, cleaning windows has given me an appetite."

She was so acutely aware of him. It was as if every nerve in her body was screaming for him to touch her. She chatted away, trying to hide her discomfort. Make that babbling not chatting. She talked about the weather, the seagulls being so noisy, how she loved the view from her window and all the time wondering if he was going to make another move on her or if she'd put him off running away like that last night.

Reece answered back in the same light, friendly manner as they sat down at the table, ate the toast, sipped their coffees but she could feel his dark eyes on her and sensed the sexual undercurrent. Finally, he put his cup down and placed his hand on hers. "Did I step over the line last night? You left fairly quickly." His eyes met hers. "Do you want to keep it platonic?"

"No, it's not that." *That's right, Ellie, let him know that you do want to go to bed with him.* "I mean ..." She hesitated looking for the right words. "We were on the beach."

"So it was the location that put you off - not that you don't fancy me?" he asked softly, his finger lightly tracing the back of her hand.

"Well, I wasn't expecting things to move so fast."

"Me neither. Do you want to slow it down?"

She couldn't think straight with his finger tracing around her wrist like that, "Er…no," she stammered.

"Good. Neither do I." he leaned over and held her face in his hands then kissed her gently on the lips. Then deeper. And deeper.

Chapter Twelve

"I knew it! I knew there was something going on with you two!" Mandy almost squealed in delight as she stood in the doorway.

Reece released Ellie and grinned at Mandy. "There wasn't," he said. "But there is now." He kissed Ellie on the forehead. "See you later, Ellie."

"I knew he had the hots for you. That's why he's been so helpful," Mandy said as soon as Reece had left the kitchen. "Oh, you make a *lovely* couple."

"Don't get too carried away, Mandy. We've agreed to date, see how we get on, that's all." Mandy was such a romantic, she'd be ordering a hat for the wedding given half a chance.

"You're right for each other. I can sense these things." Mandy touched the side of her nose. "I've got the gift you know, lovey."

Ellie was well aware of Mandy's 'gift', the inner-sense that she believed guided her. According to Mandy, her gift had warned her to not go on a bus that subsequently crashed, that her husband was the man for her the very first time she saw him, and that she'd be happy working at Gwel Teg as soon as she walked into it. She was quite a character and both Ellie and her mother were very fond of her. Although Dad had often pooh-hooed her as airy-fairy she knew that he'd been fond of her too.

"Anyway, lovey." Mandy sat down in the chair Reece had just vacated. "I've had a brilliant idea." She leaned forward and patted Ellie's hand. "You know how we need extra staff at the hotel, especially with Sue having to take things easy for a while?"

Ellie had been worrying about that. It could take Mum a few weeks to feel strong enough to work full time again and if the newly updated website and Facebook page did bring in more bookings she might struggle to cope. Perhaps she should have waited until her mother was stronger before embarking on a Social Media campaign. "We can't afford extra staff though,

Mandy," she pointed out.

"I know, lovey. But I've had an idea that might help. My niece Sara is looking for somewhere to do a week's work experience in a couple of weeks. So how about she does it here? She's a bright girl and a hard worker. It wouldn't cost you anything and would give her valuable experience. She wants to work in the hotel trade. She could help out on Reception perhaps, or in the dining room, serving the meals?"

"That's a fantastic idea. It will give Mum extra help when I go back home. Thanks, Mandy." Ellie said, relieved. She didn't feel so bad about going back home if her mother had someone else to help her, even if it was only for a week. If Sara was good at her job and things did pick up perhaps they could even arrange for her to work a few paid shifts. That would certainly help.

"Morning, dear." Mrs Smythe waved, stepping out of the lift, closely followed by her husband who was pulling the new suitcase Reece had provided. "We're off now. We've had a lovely time."

"I'm glad to hear it," Ellie smiled as she walked over to them. "I hope you've been comfortable in the Silver Room."

"Very comfortable, dear," said Mrs Smythe happily, "Aren't we, Tony?" She turned to her husband who nodded in agreement. "We want to thank you for making our stay so wonderful. The meal last night was delicious and flowers and champagne were a lovely touch. I've had to leave the flowers behind, of course. Perhaps you can put them in another room – or in here."

"I will. "Ellie told her. "I'm just so sorry that you had to change rooms."

"Think nothing of it," Mr Smythe told her. "These things happened. You couldn't have done any more to make amends."

Thanks to Reece.

"And how is your mother?" Mr Smythe asked.

"She's much better, thank you. She'll be home in a day or two."

"That's good. She's lucky to have a daughter like you," he smiled.

"Goodbye, dear." They both gave a little wave and walked off arm in arm.

"Goodbye, safe journey," Ellie called. What a lovely couple, yet it could have all gone so drastically wrong.

"We're lucky that Mr Mitchell decided to stay on a bit longer, he's saved the situation there," Mandy remarked.

"He certainly did." Ellie agreed. "If Mum could afford a manager I'd tell her to hire him."

Mandy looked surprised. "Is that what you think he is? A manager?"

"Don't you?" Ellie looked at her curiously. "He's got good people skills and is obviously used to taking charge."

"Sure but did you see that suit he was wearing the day he arrived? That was designer. And he drives a Mercedes."

So he did. She'd completely forgotten, even though it was parked out in the hotel carpark.

"I reckon he's got a much more important position than manager," Mandy said. "More like a director."

She could be right, Ellie realised. Reece hadn't actually said what his work was. Not that it mattered. "I'm going to hunt out the spare curtains and cushion covers now. Are you okay to cover reception whilst I do that?"

"I'll help you, lovey. It's all quiet here," Mandy told her. "Two pair of hands can get more done than one. And I'll be able to hear the phone from here."

"Hang on, I must phone the insurance first," Ellie said, remembering that she'd intended to do that first thing.

Luckily the insurance advisor was very helpful and when Ellie explained about her mum being ill in hospital she agreed to accept Ellie's authority to renew the insurance providing she paid a deposit up front and her mother phoned to confirm as soon as she was well enough. Ellie gave her debit card number and paid two months in advance. That would give her mum time to get straight, she hoped. In any case, she'd check with her that she could afford the payments and if not have them taken out of her own bank account until she could.

They spent the next couple of hours hanging curtains, polishing, cutting fresh flowers and polishing the bookcases and furniture in the reception. The phone didn't ring at all which Ellie wasn't sure was a good thing or not. It was good to have the time to clear up but they needed more guests.

"That looks *much* better," she said when they'd finished. "Let's have a coffee break then we could do the lounge. If you don't mind?" Mandy was employed as a receptionist, not a cleaner.

"Happy to help, lovey. But yes I could murder a cuppa first. Want me to make it?"

"No I'll do it. Come into the kitchen and sit down for a minute. If anyone needs assistance they'll ring the bell."

Who'd have thought he'd spend the morning cleaning windows, Reece thought as he changed into a suit ready for his meeting with Steve. Ellie was so 'can do' that he found himself helping her without stopping to think about it. She didn't seem at all suspicious about why he was willing to go so much out of his way to help a run-down family hotel. Her trust in him made him feel a little uneasy about the part he was playing.

You're helping them out, the hotel is too much for her mother to run alone and why should Ellie give up her life and career to help her? He reminded himself. And if the repairs are done the hotel will attract more guests so be a better investment.

Even so it felt a bit deceitful knowing that he hadn't been totally up front. That he had an ulterior motive for helping her.

There was one thing he wasn't being deceitful about though, and that was his attraction to Ellie. She was really getting under his skin. None of the other women he'd been with before had ever had the effect on him that she did. He was glad he was going home on Saturday. That way he could enjoy Ellie's company without worrying that she wanted to get too involved, which in his experience women often did.

Reece had no doubt that Mrs Truman would agree to the deal. She had nothing to lose and everything to gain. There was no way she could put in the necessary funds to bring the hotel up to date. He and Harry had already done a few of the outstanding repairs but to be honest the hotel needed a complete overhaul. The whole décor was dated, wallpaper in many of the rooms was faded or ripped, the plumbing was rackety, and the place needed rewiring.

It was a quaint hotel though, centuries old, and the location was ideal. Overlooking one of the smaller, more private beaches it offered a hint of seclusion and privacy. He could turn it into a five star sought-after boutique hotel in six months, he was sure of that. Yes, it would cost a lot of money but he was confident that money would be recuperated within two years, maximum. It was what he was good at, rescuing ailing hotels, and this was one hotel he was determined to rescue.

Chapter Thirteen

"I'm going to tackle the lounge now. What do you think of these curtains? Ellie held out a pair of pale blue jacquard curtains. "There's cushion covers to match too."

"Perfect," Mandy approved. "Let me give you a hand with them."

They gathered up two sets of the curtains and the matching covers and carried them out into foyer. A woman was standing at the reception desk about to press the bell. Although she had her back to them, Ellie recognised her instantly. There was no mistaking the sleek curtain of long dark hair and jumble of multi-

139

coloured bracelets dangling around her slender wrists. "Abiya!" She squealed in delight.

Abiya turned, her face breaking into a wide smile, revealing the dazzling white teeth that Ellie had always envied so much.

"Ellie! I was visiting my folks and heard about your mother being taken to hospital so I came to see how she was. I thought you'd be here. I knew you'd be straight down to look after her. You and your parents were always so close."

The two girls hugged, the five years since they'd last met melting away. "How are you?" Abiya stepped back. "You haven't changed a bit – except you look so tired."

"I am a bit. There's been a lot going on here."

"Your mother has been very ill, Ellie?" asked Abiya.

Ellie quickly filled her in. "I should have come down more often, checked on her."

"You mustn't blame yourself. Life is busy, days fly by." Abiya gave her a hug. "It is so good to see you. We have so much to catch up on."

Ellie longed to sit and chat to Abiya and catch up on her news. They'd always been such good friends but she couldn't leave the lounge like this. She had to finish tidying up first.

"Are you here for long, Abi?" she asked, reverting back to the name her friend was always known by. "Can we catch up later? I'm dying to hear all your gossip but as you can see – she pointed to the pile of folded cushion covers and curtains. "I'm in middle of sprucing up the lounge."

"Then I will help you. We will hang curtains and talk at the same time. No?"

Ellie felt her spirits lift already. It was so lovely to see Abi again. She was her oldest friend – apart from Zoe. The three of them had gone around together since their first day at the local school. The TT's they'd been called. The Terrible Triplets. Then Zoe had smashed their bond. Ellie had left then Abi a year later, going to live in London to follow her dream of working on a fashion mag. Ellie and Abi had kept in contact at first via text and email, promising to meet up one weekend when they both visited their folks in Cornwall but they had never managed it, and eventually their contact fizzled out as they were both so busy with their work and new lives

"I'll leave you both to it and check the menus for tonight, then pop to see your mum," Mandy told her. They'd already discussed that Mandy would visit this afternoon and Ellie that evening. She handed her pile of curtains and cushion covers to Abiya. "Have fun!"

"I guess you're down visiting your folks?" Ellie asked as she and Abiya made their way to the lounge.

"Yes. Deepa is getting married soon. Can you believe

that? My baby brother is going to take a bride."

The last time Ellie had seen Deepa he was a serious teenager, intent on getting good grades to get into university.

"Wow! That's amazing. Did he get to uni? Who's he marrying?"

"Yes he did, he studied architecture. He met his fiancée Saanvi there. They are having a traditional Indian wedding in August. You must come! Bring your man."

"I'd love to come." She ignored the bit about bringing her man and cast a questioning glance at her friend. "What about you, Abi? Are you married?"

Abi shook her head. "No, to the eternal dismay of my mother. I am living with someone though, Milo, and we will marry one day. Just not yet. What about you?"

"Not married. Not living with anyone. Footloose and fancy free, that's me."

Abi's eyes rested on hers. "Is this because of Lee? I know he broke your heart but don't let him make you bitter."

Ellie felt her cheeks flush. "I'm not bitter. Yes Lee – and Zoe – hurt me but it was a long time ago. I've had lots of boyfriends since then."

"But none that have taken your heart?"

"Nope. And I intend to keep it that way."

The girls chatted happily as they hung up the clean curtains and replaced the cushion covers, then polished and dusted.

"Hey, you've done a good job here."

Ellie spun around at the sound of Reece's voice.

He was standing behind them, looking good enough to drag to bed, dressed in a pair of faded jeans and a paint-splattered grey tee shirt.

"Do you think so?" Ellie let her eyes linger down onto his tee shirt and smiled. "It looks like you've been painting?"

"Helping Harry spruce up a couple of doors." He looked over at Abi. "Good to see you've got extra help."

"This is Abi, a good friend of mine – we haven't seen each other for years but she was down visiting her folks, heard about Mum and dropped in to see how she was." She turned to Abi. "Abi, this is Reece Mitchell, a guest here. Although by the way he's been mucking in and helping out you'd think he was one of the staff!"

"Glad to help. See you a bit later. I'm going to make sure the ceiling is dry enough for the plasterer tomorrow," Reece leant over and gave her a quick peck on the cheek then was gone. Leaving Ellie's senses reeling.

"More than a guest I think," Abi murmured, her dark eyes curious.

"Well, we've got a bit close but I've only known him a few days," Ellie told her.

"He's divine. And he likes you very much. I think you like him very much too. No? Perhaps you can bring him to Deepa's wedding."

"I told you I've only just met him."

"Ellie…"

The seriousness in Abiya's tone surprised her. "What?"

"What Lee and Zoe did was a bad thing but don't let it stop you from falling in love again. Being in love, it's a wonderful feeling. My life would be so empty without Milo. Don't let Lee and Zoe ruin that for you."

"I was over Lee a long time ago and I'm so pleased you're happy with Milo. But I don't want a partner. I like being free and having fun. Reece is going home next week. We're just having a bit of a holiday romance. No strings attached." She linked her arm with Abi's. "Now let's go and have a cup of coffee before you disappear on me again. I want to hear all about your job. And Milo of course."

Abi left an hour later. She was driving back to London that evening but they promised each other they'd stay in touch. "We'll meet again at the wedding, yes?" Abi asked as she hugged Ellie farewell. "We will send you an invite. For you and Reece," she added mischievously.

"Looking forward to it," Ellie told her, ignoring Abi's teasing. She'd been to a family wedding with Abi before and it had been a colourful, luxurious affair.

Time for snack, Ellie thought, going into the kitchen. She made herself a cheese and tomato sandwich and had just popped the last bite in her mouth when her phone started to ring, a band of worry coiled itself around her stomach when she saw that the caller was Mandy. She'd be at the hospital now, was something wrong with mum?

Ellie slid her finger across the screen to answer the call. "Mandy. Is Mum all right? Has she had a relapse?" Her words tumbled out.

"She's fine, lovey. Lots better. That's why I'm phoning you. The nurse said she can come home tomorrow so can you take some clothes for her when you visit tonight. That's great news, isn't it?"

Ellie could hear the smile in the other woman's voice. "It wonderful news, Mandy. I bet Mum's over the moon." She paused. "You didn't tell her about the room flooding out, did you? I haven't mentioned it because I don't want to worry her."

"Of course not. I thought I'd leave you to tell her when she comes home. Then she can see that you've got it all in hand and not worry so much."

"Great. Thank you, Mandy."

Mum was coming home. Ellie felt a mix of relief and panic. Relief that her mum was getting better but panic at the thought of having to tell her about the flood damage.

"What's causing the frown?"

Ellie jumped as Reece bent over and kissed her gently on the forehead. She hadn't heard him come in. "Has your friend gone?" He stood behind her, wrapping his arms loosely around her.

"Yes she only came down for the weekend."

She leaned back and nestled into him, comforted by his presence. "Mandy phoned to say that Mum will be out tomorrow."

"That's a good thing, isn't it?"

"Yes, but I'm worried she'll have a setback when she learns about the flood – and how much it's going to cost. …" her voice trailed off.

Reece wrapped his arms tighter around her. She could feel his breath on her neck, smell the tang of his aftershave. "Look, you can't take all this on yourself. You've helped as much as you can. The leak's been repaired and the ceiling is dry enough to be re-plastered tomorrow morning. And you've stopped the Smythes from suing for compensation."

"You did that," Ellie pointed out, leaning back into him so that her head rested on his shoulder.

"You've done all you can, Ellie. The foyer and lounge look great, and most of the odd jobs have been done. We'll finish the rest tomorrow before your Mum comes home." Reece added, trailing kisses down her neck and sending tremors coursing through her body.

"Talking about the odd jobs, I need to settle with you for those."

"No you don't. We had the materials we needed here."

"And what about your time?"

He turned her around, his mouth just inches from hers. "I'll accept dinner as payment."

"I can't..." she started to say but his lips found hers and silenced her.

He wrapped his arm around the back of her neck, pulling her closer to him. So close their bodies were almost as one. She ran her hands up his back, feeling the contours of his body underneath his tee shirt. He groaned and she felt his arm slip down to her waist, his fingers slide under her top. She gasped as they found her bare flesh and stroked it slowly, feather-light kisses that burned her skin, stroking the flame of desire. By the feel of his body pressing against hers he was filled with the same longing.

"Ellie," he murmured as his hand snaked around to her stomach then up towards her breasts.

"TRRIIING!" Damn what a time for her mobile to ring.

"Ignore it," he muttered thickly.

"TRIING!"

What if it was the hospital about Mum? She pulled away, reached for her phone and slid her finger across the screen. "Hello?"

"Sorry to disturb you Miss Truman but no one is on reception and there's a couple here who want to book in," Henry said.

"I'll be right there." She switched off the call and looked ruefully at Reece. "Sorry but we've got guests. I need to go to Reception."

He cupped her chin with one hand and traced her lips with the fingers of the other. "We'll have to continue this later." His voice was thick with promise. "Meet you at eight for dinner?"

She nodded. Adjusting her tee shirt, she hurried over to the door. She didn't want to keep the guests waiting.

The guests were a young couple who wanted to book in for a few days.

"Could we have a sea view?" the woman asked. "I love being able to wake, open the curtains and look at the sea."

"Yes, we have one free," Ellie told her. They had a few free actually, but no need to tell them that. "The sea view rooms are all at the back of the hotel, and are very quiet. They're slightly more expensive though." She told them the price.

"That's fine. I don't suppose it has a balcony?"

Ellie glanced at the computer screen. "We do have a room with a balcony but again it's slightly more expensive."

"We'll take it," the woman said when Ellie named the price. She handed over a card for payment.

Brilliant. Unexpected guests and they've taken one of the more expensive rooms, maybe things were looking up, Ellie thought as Harry put the couple's suitcases on the trolley and led them to the lift.

Her mind wandered back to the hot embrace with Reece, and his promise to take up where they left off later. She felt her skin glow in anticipation. Yes, things definitely were looking up.

"How was your mother?" Reece asked after they'd finished their meal and were sipping Irish coffees.

"She's looking a lot better but I wish the cough would go," Ellie told him. "It's really knocking her about."

"We'll have to make sure she takes it easy." Reece sipped his coffee. "Do you know what time she'll be home?"

"She has to wait and see the doctor first so about two."

"At least the plasterer will be gone by then. And I'm free in the morning so can help you with any other jobs that need doing."

"Are you sure? It's really nice of you but are you sure you don't have anything else to do? You said you were down here on business?" She felt guilty at Reece doing so much for them. "What exactly is your job? You said you work for a hotel group and you have lots of meetings to go to, so are you some kind of consultant?"

"You could say that. I guess you could say I help struggling hotels get back on their feet again."

"Which is sort of what you've been doing here."

Ellie reached over and touched his hand resting on the table. "Thank you. I really appreciate it."

His eyes held hers for a moment and she felt the stirrings of desire fluttering in the pit of her stomach once again. "How about we have a stroll around? Have a drink in one of the other bars?"

"I'd like that. It's about time I showed you a bit of Port Medden. I bet you haven't had time to look around much, have you?"

"Nope, so would you like to give me a guided tour?"

"I'll go and grab a jacket, it can go a bit chilly in the evening. I'll only be a few minutes."

"Take as long as you need. I'll wait outside."

She did more than grab a jacket, she brushed her hair, put on a spray of perfume, renewed her lipstick then studied her reflection in the mirror. She looked tired, she acknowledged – and no wonder, she'd been working hard the last few days – but there was a glow to her eyes and a flush to her cheeks. All due to Reece. He made her feel alive. She hadn't felt this way since Lee.

Lee was history. Maybe Abi was right and it was time she let go of her hurt and mistrust. Time she gave love a chance again.

Chapter Fourteen

"Where would you like to go first?" she asked as she joined Reece outside.

"How about showing me your childhood haunts. How old did you say you were when you moved here?" he asked, slipping his hand in hers.

"Six." She remembered how excited she'd been to move from the city to this quaint seaside town. To live in a hotel right by the beach. And she'd loved it here. She'd settled in easily and soon made friends. Abiya and Zoe had come over to her the very first day at school, invited her to play with them and they'd been inseparable ever since. "Okay, we'll start with the school. It's just a few minutes' walk but I'm afraid it's uphill all the way."

They walked up the hill, chatting easily, comfortable in each other's company, until the blue railings of the primary school came into view. Strange how big the school looked when she was a pupil there but now it looked so tiny. "This is it."

"A typical village school. You were lucky to go there instead of a big city school," Reece told her.

"Did you got to a city school?" she asked.

"No I went to boarding school." Something about the clipped way he said it made her think that his school days weren't happy. She would have hated to be sent away to school. She was lucky to have grown up in a happy home. Her mother had told her how they had been trying for a child for years so had been ecstatic when she was born. "We would have liked a brother or sister for you but it wasn't to be," she'd said. Ellie would have liked a sibling but she hadn't been lonely. She'd had friends, Abi and Zoe. There had been a lot of love and laughter in her life.

"Do you have any brothers or sisters?" she asked.

Again the hooded look fleeted across his face. "I've a half-brother and sister. My mother remarried."

She could sense the hurt and bitterness there and wanted to ask him what had happened. It had obviously

153

affected him. Did he go to live with his mother or his father? Was he unhappy at boarding school? But she didn't like to pry so instead said in an extra-bright voice. "This is the park we all used to gather at when we were kids. Abi used to go so high on that swing I was sure she would swing right over the top of it."

"She was your best friend?"

"Yes, right through the High School too. Her and Zoe," she added quietly.

"And where is Zoe now?"

"I haven't seen her since she ran off with Lee, my boyfriend, six years ago. They went to live in Bristol, got married and had a couple of kids."

Reece whistled. "That's tough."

"It was at the time." She shrugged. "It's history now."

He squeezed her hand and looked down at her. "Let me guess, and there's been no one serious since?"

"Not serious, no. I like being a single girl. Footloose and fancy free, in charge of my own destiny," she quoted. "People give up too much for love. They lose sight of who they are, of what they want to do with their life. I don't intend to do that." She met his eyes. "What about you?"

"There's never been anyone serious in my life and I intend to keep it that way." He bent down and kissed her. "Good to know we're on the same wave length."

She showed him around the small Cornish village, with its cobbled streets and old fisherman's cottages, pointing out the rickety stone cottage where Sandy Mather, the famous painter lived, the Grade 11 listed dwelling where the smugglers used to meet and the haunted pub where the ghost of a murdered pirate was said to come back in the early hours of the morning for his last drink. "You sound like you loved living here," Reece said. "Do you ever regret moving away?"

She thought for a moment. She did love Port Madden but if she was honest she'd felt a bit stifled here, she'd needed to spread her wings a bit. Lee and Zoe had given her the push she needed to do that.

"I enjoy my job and the buzz of the city, but I have to admit it's good to be back. Nothing quite beats the sound of the seagulls on my roof in the morning, opening the curtains and seeing the sea, the smell of salt in the air." She laughed. "Hark at me! I sound like a holiday guide."

They were standing outside the Old Sea Dog now, an old pub which was a favourite with tourists. "Fancy a drink?" she asked.

"Sure." He looked at the black and white pub with its crooked windows and faded sign portraying a wrinkled fisherman. "I'm guessing this used to be a fisherman's haunt?"

"You've got it. According to legend, smugglers used

to gather and sell their contraband cargo."

"Fascinating." He pushed open the door.

"Watch your head!" Ellie shouted, suddenly remembering the low ceilings. Reece ducked just in time. "The floor's a bit wonky too," she added.

"You're not kidding."

The pub was crowded, as always. With all the nautical bric-a-brac such as cannons, ships' figure heads, fishermen's nets, anchors and even a ship's wheel it was a target for tourists. The stone floor, granite fireplace in the bar and dark beams all added to the atmosphere, as did the various paintings of smugglers on the walls.

"Love it," Reece said approvingly. He fished his wallet out of his pocket. "What do you want to drink?"

"It used to be half a cider," a voice said behind them.

Zoe's heart skipped a beat. She'd recognise that voice anywhere. She turned slowly.

"Hello Ellie."

Lee.

She'd been dreading this moment for years. Would have done anything to avoid it. As she looked at Lee, memories flashed across her mind. Her and Lee surfing, sunbathing, at a beach barbecue, racing around in his battered mini. Making love. Lee had been her first lover and she'd thought they were forever. So many years of memories then nothing. It had been six years since she'd last seen him, when she'd walked away heartbroken to build a new life in the Midlands.

"You look good," he said in the soft, seductive voice she knew so well.

So did he. He was older, of course, his long sun kissed blond hair now darker and cut short, his usual dress of bleached cut-off denims and tight vest replaced by chinos and a black shirt but he still oozed sex appeal. He looked quite smart, as if he'd done all right for himself. She guessed that he and Zoe had a house in a suburban street, 9-5 jobs, two children, a normal life. Were they happy, she wondered. They had hurt her so much but it no longer mattered. Looking at him now she felt nothing. He'd been her world once but now he was a stranger.

"Hello, Lee. Are you down visiting your folks?" she asked coolly.

"Back down here for good. Me and Zoe have split up." His gaze swept over her. "What about you?"

"Just a quick visit." She nodded. "Nice to see you again." Then she linked arms with Reece. "Shall we sit down by the window?"

Lee looked a bit stunned. Did he think she was still carrying a torch for him? Expect her to fall at his feet just because he'd announced he'd split from Zoe. Had he cheated on Zoe too? Walked away and left her with two small children to look after? A few years ago she'd have been pleased to hear that they were no longer together but now she felt sorry for her former friend.

"Sure, you grab a seat and I'll bring the drinks over. White wine spritzer right?"

She nodded. "Thanks." She kissed him on the cheek then turned away. She could sense Lee's eyes following her as she wove her way through the crowd over to the table but refused to give him the satisfaction of looking back.

Ellie sat down, her mind racing. Lee said he was back for good and he and Zoe were finished. She thought of her former best friend with her honey gold pixie cut, huge blue eyes, high cheekbones. It was always Zoe the boys looked at. She was so full of life, sparkly, fun. No wonder Lee had fallen for her. How would Ellie feel if she saw her again? Zoe had hurt her more than Lee. Zoe's betrayal had been like a knife in her back.

"You look thoughtful." Reece placed the glasses down on the table and sat down beside her. "And your friend is standing at the bar watching us. I think he'd like to catch up on old times? Do you want to talk to him? I don't mind making myself sparse."

"No, I don't. I've nothing to say to Lee." She took a sip of her spritzer. It felt cool and refreshing. "It was all a long time ago and I'm well over him but I'd prefer not to sit sharing pleasantries with him."

Reece placed his hand on hers. "Do you want to go somewhere else? Is he making you feel uncomfortable?"

She shook her head. "No it really doesn't matter to me. Like I said it was a long time ago." Let Lee see her with someone else, especially someone as hot as Reece. That would show him she was so over him.

She placed her hand on Reece's and leaned in closer. "Thank you for all your help today."

"It's no big deal. I'm pleased to help, you know that."

"It's very kind of you." She kissed him on the cheek. "Now that's enough about me. Let's talk about you." He'd been so helpful and supportive to her, she could at least show some interest in his life. She hadn't even bothered to ask him what he was doing down here, what his business meeting was about. "What made you come to Port Medden? I wouldn't have imagined a little village like this was your territory."

"I've had some business in Truro and was going to stay at a hotel there but I wanted somewhere not so busy. I like to get away from it all once in a while and this looked a quaint village," he replied, taking a sip of his drink. "Take this pub for example. It's fascinating. Tell me a bit more about its history. I love the whole smuggling thing." He pointed over to a ship's figure head of a mermaid hanging just above their head. "Is that a genuine ship's figure head?"

"Yes, apparently it came from a local ship, The Siren, which was captured by pirates in the eighteenth century." She related the story to him. "The pirates sunk the ship, taking the crew prisoner and stealing all the goods. When the sunken ship was recovered the figurehead was hung on the wall in this pub as a sort of homage to the crew that was lost." She turned and pointed to a ship's wheel. "That was taken from a smuggler's ship that was grounded by the Customs men. Cornwall is proud of its smuggling heritage."

"I can see that. And what about that picture there? Who's that?"

Reece listened intently as Ellie told him the old smuggler legends. She was gorgeous. Not carefully coiffured, manicured and groomed to perfection like the women he usually met, but a natural beauty. Her skin glowed, she wore the minimum of makeup, her glossy hair hung carelessly around her bare shoulders which had a hint of a golden tan and when she laughed it was like the tinkle of silver bells. No wonder that guy – Lee – couldn't keep his eyes off her.

Out of the corner of his eye Reece could see Lee staring at them. Ellie had been insistent it was over and she didn't want to talk to him, and who could blame her.

But Reece had a feeling that it wasn't over for Lee. He'd made it immediately clear that he was no longer with the woman he'd left Ellie for – her best friend. No wonder she'd left for the Midlands. She must have felt betrayed. Heartbroken. He wondered if Ellie still had any feelings for him? He'd heard the gasp of breath when she saw him, noted the stiffness of her body. She'd loved him. He must have been her first real love if they dated while they were still at school. Wasn't your first love supposed to be the one you remembered most? Not that he'd know, he'd never fallen in love with anyone. Never allowed himself too. As soon as he felt he was getting in a bit deep he'd walked away. Yes, sometimes it had taken a bit of willpower to do that but he preferred a little hurt to a broken heart. No one was going to capture his heart then destroy it. Not like his Mum had done to his Dad.

That guy definitely still had feelings for Ellie though. Did he regret finishing with her? Not that Reece was jealous. And the fact that he knew Lee was watching them had nothing to do with why he kept reaching for Ellie's hand, touching her arm, leaning forward and kissing her on the cheek. Nothing at all.

The evening passed so quickly. There had been one dicey moment when Ellie had questioned what he was doing here but he'd soon got her off the subject by asking more questions about the old smugglers' legends. He could tell she loved Cornwall. Would she ever have left, he wondered, if Lee hadn't gone off with her friend? And now he was back would she want to stay?

Well, if she did it was nothing to do with him. He'd be moving on in a few days, onto another deal, another success. Once he'd wrapped up this one. He'd sent his report over to Steve and had a meeting booked in with him to discuss it tomorrow.

"Would you like another drink or are you ready to go?"

Ellie's voice cut through his thoughts. He focused his attention on her and smiled. "Sorry I was miles away then, imagining myself back in the smuggling days. You tell the tale so vividly I almost felt I was there." He straightened up in his chair. "Actually, I'm ready to go. It's a bit stuffy in here. If that's okay with you?"

She nodded and pushed back her seat. "I could do with some fresh air too."

A quick glance at the bar as they stood up showed that Lee was still propped there watching them. He raised his hand in a salute when he saw Reece look his way. Reece nodded in acknowledgement but Ellie ignored him

"I think your ex might be hoping for a reconciliation," Reece said as they left the pub arm in arm.

"Well he's got no chance," Ellie said firmly. "He's history." She tugged at Reece's hand. "Come on, let's

162

have a walk down to the seafront. It's only a few minutes."

He rolled his eyes. "You and the sea. I'm beginning to think you're a secret mermaid. It's a wonder you could bring yourself to move away."

"It was tough, but I don't regret it," she said firmly. "I intend to make the most of it while I'm here though."

Laughing, she half-pulled him down the hill towards the sea front and they walked along hand in hand.

"We must come here in the daytime then I can show you the smuggler's caves," Ellie said. "Well, everyone says the smugglers used them."

"I bet you used to go exploring them hoping to find treasure," Reece teased.

"I did! How did you guess? Once we found a secret passage and went down it. We found a wooden crate, all broken and dirty and carefully carried it all the way up the hill. Then Abi noticed a name written on the side, it was from the local fruit shop."

Reece chuckled. "I bet you were really disappointed." He slipped his arm around her waist and pulled her closer, kissing her on the forehead. As she turned her head up to look at him the usual spark flared up in his groins and he bent down to kiss her mouth. A deep, long, kiss that stirred the spark into a flame.

"How about we go back to the hotel and have a

nightcap?" he suggested when they both finally came up for air.

She nodded. "Sounds like a good idea."

They held hands and walked back in companionable silence. He'd never felt so comfortable with a woman, Reece thought. It was as if Ellie was the ying to his yang, they slotted together so perfectly.

Whoa! Hang on there. This is supposed to be a holiday flirtation, a bit of fun. Fancy her yes, but don't get going ga-ga over her.

"Another spritzer or something stronger?" he asked as they entered the hotel.

Ellie slipped her hand out of his. "Actually, I'd prefer a hot chocolate? Do you mind?"

"No, not at all. I wouldn't mind one myself."

"Let's go into the kitchen then and I'll make us one." She carried on ahead, leaving him to follow. He watched her retreating back thoughtfully. He'd been on the brink of suggesting they have a brandy in his room, but the closeness they seemed to have suddenly was gone. It was as if Ellie was trying to put their relationship back on a more impersonal footing.

Hot chocolate in the kitchen wasn't exactly impersonal.

No but it wasn't up, close and personal either.

The question was, was Ellie trying to put a bit of a

gap between them because she was thinking about her mother coming home tomorrow. Or was it because seeing her old flame Lee again and learning that he was free had rekindled her love for him?

Chapter Fifteen

Ellie was up bright and early the next morning. She wanted to make sure everywhere was spotless before she went to the hospital to fetch her mother. She found Reece already up, fixing the door handle of a cupboard in the staff kitchen.

"Morning," he said as she walked in. "Fancy a cuppa?" He stood up, leaned over and kissed her on the cheek.

"I've just had one, thank you." She touched his face with her hand, running her fingers over the stubble. "Thank you for fixing that. Harry's done his best to get through the list but he hasn't had enough time to do it all."

"We're nearly through now." Reece took the list out of his pocket. "There's a curtain rail to fix in one of the rooms, a lampshade to be replaced, the blind in the lounge to rehang and that's about it."

"I'll fix *you* a cuppa, shall I?" She went over to the kettle and filled it up. "Mandy's coming in early so we can make sure everything is sparkling and fresh for Mum to come home." She turned to Reece. "You must have been up with the seagulls."

He took a mug from the stand and spooned coffee into it. "No, I've only been up about an hour. I wanted to do these few jobs first then I'll have a quick shower and change before I go out."

"Ah, that explains the stubble." She plugged the kettle in. "I was wondering if you were growing a beard?"

He came behind her, wrapped his arms around her waist and nuzzled into her neck. "Do you like beards?"

"Not really, to be honest. I don't mind a bit of stubble but beards don't do it for me."

"I'll be smooth-shaven soon," he promised.

He pulled Ellie around and kissed her soundly. She returned the kiss for a few moments then slid out of his grasp as her phone rang. It was Harry to tell her that the plasterer had arrived. "Show him up to the Honeymoon Suite, will you, Harry?" she said.

Reece had made the coffee. "Any more news from the hospital? Does your mum have to wait to see the doctor before she can come home?"

"Yes but the sister said that's just a formality and she'll definitely be coming home. So I'll get to the hospital for two. Mum won't want to stay in there a moment longer than she has to. She'll be itching to come home. And to get straight back to work if I don't keep an eye on her."

Reece grinned. "It sounds like your Mum is a bit stubborn."

"It's stubbornness and hard work that keeps her going, especially since Dad died." Ellie sighed. "I just hope I can persuade her to slow down a bit."

"I'm sure you'll do your best." Reece kissed her on the forehead. "I'll take this coffee up with me. It's time I showered and got changed now. Don't go working too hard yourself. The hotel looks fine. You've done wonders in the few days you've been here."

"With your help. And Mandy's and Harry's." Ellie reminded him.

She took down the kitchen curtains, put them in the washing machine, cleaned the windows, then decided to tidy up the flat and put clean sheets on Mum's bed. First though, she'd check how the plasterer was getting on.

She paused in the doorway of the Honeymoon Suite. The furniture, bed and carpet were all covered in dust sheets and a man was standing on a ladder plastering over the now-boarded up hole in the ceiling.

"Afternoon. Are you Mrs Truman's daughter?" he asked.

"I am. Do you know my mum?" she asked.

"Aye, I've done a few jobs for Sue – and Pete, God Rest His Soul – over the years. I heard Sue is in hospital. How is she?"

Ellie had forgotten how quickly news spread around Port Medden. "A lot better, she's coming home this afternoon." She looked up at the half-plastered ceiling. "Will this take long?"

"I'll be done within a couple of hours," The man put some more plaster on his trowel. "But it'll take a good few days to dry. I'd say leave it until after the weekend before you paint."

That long. Still at least she could do it before she went home. "I will, thank you. Would you leave your bill at Reception so Mum can settle with you as soon as she feels a little better?"

"Certainly, Miss. No rush tell her. Sue's word is always good."

Ellie spent the rest of the morning cleaning, polishing and shining the living quarters. She changed the sheets on her mother's bed and vacuumed but was careful not to touch anything. Mum was big on privacy. By the time she'd done all that it was almost twelve so she showered and changed then went downstairs to see how the hotel was looking. Jenny and Pat, two of the cleaners, had promised to give it a good overhaul.

"It's wonderful," she told them. "Mum will be so pleased when she comes home. Thank you both so much."

Reece was right, they had done wonders in a few days. And she still had over a week left so surely that was enough time to get it all straight. Then she'd be able to go back home with a lighter heart.

Ellie's mother was delighted when, holding onto her daughter's arm, she walked into the newly-spruced up foyer, although she scolded them all for working so hard. "Especially you, Ellie. You should be taking it easy, having a holiday not cleaning the hotel for me."

"I came down to look after you, and that's what I'm going to do," Ellie told her.

"Well it all looks lovely. I know I've let things go a bit since your dad died but I'm going to get Gwel Teg back on its feet again as soon as I'm feeling stronger." Sue Truman said as they all walked through into the kitchen. "I've been thinking about it in hospital. Pete wouldn't want me to let the hotel go to ruin like this. It

170

was our dream come true moving here."

"Dad wouldn't want you to wear yourself out, either Mum. He'd want you to look after yourself. And if Gwel Teg got too much for you he'd want you to sell and buy yourself a little bungalow," Ellie said gently.

"I will *not* sell up. This is my home," her mother said indignantly. She paused as a coughing fit overcame her.

Ellie watched worriedly as she sank down on a chair, bent almost double, the coughs wracking her fragile body. "Can I get you anything, Mum? A glass of water?"

Sue waved her hand dismissively. Finally, the coughing subsided. She sat up, her face pale but resolute. "I'm quite capable of running this place. I've just had a blip, that's all. By next summer it'll be full of guests, just like it used to be."

It did too. Ellie remembered times when she was younger when they'd had to turn people away in the summer months. With its white pebbledash exterior, pretty window-boxes full of flowers and prime location next to the beach, Gwel Teg had been a magnet for holidaymakers.

Mum was looking around, her eyes scanning the kitchen. "I see you've been busy in here too. The drawer handles have been fixed, and the cupboard door. I'd been meaning to ask Harry for ages."

"Reece fixed them. He's …er…one of the guests." Ellie floundered for a minute trying to think of a way to explain her relationship with Reece.

"A guest has been doing repairs in the kitchen?" Sue stiffened. "Perhaps you should explain, Ellie."

"Now don't worry, you'll like Reece. I know he's a guest but he's become a good friend too. As soon as he found out you were in hospital he's been helping out. Sit down and let's get you a cup of tea then I'll tell you all about it." Ellie flicked the kettle on and reached for the teabags. This was going to be difficult. She wasn't looking forward to telling Mum about the flood in the hotel room and the lapsed insurance.

"Oh my goodness. I am so sorry to leave you with all that to sort out, Ellie." Her mother said when Ellie had finished. She looked quite shaken up. "I'd had a reminder about the insurance and meant to renew it but I forgot."

"I didn't know what to do, Mum. It if wasn't for Reece I'm sure the Smythes would have sued us."

Sue frowned. "I know you meant well, Ellie but I don't like a stranger – and a guest at that - involved in this way. Knowing our private business."

Ellie bit her lip. She didn't want to upset her mum, and knew how proud she could be but honestly, Reece had been a godsend.

"I know, Mum, but I didn't know what to do. Everything was such a mess, and the guests were so upset. Reece could see I was out of my depth so he stepped in and dealt with it for me."

Her mother gave a tight smile. "Yes, I know you were just doing your best and I'm grateful and it was kind of him." She sighed again. "Although why he should put himself out like that is beyond me." She glanced shrewdly at Ellie. "Are you and he . . . ?"

"We're friends – okay I guess you'd call it dating now. He's been so kind, Mum. A real rock to me. He's been doing the repairs with Harry too. He's even stayed on an extra few days to help me."

"Dating." Another silence. Ellie was beginning to feel distinctly uncomfortable as she realised how it must look to her mum. Ellie had only been here a few days and was already so close with a guest that he was doing odd jobs for them. "Not like that," she murmured. "We're not…"

"I really don't want to know your personal business, Ellie. I'm not trying to pry, I'm just surprised you've got so friendly with this man in such a short time." Mum put her cup down and stood up. "I'd better take a look at the Honeymoon Suite and see how bad the damage is."

"It looks worse than it is, Mum," Ellie said as she followed her out to the lift. "As soon as the plasters dry I'll repaint the ceiling. You'll need a new carpet and bed but Reece has contacts and can get us a massive discount so it won't be that expensive."

"I see. I must say it's a bit of luck that he was staying here when it happened, wasn't it."

Ellie detected a frosty tone to her voice. Mum was fiercely independent, resented anyone 'taking over' and thinking she couldn't handle things. Of course she wasn't very happy to know that a *guest* had to come to their rescue.

Ellie bit her lip as she turned the key in the lock and opened the door, praying that her mum wouldn't be too upset. She held her breath as Sue stepped in, looked up at the ceiling, then around the room.

"Well, it doesn't look too bad," she said. "I'm presuming the rug is hiding the water-stained carpet?"

That had been Ellie's idea. She hadn't wanted her mum's first reaction to be one of shock so had tried to hide the damage. A throw over the bed, a rug over the carpet. She couldn't disguise the newly-plastered ceiling though.

Ellie watched as her mum bent down and rolled back the rug, revealing a huge dark stain, nodded and replaced it again. Then she walked over to the bed and turned back the throw. "Yes, I can see that the bed and carpet do need replacing. Well, it's my own fault. I should have renewed the insurance." She turned around and Ellie could see the worry etched on her face although her mum was trying hard not to show it. "I'll just have to see if the bank will extend my overdraft a bit. If not, we'll have to close this room down for a while. We'll manage." She reached out and squeezed Ellie's hand. "Thank you for tidying it all up, dear. I feel awful that you've had to cope with all this. I should be glad that you've had someone to help you instead of complaining about it. It's very churlish of me to complain."

"It's okay, Mum. I can help you out with the money. And I told you, Reece can get us a big discount."

She saw Mum straighten her shoulders and tilt her chin. "That won't be necessary. I think you've both done enough."

Ellie took a deep breath. She hated having a confrontation with her mum but needs must. "Mum don't be stubborn," she said gently but firmly. "The important thing is to get Gwel Teg back on its feet. You can pay me back later and using Reece's business account will save us a great deal of money. The Honeymoon Suite is your best room, you can't afford it to be out of action."

Sue hesitated, Ellie guessed she was having an inner battle with her pride and her common sense. Finally, she smiled. "You're right, dear. And it is very kind of you. Both of you." She titled her chin determinedly. "Now you'd better introduce me to this

Reece of yours so I can thank him."

"I'm not sure he's back yet, he's had to go out on business," Ellie explained, shutting the door behind them and locking it.

"What sort of business is he in?" Mum asked as they walked over to the lift.

Ellie paused, realising that she didn't know what Reece did. How could they have talked so much and not discussed that? She had asked him a couple of times, she remembered, but he'd dismissed it. "Something to do with the hospitality sector," she replied, pressing the lift button.

The doors slid open and they stepped inside. When the doors opened again she saw Reece strolling towards them carrying a big bunch of cream roses mixed with purple irises. Her mother's favourites. How had he known? Had she mentioned it to him during one of their many conversations?

"Hello, Ellie. This must be your mother." He flashed a devastating smile at them, then handed the bouquet to Sue. "Welcome home. I hope you're feeling better, Mrs Truman."

Ellie was astonished to see her mother flush, then take the bouquet from him. "Thank you, Mr ...."

"Call me Reece, please." He smiled again. "Have you been to look at the flood damage? It's not too bad, is it?

A couple of weeks and it will be ready to let out again." He casually put his arm around Ellie's shoulders. "Ellie's worked so hard to get everything sorted for you. I don't think I've ever come across anyone who cares so much for her mum."

Ellie saw her Mum's aloofness crumble. A big smile spread over her face. "We've always been a close family. She's got a good heart has Ellie." She looked at the flowers. "I'll go and put these in a vase of water. Won't you join us for a cup of coffee? I believe you know the way to the staff kitchen?"

"Thank you."

Within five minutes of meeting, her mother Reece had effortlessly charmed her so much she'd forgotten all about her objections at a guest being allowed 'behind the scenes' at Gwel Teg, and to do odd jobs.

Just like he'd charmed the Smythes. And charmed her too. For some reason that made Ellie feel really uncomfortable.

Was Reece a little too smooth and charming?

Chapter Sixteen

"I hear that you've been very helpful to Ellie," Sue said as they all went into the staff kitchen for another cup of coffee. Ellie noticed that she didn't make any objection to Reece taking the flowers off her and putting them into a vase of water or whisking out a packet of shortbread biscuits (did he remember everything she told him?) and putting them on a plate. "I must say, it's very good of you," she looked at him sharply. "My guests are often pleasant but never to the extent that they work for me for free."

Reece leaned back against the worktop, crossed his arms casually and met her gaze, smiling disarmingly.

"It's a poor world if we can't help each other." Then the smile was replaced by a look of concern. "I hope it didn't upset you to see the flood damage in the room. These things can look worse than they are. It'll look a lot better once the ceiling's painted."

"I know. Although I can see that the entire room needs redecorating as well as a new bed and mattress." A coughing fit seized Sue again. Ellie pulled out a chair and gently eased her Mum into it. "I'll go and fetch you a cushion."

"Allow me." Reece was out the door before she could object, returning a couple of minutes later with a cushion from the lounge which he passed to Sue. She held it to her chest for support, bending over as the cough consumed her.

Ellie watched in concern, a glass of fresh water at the ready.

Finally, the coughing ceased. Ellie handed her mum the glass of water.

Sue drunk half of it then placed the glass down on the coffee table. "Sorry about that. The cough is so annoying, it comes on without warning."

"And painful too, I can see." Reece said gently. "Please don't stress about the cost of refurbishing the room. I can help with that. As I told Ellie I deal with hotel refurbishments a lot so whatever you need you can order through my account which will get you a very good discount."

"Thank you, that's very kind." Sue rose shakily to her feet. "I think could do with a rest now. The journey was rather tiring."

"Let me help you, Mum." Ellie stepped forward and took her mum's arm, gently supporting her. "You're bound to feel weak at first. You've been very ill."

They had just reached the lift when Sue was seized by another bout of coughing. That cough sounds awful, Ellie though worriedly. How could she go back home and leave her mum like this?

Ellie placed her arms around her mum's shoulder as they went up the lift and into the private quarters and Sue seemed grateful for the support until they reached her bedroom door when she shooed Ellie away. "Thank you dear, but off you go. I'm not that ill that I can't undress myself and get myself into bed."

"Are you sure? I don't mind?" Her mum looked so weak Ellie was worried she might faint.

"I do." Sue patted her arm. "Really, I'll be fine, love." She walked in and closed the door firmly behind her.

Ellie listened anxiously as she heard the coughing again. It was frightening seeing her mum like this. The doctor had said the cough would linger for a while, and that Mum would be weak for some time, she reminded herself. She had to be patient.

But what if she was still ill when Ellie was due to go home next week?

Deep in thought, Ellie went down into the kitchen where Reece was finishing his coffee. He walked over and wrapped his right arm around her neck, pulling her into him and tenderly kissing her forehead. "She'll be a lot better when she's had a rest."

Ellie felt like bursting into tears but she held them back. She was being silly. Mum was getting better. She wasn't going to die like Dad had. She snuggled into Reece's shoulder for a few minutes, silently basking into his embrace, grateful for his presence. Then she pulled away and smoothed back a strand of hair from her forehead. "The trouble is she's realised that the entire room needs redecorating and I think that's really worried her." She bit her lip. "She looks so weak. I can't see how I can go home next week and leaver her to cope alone. I'll have to book another week off."

"Can you do that? Do you have an understanding boss?"

"I do, but there's an important conference on the Monday, and I'm supposed to be doing a presentation for it. I'm not sure if my boss can get someone to replace me. She bit her lip. "Perhaps I could go back for the conference then come back down again and stay for the rest of the week. I can do some of my work down here on my laptop." She felt exhausted herself. It had knocked her seeing Mum like this. She was scared to leave her. She closed her eyes for a moment to compose herself.

"Hey." Reece pulled Ellie close to him again and wrapped his arms around her. "We'll sort something out. A lot can happen in a couple of weeks."

Ellie nestled her head on his shoulder, taking comfort in his warmth and support. Reece really was a nice guy. She wished he wasn't going home at the weekend. It felt so good to have someone to turn to.

"Is Mandy still here?" asked Reece.

Ellie nodded. "She's on until six."

"Then let's go for a walk. I've got a couple of hours to spare and the fresh air will do you good."

Ellie hesitated. "There's so much to do here."

"Nothing that can't wait." He kissed her on the cheek. "Come on, a quick stroll along the beach. That always cheers you up."

He was right. She needed to clear her head then she might come up with a solution. Her dad used to say that there was always a solution, it might not be the one you want to take but there was a way to solve every problem if you put your mind to it.

Maybe the solution to this problem was the one she'd first thought of. To move back down here.

Could she handle that now that Lee was back? She

could tell by the look in his eyes last night that he was still interested in her, she'd felt him staring at her all evening although she'd pretended she hadn't. She'd been glad that Reece was with her, hopefully Lee would think they were an item and keep his distance.

Lee walked in later that evening when Ellie was doing a stint on reception. He walked boldly up her, a friendly smile on his face, as if he'd never cheated on her, never broken her heart.

"Hi Ellie. I heard your Mum was in hospital so thought I'd pop in and see how she was doing." He flicked back his floppy fringe and smiled wide enough to show off his dazzling white teeth. Still the same old Lee, thinking he was God's gift. Well he didn't dazzle her any more. She knew that behind that handsome exterior was a liar and a cheat. Still, they were adults. She would be polite. She eyed him levelly.

"She's out of hospital now, Lee. She came home this afternoon. Thanks for asking though."

"That's okay." He leaned against the counter a bit too close for her liking. She took a step back. "I've always admired your Mum and Dad. They were kind to me. I wanted to come and offer my condolences when your Dad died but I wasn't sure if you'd want that. The last thing I wanted to do was upset you."

You mean you were still with Zoe and now you're not, Ellie thought. Zoe hadn't bothered to come and see her either. Hadn't even sent a sympathy card, yet she and Ellie had been best friends for years. Zoe had practically lived at Gwel Teg during the summer holidays, Ellie's parents had been glad for her to have some company as they were always so busy with the hotel. Ellie had thought that maybe Zoe hadn't heard about her dad dying seeing as she no longer lived in Port Medden, but it sounded like she had known. What did it matter now? It was all so long ago she reminded herself. "It doesn't matter," she replied. "I didn't expect you to."

Lee fixed his oh-so-blue eyes on her. He and Zoe had the same colour hair and eyes, the same suntanned lithe figure. They'd been the ideal match, the 'in' couple, both loving surfing when Ellie couldn't even lie on a surf board, never mind stand up on one. Small wonder they had found each other attractive. Ellie had felt so awkward around them that she'd taken secret surfing lessons. She could still remember the stunned look on Zoe's face as she watched Ellie ride waves higher than even she dared to tackle.

"Look, I'm sorry. What me and Zoe did was terrible. We really hurt you. But we were just kids. We let our hormones rule our heads." He gave her his 'little boy sorry' smile "It didn't work out though. We soon realised that we weren't suited. I guess you could say we got what we deserved."

Why didn't it work out? Who cheated on who? Did Lee find Zoe boring when she was tied down with two little kiddies, maybe a little fatter than she used to be and a lot more tired? Or had Zoe got fed up with Lee's selfish ways, of him wanting to always be put first. She shrugged. "Forget about it. I did. Years ago." She nodded towards the computer. "Thanks for popping in, Lee, but I really must get some work down. I'll tell Mum you called."

Lee leant closer, his eyes holding hers. "I was wondering if we could maybe have a drink together? For old time's sake? Give me chance to apologise properly and for us to catch up on each other's news."

Reece stood in the doorway watching them. Lee was leaning over the counter, his head almost touching Ellie's. He couldn't see Ellie's face but he would bet any money Lee was on full charm offence. It had been obvious the other night that he wanted Ellie back.

Should he join them or leave them to it? He didn't want to come over all possessive but he and Ellie were supposed to be dating. Not that it meant she couldn't talk to another guy. Reece prided himself on not being the possessive type.

To be honest, he'd never cared enough to feel either jealous or possessive about them.

He hesitated for a moment, then saw Ellie turn her head. Her eyes met his and she waved. Was that relief on her face? "Oh Reece, I could do with some help over here!" she called.

"Sure."

As Reece made his way over to her, Lee straightened up and turned around. He glanced at Reece. He nodded, then shoved his hands in his pockets and sauntered nonchalantly over to the entrance.

"What's up?" Reece asked. "More problems?"

Ellie grimaced. "I wanted to get rid of Lee. Can you believe he's asked me to meet him so we can catch up? Honestly, the nerve of the guy!"

"He came in to ask you that?" Ellie looked agitated. He was trying to figure out if she was annoyed or upset.

"I reckon so. Although he made out he'd come in to ask how Mum was. As if he cares!"

"I'm guessing you didn't take him up on his offer?"

"You must be kidding. No way do I want to sit and have a conversation with that jerk. I'll be polite to him, but that's it." Bright spots of anger dotted each cheek. "Do you know what, I reckon he's only asked me because Zoe's dumped him and he thinks he can take up where he left off all those years ago? Talk about conceited!"

"Exes, eh?" Reece said lightly, as if he didn't care whether she went out with Lee or not although he was actually ridiculously pleased that she didn't want to. "Now what time are you finished here?"

"Not until ten I'm afraid," she said apologetically. "Don't hang around for me if you've got things to do or want an early night."

"I do have things to do but I'll be finished by ten so perhaps we could have a drink together then."

"I'd like that," she agreed.

"How about a nightcap in my room?" he suggested. "We'll have access to my laptop then and can check out the company we get our supplies from, take a look at the carpets and beds. You've probably got a good idea of what your mum would like so we could narrow it down to a shortlist to show her tomorrow, letting her have the final choice?"

His room? That sounds a bit…personal.

He grinned. "I promise to be a gentleman – unless you don't want me to be, of course." He leaned over and kissed her tenderly on the lips. Slowly. "Do you?" His voice was soft, almost a caress.

Did she? "Of course," she said. "I'll bring the wine."

It was on Ellie's mind for the rest of the evening. Should she suggest that they meet in the lounge instead? Was going to Reece's room giving him some sort of message? Saying she was prepared to take the next step?

Was she prepared to take the next step? She'd guessed that was what he had in mind when he'd mentioned a nightcap last night, but seeing Lee had reminded Ellie of how much he'd hurt her. She didn't want to get that close to anyone again. Mind you, there would be no chance of that when Reece was only here until Saturday. She had to admit she fancied him like mad and he'd made it obvious he felt the same way. What harm would it do?

In the end Ellie decided to wait and see how she felt but just in case, she hurried up to her room and freshened up before heading to Reece's room with a bottle of white wine.

The tang of after-shave wafted over to Ellie as soon as Reece opened the door. So he'd freshened up too. "I forgot to ask you if white was okay?" she waved the bottle at him, feeling a bit awkward now she was here. "It's straight out of the fridge so cold enough to drink."

"White is perfect. Come in." He pushed the door open and stepped to one side so she could walk past him. Her eyes immediately went to the door of the ensuite and an image of Reece's naked body flashed across her mind. *Sexy*.

He caught her glance and a smile tugged at the corner of his lips. "Shall we sit on the sofa? I've pulled the table up to it."

He'd remembered it too. She walked over to the two seater sofa by the window. Reece's laptop was open on the wooden coffee table in front of it, and a notepad and pen were placed beside it.

"I see you're all ready for action," Ellie quipped as she sat down. Then she realised that could be construed with a double meaning and wished she'd chosen a different phrase. Great. She placed the bottle of wine down on the table and hoped she didn't look as awkward as she felt.

Reece picked it up, took it over to the sink to uncork it and poured it into two glasses. Then he put the bottle in the fridge.

"We can get an idea of the cost tonight then show your mother tomorrow that it's all in hand and achievable," he said, handing a glass to Ellie.

He opened his laptop which immediately sprung into life. "I've already logged onto the website of the company we use for carpeting. Have a browse and star any you think might be suitable."

Reece swivelled the laptop around so that Ellie could

see the screen. The website belonged to a commercial carpet company and she was astonished to see that there were pages of carpets to choose from, in different colours and designs. At the top of the screen was the name Reece Mitchell. Reece had obviously logged in.

"I thought you'd have to log in with your company name," she remarked.

"What?" he looked blank for a moment but when she pointed to the log-in name he nodded. "Oh no. I'm the one who deals with this sort of stuff so I log in with my own name."

"Well it's an easy user name to guess so I hope you change your password frequently."

"I do, Miss Security," he grinned. "Now what do you think of this carpet?" He leaned over her and pointed to a golden beige material. "It's neutral looking so will go with any décor, hard-wearing but soft on the feet so feels very luxurious." Or this," he pointed to a fawn carpet in a mottled pattern.

"They're certainly possibilities. The Honeymoon Suite is gold so any of those carpets would go with the décor." Ellie flicked through more carpet designs, starring any she liked. She ended up with a shortlist of ten. "These all seem fine, so let's get down to the nitty gritty. What will they cost?"

"Let's put in the measurements. You wrote them

down, didn't you?"

"Yes." Ellie grabbed her bag and searched for her notebook. "Here you are."

Reece keyed in the measurements and selected the quote option. "There you are. What do you think of those prices?"

Ellie stared at the figure in relief. "Really? That's definitely not as much as I thought it would be."

"I told you I could get you a good discount." He looked very pleased with himself.

She stared at him. "How come you get such a massive amount off? Are you the buyer for a hotel chain?"

"Not exactly." There was a pause before he continued. "I told you, I'm a sort of advisor. I tell hotels how they can improve their image and increase their clientele."

"So that's why you knew how to handle the Smythes and have so many connections. Well, thank you for sharing your expertise with us." She glanced back down at the screen. "I'll jot some of these figures down so I can give Mum some idea of prices before she takes a look for herself. She'll be reassured when she sees this. I can see that she's worried sick at the moment, although she's trying not to show it." She reached for her handbag to take out her notebook and pen then started scribbling down a few of the prices.

"I'll save the selections too. Your Mum might want to choose different designs, which is fine. The main thing is that she's got something to go on."

"I really can't thank you enough," Ellie said softly. "It's so kind of you to help out like this."

"Think nothing of it," his voice was almost like a caress and his eyes held hers intently. She held her breath as his head come nearer, one hand reaching out to close the laptop and the other hand encircling around the back of her neck. "You're a lovely woman, Ellie Truman. It's a pleasure to help you."

As Reeces's kisses deepened – Ellie knew that this time they wouldn't stop at a kiss. Tingles coursed through her body at the promise of what was to come.

Chapter Seventeen

Someone's holding my hand!

Ellie woke in a panic, her heart pounding, her eyes frantically trying to focus. A cold chill ran through here. She wasn't imagining it. There definitely was a strange hand holding hers.

Then she became aware of a soft snoring and a body curled up next to her, the memories flooded back and the panic disappeared. She remembered who the hand belonged to. *Reece*. She'd spent the night with him.

And what a night it had been.

She had never had such hot sex in her life. Her cheeks burned as she remembered some of the things Reece had done to her. And wow, how she'd enjoyed it.

A light kiss on her shoulder made her jolt. "Morning sweetheart." Reece pulled himself up onto his elbow and leaned over her. "Did you sleep well?"

She turned onto her back and smiled up at him. "Very well. And I don't have to ask if you did, you were snoring when I woke up."

"It's called breathing heavy. That's the effect you have on me." He kissed her on the nose. The lips. Made a trail of kisses all down her throat. Then they were wrapped in each other's arms again, bodies melting into each other, fusing as one.

It was much later before their passion was sated and they finally pulled apart.

"I don't mean to be rude and kick you out but I need to get showered and dressed. I've got a meeting this morning," Reece said ruefully.

Shit! She was still wearing yesterday's clothes. Well not actually wearing them, they were strewn all over the floor where she'd left them after they'd feverishly undressed each other last night.

And she still had her contacts in. No wonder her eyes were stinging like mad.

Ellie rolled over and squinted at the clock. Eight o'clock. Mum would be up by now and was bound to have called her to see if she wanted a cup of tea, gone into her room when she didn't answer and have seen the unmade bed. She groaned and buried her head in the pillow. Why the hell hadn't she sneaked out in the middle of the night and gone up to her own room?

Because by the time they'd finished their sexual gymnastics she'd been worn out and had fallen asleep.

"I didn't think you'd miss me that much."

She pulled her head out of the pillow. "I'm not groaning about that. I'm wondering how I'm going to sneak into the apartment in yesterday's clothes without Mum spotting me. I bet she's already been in my room to see where I am."

Ellie sat up and wrapped her arms around her shoulders. "It was her first night home too. I should have been there. What if she needed something?"

"I'm sorry to have put you in such an awkward position." Reece leaned closer and nibbled her ear. "I hope you think it was worth it because I definitely have no regrets."

She wound her arms around his neck and kissed him. "Neither do I." She gently pushed him off her. "Now I'd better get out of here and leave you to shower." She swung her legs off the bed, sat on the side and yawned. That was some night!

Reece leaned over and trailed kisses down her back. "I'll see you later won't I?" He propped himself up on

195

one elbow. "Maybe we should exchange numbers so you can let me know when you're free." He reached for his phone off the bedside table. "What's your number?"

He punched the numbers into his phone as Ellie recited them. Two seconds later a message pinged from her phone in her bag beside the bed. She fished it out and opened the message.

"Thanks for a great night, Sexy xx"

She looked up and saw Reece's eyes twinkling at her. He was waiting for her to get off the bed and walk to the bathroom. Damn, she wished she had a gown to slip on. It was one thing being naked in front of him in the throes of passion last night, but another thing entirely in the bright light of the daytime with bed hair, no makeup on and red eyes. She needed to get these perishing contacts out.

"You're tempting me to forget about my meeting and entice you back into bed for round two. Or is it round five?"

His voice was tender but laced with amusement.

"Stop bragging, it's unbecoming," she told him as she bent down, scooped up her clothes and hurried to the bathroom.

Once inside she closed the door behind her and leaned against it. Boy, did he have something to brag about. That was the best night's sex she'd had in her entire life.

He'd known Ellie was hot the first time he'd seen her, and he was right. That day on the beach when her wet skirt had clung enticingly to her legs, show-casing her gorgeous figure had kindled the stirrings of desire he felt for Ellie as soon as he saw her.

Ellie was like a breath of fresh air, as warm and giving in her lovemaking as she was in her life. Beautiful inside and out, that's what his Gran would have said.

He didn't want to hurt her.

He'd never felt like this about anyone before. Wanting to protect them, to look after them. The women he usually dated were as worldly as he was, they knew the score. Ellie, although she'd made it evident she wasn't looking for a relationship and certainly wasn't clinging to him, was softer, kinder. And she cared deeply about her mother.

Reece was now beginning to feel uncomfortable about his plans. He still intended to go ahead with it, he had a business to run, but he needed to be careful how he did it. This hotel was more than a business to Ellie and her mother. It was their home.

Ellie turned her key in the lock, pushed the front door open and listened carefully. It was all quiet. With a bit of luck Mum was still in bed. She slipped off her sandals, closed the door quietly behind her and tiptoed down the hall. As she passed her mother's bedroom she heard coughing. She could imagine Mum sitting up in bed, her body heaving, holding the pillow to her chest to try and numb the pain and felt a wave of compassion for her. Poor Mum. She was a doer, always dashing about, never one to sit idle. Apart from the coughing and pain, the weakness must be driving her mad. She wondered if she felt old and vulnerable. She would be sixty two this year, the same age as Dad when he died.

Ellie crept past the door and along the corridor to the door that led to her attic, opening it and stepping inside just as she heard her mother's bedroom door open. Pushing the attic door to, she listened to her mother's footsteps patter along the hall, then disappear into the kitchen before she clicked the door shut. That was close! She tiptoed up the stairs, then collapsed on her bed in a fit of giggles as the ridiculousness of the situation hit her. She was almost thirty for goodness sake, yet here she was sneaking in like a teenager who'd stayed out too late.

The trouble was, living back at home with her mother made Ellie feel like a teenager again. It was always the same, they fell back into their old relationship of mother and daughter, with Ellie trying hard not to do anything to upset her mum. Not that Mum was difficult to live with, but she had different views, she was set in her ways. Although she wouldn't outwardly voice her disapproval, Ellie knew that she wouldn't be happy about Ellie spending the night with Reece, a man she only met a few days ago.

Not that Ellie was in the habit of doing that. But there was something about Reece that made her feel she could trust him. It was only a holiday romance, she knew that, but he made her feel good. Looked after. As if she had someone to rely on. And right now she needed that. They both knew the score, were free agents and had used protection, so who was she hurting?

She took out her contacts, had a quick shower, pulled on some fresh clothes and quickly applied basic make-up, then slipped on her tinted glasses. She needed to get down to reception, she was on duty today, but first she wanted to check on Mum.

She found Sue sitting at the kitchen table nursing a cup of tea. She looked pale but to Ellie's relief was no longer coughing. Ellie pulled out the chair next to her and sat down. "How are you feeling, Mum? I heard you coughing earlier."

"I didn't keep you awake did I, dear? I'm afraid I was coughing most of the night and I was worried that I might disturb you." Ellie could hear the strain in her voice.

She gently touched her mum's hand. "No, I slept fine. You mustn't worry about disturbing me, just concentrate on getting better. Why don't you go back to bed for a bit? The doctor said you needed plenty of rest and you look done in."

"There's so much to do here."

"I can deal with that. I've got Mandy and Reece to help me. Rest for another hour or so. If you overdo it you'll end up back in hospital and you don't want that do you?"

"Perhaps I will. Are you sure you can manage?"

"Of course. It's no problem at all."

Ellie watched worriedly as Sue stood up and shuffled out of the kitchen, almost huddled over. She looked so frail. How on Earth could she run this hotel on her own?

Her phone bleeped, announcing an incoming text. Ellie took it out of her pocket and glanced at the screen. It was Martin. She swiped across to read the message.

Hi Ellie. How's your mother? I hope she's a lot better now. I don't want to nag, I'm sure you have enough on your plate but I'll need to know by the middle of next week whether you can return to work in time for the presentation. If you can't, let me know and I'll arrange something.

Regards Martin

It was good of him to even consider giving her another week off. What should she do? At present, Mum didn't look well enough to leave but she might be a lot better in a few days. Ellie didn't want anyone else to do the presentation if she could avoid it. She loved her job and wanted Martin to think she was indispensable. Even if Mum was still ill, surely she could drive back for a couple of days? It wasn't as if she lived here alone.

Ellie sent Martin a quick reply back thanking him and saying her mother was home now and recovering well so she expected to be back.

No sooner had she sent it when another text came in. *How's your mum, gorgeous? Did you manage to sneak in without her spotting you? See you later. Xxx R*

She smiled as she read it. It was so sweet of him to ask about her mother first. He really was a thoughtful guy. Three kisses this time too. She read it again, butterflies dancing around her heart. Did he really think she was gorgeous?

God, she was smitten.

No she was not. She pulled herself together. He was a nice guy, they had fun but it was a holiday romance. End of.

She sent him a quick text back telling him her mum was coughing badly and yes she had – thankfully - managed to slip in unnoticed. She hesitated for a moment then added three kisses. Best to do the same as him. No more. No less. That way she wouldn't look too keen or too cool.

Humming softly she fixed herself a cup of coffee and a bowl of cereal. Then she went downstairs to take over reception.

Ellie's social media onslaught had worked and she was pleased to see quite a few queries on the Gwel Teg Facebook page, a handful of emails, and a few Pinterest board shares. She replied to the Facebook queries first, knowing that a quick response rate gave them a better ranking, then moved onto the emails. She'd just finished replying to them all when her mother came into the foyer.

"Let me take over, Ellie. You go and have a break," Sue said opening the hatch and stepping behind the desk.

Ellie quickly assessed her. She had more colour in her cheeks now and seemed quite sprightly. Maybe she'd be glad of something to do. She knew how her mum liked to be kept busy. "Are you sure?" she asked. "I don't mind waiting until Mandy comes on duty." She glanced at her watch. "It's only another hour."

"No really. I'm bored out of my mind." She frowned as she took in the computer screen. "What are you doing?"

"I've updated the Facebook page and it's generated a

lot of enquiries," Ellie told her proudly. "We've at least another two potential bookings."

"Facebook? Oh I can't be bothered with that, Ellie. It's so time consuming and surely no one bothers with it. If they want to know anything they'll phone or email."

"Social networking's important, Mum. People expect all businesses to have an up to date Facebook site now. I can show you how to manage it so it doesn't take up too much time. And Mandy will help too."

She could see her mother looked flustered. She was fine with basic computing but hated learning anything new. "Honestly, you'll pick it up in no time," Ellie assured her.

"You look busy?" Reece's voice sent goosebumps down her spine as she remembered their night together. She swivelled around and greeted him with a smile. "I am. The Facebook page has generated a lot of interest. We've had lots of enquiries and comments."

"What did we do without Social Media?" Reece leant towards her and kissed her on the cheek. Then he smiled at her mother. "How are you today, Mrs Truman? You look like you've got a bit more colour in your cheeks. There's nothing like being in your own home to make you feel better, is there?"

"I am feeling stronger, thank you. Let me take over for a while Ellie. Mandy will be here soon. Go and have a coffee. You've done so much here, I don't want you falling ill too."

"I'm fine, Mum, but if you're sure I will go for a coffee break." Ellie agreed, knowing that it would pick Sue up a bit if she felt she could still be useful around the hotel.

"Fancy joining me for lunch later?" Reece asked. "I noticed a quaint little café on the harbour front. I wouldn't mind having a coffee and sandwich there."

"Sure." She hoped she sounded natural because she certainly didn't feel it. All she could think of was last night. Was he remembering it to? The way they'd kissed, torn off each other's clothes, made love so wildly.

Was he thinking, like her, that he didn't want to say goodbye?

Chapter Eighteen

"So no regrets about last night?" Reece asked as they sat facing the harbour with their coffees and ham salad sandwiches.

Boy did he believe in getting straight to the point. Did that mean he had regrets? He certainly hadn't this morning, she thought, remembering how he'd tried to entice her back into bed. She shook her head, her eyes fixed on his. "How about you?"

"Absolutely not. It was an amazing night." He leaned over and kissed her on the cheek. "Besides, I don't believe in regrets."

"Really?" She tilted her head to one side

questioningly. "You've never done anything you regret?"

Reece leaned back, elbows on the arm of the chair, fingers loosely linked. "No, I make a decision and that's it. If things work out different to how I expected I just move on. I don't see the point of chewing over things. You do what you do and have to take the consequences."

He sounded remarkably in control and confident. Maybe too much in control? "And is that what you do in your personal life too? Move on when things get difficult?"

His gaze flicked lazily over her face, resting on her lips for a few seconds as if he was remembering how he'd kissed them last night. Well if he wasn't remembering she certainly was. "I move on *before* things get difficult. Don't you?" His eyes were suddenly sharp, probing. "I thought your motto was 'footless and fancy free' too?"

So last night hadn't had the same effect on him as it had on her. For a brief moment she felt a stab of disappointment but she quickly shook it off. That was a good thing. This was a holiday romance and that was the way she wanted it to stay. Okay, so sex with Reece was so flaming hot it went right off the Richter Scale, but that didn't mean she wanted to get all clingy and couply. Reece's words were just what she needed to make herself get a grip. "It sure is. Just checking we're on the same page," she said nonchalantly. "How did your business meeting go this morning?"

"Good. We're almost wrapped up," He nodded but didn't enlarge any further.

Ellie frowned. He wasn't very forthcoming about his work. But then why should he be? Three more days and they'd be parting company, she didn't need to know all his business. Even so...

"What made you change your plans? Did something come up you weren't expecting?" It would be flattering to believe that he extended his stay because he was mad about her but she suspected it was purely business. Reece looked like the kind of guy who would put business first each and every time. That's not fair. She reminded herself of how much he'd helped her, without asking for any payment.

He studied her, his expression giving nothing away. "What do you mean?"

"You originally only booked in for one day, and then decided to stay for an extra week. So I'm guessing the 'business' was a bit more complicated than you thought."

He shrugged. "Let's just say it took an unexpected turn but that's not a bad thing. It's all working out well."

Sensing he didn't want to say anymore, Ellie changed

the subject. "I was wondering if we could let Mum have a look at those carpets this afternoon? It would be good if we could arrange for them to be delivered after I've painted the ceiling next week.

"Yes that'll be no problem. I'll bring my laptop down into the lounge if you like and we can take a look at some carpets there?"

"That would be great. I'll tell Mum as soon as we've finished lunch." She took a bite of her ham sandwich.

They chatted easily as they ate, then held hands and walked along the harbour front for a while. Ellie snapped a few shots with her phone.

"I want to put these on the Facebook and Pinterest pages," she said. "Photos are a good way to generate interest."

"You're really serious about this aren't you?"

"I am. I'm going to get Gwel Teg back on its feet again if it takes me the rest of this year." She glanced at the time on her phone screen. "I ought to be getting back. I don't want to leave Mum too long. She's still very weak."

"I think I'll hang around for a bit longer," Reece replied. "I'll see you in an hour or so." He snaked an arm around her waist and pulled her to him. Then they kissed. A long, lingering kiss that made her want more.

When she returned to the hotel, Ellie's mother was talking animatedly to Mandy. She looked much brighter, her eyes were almost sparkling and there were two pink blotches on her cheeks.

"Mandy's shown me how to update the Facebook page," Sue said. "It's not difficult at all. We think we might even start an Instagram page next. Mandy said it's easy, all you have to do is post photos. I could take photos of the hotel, the rooms, the beach, show people how lovely Port Medden is. What do you think?"

That's exactly what I've been trying to tell you! Ellie smiled. It was good to see Mum so elated. "It's a great idea, Mum. I've just taken some photos of the harbour so I'll post those in a little while."

"We've had another booking too. A young woman, she's coming to stay tomorrow for a few days. Things are definitely looking up." Her mother's smile was suddenly replaced by a look of pain as she started coughing again. Ellie grabbed a cushion off the sofa and passed it to her, knowing that hugging the cushion to her chest helped deaden the pain. "Bother this cough!" Sue gasped when it had finally stopped.

"What you need is one of my special drinks," Mandy told her. "I've brought the stuff to make it with me. You hold the fort here for a few minutes while I go and do it. She picked up her bright red patent handbag and tottered off to the staff kitchen.

"What would we do without, Mandy," Sue said, the corners of her lips lifted up into a smile. "I do feel bad though, she's worked so much unpaid overtime just lately. At least she's had you to help her this week. And I'm sure I'll be a lot better by the time you go home. Between us we'll manage."

Ellie suddenly remembered Mandy's idea of her niece helping out for a week as work experience. "You won't need to for the first week," she said, explaining about Sara. "What do you think? It sounds like a good idea to me?"

"Oh yes, I've met Sara she's a lovely girl. She'll be a big help. And if we keep getting the bookings coming in we might be able to afford to take someone else on."

Mandy was making her way back, holding a mug of steaming liquid.

"What's in that?" Ellie asked. She could smell herbs and something else, something she couldn't quite put her finger on.

"It's herbs, honey, blackcurrant and a touch of brandy," Mandy told her. She placed the mug down on the counter. "There you are, sip it slowly, mind. It's hot."

"Brandy? Are you trying to get me drunk and so early in the day?" Mum said in mock-horror.

"It's only a teensy bit. I'll make you another one

210

before I go home. That'll help you sleep tonight."

"Knock me out more like," Mum retorted. She picked up the mug and took a sip then pulled a face. "My goodness, that's strong!"

"Get it down you, lovey. It'll do that cough the world of good," Mandy told her. She walked behind the counter. "Now be off with you, this is my shift. Go and put your feet up."

"You know, I sometimes wonder who's the boss here," Mum told Ellie but she picked up her mug and walked around the Reception desk.

Reece returned a little later. "Do you think your mother would like to take a look at some carpet samples now?" he asked Ellie after greeting her warmly with a kiss, his eyes twinkling a promise of more to come later. "If I order them today I can arrange for them to be delivered, and fitted, next week.

"What do you think, Mum?" Ellie turned to her mother who had now returned, saying she couldn't bear sitting around doing nothing.

"Yes, thank you." Mum shot him a grateful look. "We could do with more guests like you."

Reece glanced at Ellie, a smile curving his lips. "I hope I'm a bit more than a guest." He turned his attention back to Sue. "Shall we sit over there?" He nodded

211

towards the sofa in the corner of the reception, "or do you prefer to go somewhere more private?"

"This will be fine. We're unlikely to be disturbed but will be on hand if Mandy needs us." Mum walked, a little unsteadily over to the sofa and sat down in the middle of the two cushions.

She's still weak, but she does look a lot better, Ellie thought in relief.

Ellie and Reece sat down either side of Sue, then Reece opened his laptop and logged on. A few clicks on the touchpad and he was on the site they'd looked at the other night.

"This is impressive," Mum said. "Is it a website especially for hotels? Can I open an account myself and get a discount whenever I want to order anything?"

"You have to be part of a large hotel group I'm afraid," Reece told her. "I'm happy to order anything you need through my account though, so you can get the discount."

"That's very good of you. Are you sure it won't get you into trouble? Won't your boss wonder who the purchases are for?"

"It won't be a problem at all" Reece clicked a link and a page showing numerous carpet samples opened. "Take a look at these. Ellie chose a few she thought you might

212

like last night – we've saved them –do you want to see those first?"

Sue leaned forward, her eyes resting on the screen as Reece flicked up a section. "It might be interesting to see if we chose the same ones. Now let me see. I like that one."

"That's one I chose too," Ellie said. "It looks classy doesn't it and would go with any colour scheme."

After careful consideration her mother chose six she liked, three were ones Ellie had chosen too. They called Mandy over to help them make their final decision.

"That one," she pointed to a mink and brown patterned carpet. It looks classy."

"I agree," Ellie said.

Sue hesitated. "I quite like this beige floral one. Oh goodness, I can't make up my mind."

"I think the main thing to consider is whether you want a busy carpet that attracts the eye or one that provides a background to compliment the other features in the room," Reece said.

Ellie shot him a mischievous glance. "That sounds like salesman spiel. I can see you're used to this."

He grinned. "I sometimes advise people yes." He turned to Sue. "Are you changing the colour scheme of the room at all? Or are you keeping it as a 'gold and white room?"

"Gold and white, definitely. They're good colours for a honeymoon suite. And I want the carpet to look classy but not be the main thing you notice when you walk into the room."

"Then can I suggest something." Reece flicked back a couple of pages. "This light beige/gold fleck twist would be ideal. It's easy on the eye, the gold flecks give it a hint of luxury and will complement the rest of the décor." He looked up. "The idea is to give an ambience of luxury without going over the top. CBS I call it, classy but subtle."

It was one of the carpets Ellie had chosen. She'd liked it immediately for the same reason but it hadn't been on her mother's favourite list.

"It is nice. Plain but nice," Sue agreed. Ellie sensed she preferred the floral one. Her mother liked flowers and favoured chitzy floral curtains and cushions. But Reece's choice of a plain twist with a bit of a fleck was classier.

Finally Sue nodded. "You know I think you're right. I probably need to tone down the florals a bit." She glanced at Ellie. "I noticed you changed the curtains in the lounge to the pale blue ones. A perfect choice. It changes the whole atmosphere in here."

"So we're agreed then." Reece selected the carpet. "Ellie and I measured the room the other day so we know what size carpet we need."

Sue glanced over as the price came up. "Goodness that is a big discount. Your firm must place a lot of orders to get that."

"We do quite a lot of business with them," Reece told her. "Now let's take a look at beds."

For the next half an hour they checked out the beds with Sue finally choosing a luxurious king sized white divan bed with a padded gold headboard.

"I can't believe how much money you've saved me," she told Reece. "I'll go and write you a cheque now."

"There's no need. I'll arrange for an invoice to be posted to you, then you can pay by cheque or credit card if you prefer."

"If you're sure. Thank you." Ellie could see that her mum looked relieved. She guessed she was planning on asking her bank manager to extend her overdraft but there was no need. Ellie would talk to her tonight about her plan to have an interest free balance transfer from her credit card. Mum could pay her back when she was on her feet again.

The sound of the bell announcing that someone was coming in made them all look up. A young couple entered, pulling suitcases behind them.

"This must be the couple that booked in earlier. I'll look after them." Beaming, Mandy walked over to them.

"You must be Sandy Holmes and Nick Carter?"

The woman nodded. "That's right, we phoned this morning."

"What a lovely location. You're right by the beach," The man added.

"Yes, we have one of the best locations in Port Medden," Mandy smiled at them. "Do come over to the reception desk and sign in, then I'll give you your keys." She looked at the cases. "Do you need any help with your luggage?"

"No, thanks. We're fine," the man replied as they followed Mandy to the desk, wheeling the cases besides them.

The cases looked a bit battered, and had quite a few labels dangling from the handle. A well-travelled couple by the look of it. She wondered what had brought them here. Whatever it was she was glad of it. Mandy said they'd booked in for two weeks. That was much needed funds.

"Right, I've just had confirmation that both the carpet and bed will be delivered next Tuesday. The carpet will be here first thing, with the fitters arriving a little while later. That way it should be all ready by the time the bed is delivered in the afternoon." Reece closed down the computer screen. "Now I'll take this upstairs. I've got some work to finish. Perhaps we could meet later, Ellie?"

"Sure. Text me when you've finished and I'll see how I'm fixed," Ellie told him. "I've got a couple of jobs I want to do here."

Reece leaned over and feather-kissed her on the cheek. Then he smiled at her mother. "See you later Mrs Truman."

"What a charming man," Sue said as Reece walked away. "I can see why you trusted him so readily, Ellie."

Reece was really nice, Ellie thought. What a shame he was going home on Saturday. She was going to miss him. A lot.

Chapter Nineteen

"So you're not mad at me any more for telling him our business?" Ellie teased.

"I wasn't cross..." a bout of coughing interrupted Sue's flow. "Not really," she continued when it had subsided – and a lot quicker this time Ellie noticed – "I was embarrassed. I don't like people to know how I've let things go. I've let your father down." Her voice wobbled a little.

Ellie put her arm around her mother's shoulder. "Of course you haven't. This hotel is a lot for you to run by yourself. And you've been grieving too. Don't be so hard on yourself." She was repeating Reece's words to her a few day's previously, she realised. "I should have helped you more, and I will now. I promise. I'll come down at least one weekend a month, more if I can. We'll soon get this place up and running again."

"It's really kind of you, dear, but you've got enough to do without driving up and down the motorway to take care of me."

"I haven't." She gave her mum's shoulders a squeeze. "Besides, it'll be nice to spend some time down here. I miss Cornwall." She stood up. "Do you feel strong enough to take a short walk? The fresh air might do you good? We could walk to the wall overlooking the beach."

"I'd like that." Her mother got rather unsteadily to her feet. "I've been cooped inside for too long. Let me get my cardi from the kitchen and I'll be ready."

"I'll fetch it for you."

Ellie dashed through to the kitchen and soon spotted the cream cardigan hung over the back of the chair. When she returned, her mother was chatting to Mandy and looked a lot sprightlier.

"Ready Mum?" she hoped this was a good idea. It was only a short walk so hopefully it wouldn't tire Mum out."

Her mother definitely had a spring in her step as they walked down the hill. When they reached the wall overlooking the beach she leant against it for a while to catch her breath.

"You know, it was this beach that made me and your Dad buy Gwel Teg," She told Ellie. "I've always wanted to live by the sea, right from when I was a young girl. Pete said it was an ambition of his too. He was working long hours, we hardly saw each other, and one day we decided to go for our dream. We knew we'd need an income though, permanent work is hard to get in seaside towns, so we thought a small hotel would be the best decision. We spent months looking around." She looked almost wistful as she gazed down at the golden beach below. "We liked Gwel Teg as soon as we saw it but it was this beach that decided it for us."

Ellie listened in surprise. Her mother had never told her how they'd come to buy Gwel Teg and she'd never asked. She'd been young when they moved here and accepted their decision without question. It had been an adventure for her. And a wonderful childhood living in a small seaside town. It was only as she got older that she began to get restless and hankered after city life.

Especially after Lee.

Realising that her mother was still talking, she turned her attention back to the present.

"When I saw this just a few yards away, I knew this was the place I wanted to live. And I've never regretted it." Ellie heard the catch in her mother's voice and shot her an anxious glance. Mum's eyes were glistening with tears.

"Oh Mum." She said softly. She knew Mum still missed Dad terribly. She did too. It was like a deep wound that they could cover up but would never heal. She reached out and took her Mum's hand in hers.

"Don't mind me, dear. I have a cry about your Dad now and again but I'm fine. I've got good friends here." She took a hankie out of her pocket and dabbed her eyes. "I'll get the hotel back on its feet again. You'll see."

This is Mum's life, Ellie thought, as they slowly headed back up the hill. It's where she wants to be.

On the way back one of the neighbours stopped to chat to Mum for a few minutes. Ellie noticed how her mum immediately perked up, her face sparkling as she talked. Mum liked people, always had. So had Dad. That's why they had both wanted to buy Gwel Teg, it would allow them to work together and the opportunity to work with people too. They'd made ideal hosts. Mum would miss all this if she left. She'd wither away in a bungalow or flat somewhere with nothing to do and no one to talk to.

She had to make Gwel Teg a success again. If Mum had to sell it would destroy here.

When they returned, Mandy called over. "We've had a couple of enquires through the Facebook page. That was a brilliant idea of yours, Ellie."

"I'm going to contact some travel sites too," Ellie told her. "See if they'll add Gwel Teg to their list. That might get us even more bookings."

"Good idea." Mandy picked up her bag. "See you tomorrow then."

"I'll take over for a while, you go and put your feet up," Ellie told her Mum. And for once Mum didn't argue!

Ellie sat on the chair and clicked on Google. She wanted to do a bit of research on some hotel sites, see if she could add Gwel Teg to a few lists that would increase their profile, and hopefully bring in more guests.

"Can I tempt you away from the computer for a while to have dinner with me?"

Ellie nearly jumped out of her skin. She'd been so engrossed she hadn't heard Reece approach. She glanced at her watch. "Is it that time already?" she shut the screen down. "Have you seen Mum?"

"She's pottering about in the garden," Reece told her. "She looks much brighter now."

"I know. We had a short walk to the beach earlier on and that really seemed to cheer her up." Ellie brushed a stray lock of her hair behind her ear. "She's going to be okay. She's determined to get Gwel Teg back on its feet again and I'm going to help her. We've both been talking about it this afternoon."

A strange look came over Reece's case, she couldn't quite put her finger on it but then it was gone and he was kissing her. "I'm glad she's feeling so positive. Now how about we eat out?" I noticed a seafood restaurant on the harbour front when I was walking along there today. Do you like sea food?"

"I love it. And yes, I can recommend that restaurant. Their prawn risotto is delicious and they do a wonderful selection of seafood platters. And oysters and fresh lobster, of course."

"That sounds perfect. Shall we say half an hour? I'd like to freshen up first."

"Me too." If they were going to the seafood restaurant she'd like to change into something dressier. A maxi dress perhaps.

She decided on a halter neck, high split maxi dress in a burnt orange and black print. She knew the colour suited her, and showed off her golden tan. When she walked into the foyer and found Reece waiting for her, looking very handsome in pale blue chinos and a slim fit white shirt, she was pleased she'd made an effort.

"Breath-taking," he told her, sweeping his gaze over her in admiration. He hooked his arm. "Ready?"

She slipped her arm through his. "Lead the way."

It was a warm, balmy evening and the town was bustling with holidaymakers. Ellie soon had to let go of Reece's arm, it was impossible to walk together amongst the crowds but he held out his hand behind him so they could link hands as they weaved in and out of the mass of people.

As they approached the restaurant, Ellie spotted a table free right at the front. She increased her pace, wanting to grab it before someone else did. They'd have a lovely view of the harbour there.

"Don't worry, we'll get it." Reece covered the distance in a couple of long strides, pulling out a chair for Ellie to sit down in before sitting down himself.

"I presume you'd want to face the harbour," he said.

"Move your chair around and we can both face it." Ellie shuffled her chair to make room. "It's a shame for you to sit with your back to it." The view across the bay was spectacular, the shimmering ball of the setting sun glowing in an orange and purple streaked sky, casting shadows over the silhouetted boats bobbling on what was now an almost indigo sea.

'It makes you want to take a photo, doesn't it?" she

said. 'But no matter how much I try, my photos never seem to capture the true splendour of the sunset."

Reece nodded. "I can see why the town has inspired so many artists. It's stunning."

"Good evening." The waiter smiled at them pleasantly, handed them a menu each and lit the candle standing in the middle of the table. "Would you like a drink or to order first?"

"Probably best to decide what we're eating first, don't you think?" Reece looked questioningly at Ellie.

"Oh I don't need to look at the menu, I know what I want. A seafood patter. I've had one here a few times and they are really delicious."

Reece's eyes twinkled in the candlelight. "In that case, I'll have the same. And how about a light, white wine to go with them? A Sauvignon Blanc, perhaps?"

"Sounds perfect."

The restaurant was quite full already but the service was fast and efficient. As they chatted easily, Ellie marvelled at how comfortable it felt to be in Reece's company. She felt as if she had known him years rather than a few days.

"You were right, that was delicious." Reece pushed his empty plate away and rubbed his stomach appreciatively. "Would you like a dessert?"

"Not right now, I'm stuffed. How about we walk

around for a while then have an ice cream? There's an ice cream parlour a little further along that does fifty flavours of ice cream and all sorts of different toppings."

"Fifty flavours!" Reece beckoned the waiter to bring over the bill. "I wouldn't think they could possible think of fifty different flavours."

"You'd be amazed by what they come up with," Ellie told him. "As well as the usual ones such as chocolate, strawberry and mint there's Cointreau, banoffi and mango and passion fruit."

"Cointreau sounds good," Reece took out his wallet to settle the bill but Ellie reached out to take it off him.

"Please let me settle this. It's the least I can do after all the help you've given us."

"I insist. I'm old-fashioned that way," Reece handed the waiter some notes. "Besides, you supplied the meal yesterday."

"As a thank you for your help," she reminded him. "And I like to pay my way. I'm not the kind of woman that expects – or wants – a man to pay for everything."

"In that case how about you buy the ice cream?"

"Deal," she agreed.

They spent the rest of the evening wandering around, holding hands, talking and laughing.

I can't believe how well we get on, Ellie thought. She felt as if she'd known Reece forever.

As they headed back towards the hotel Ellie started to feel awkward. What happened now? Reece too, had gone quiet. Was he wondering, like her, what the arrangements were for this evening? Last night they'd had sex for the first time. Was he expecting her to go back to his room tonight? And did she want to?

Yes!

But should she?

Reece paused outside Gwel Teg and snaked his arm around Ellie's waist, pulling her to him and kissing her soundly on the lips. "How about a nightcap in my room?" he suggested.

She returned the kiss with fervour, revelling in the closeness of his body.

"Just a nightcap?" she asked when they finally pulled apart.

He grinned. "How about breakfast as well?"

"Breakfast? At this time of the night?" she glanced at her watch. "Who eats breakfast at ten o'clock?"

"You could eat it at 10 am," he teased. His eyes darkened and he nuzzled into her neck. "Spend the night with me again, Ellie."

Should she? What if her mother woke coughing and needed her?

"I can't stay all night," she said. "If Mum woke in the

227

night and needed me…" she frowned. "It wouldn't be right."

"Stay half the night then," he suggested, gazing down at her. "We'll put the alarm on for three o'clock and you can sneak off."

She met his gaze, saw the longing and passion there. Saw something else too, something soft, gentle, caring.

"If you put it like that." She smiled. "Okay."

He nibbled her ear. "I promise you it'll be more than okay."

Chapter Twenty

The alarm buzzed through her deep sleep. Ellie groaned and reached out for her phone to turn it off. Besides her Reece slept soundly, spooned against her back, one hand cupping her breast. She yawned, longing to lie there, snuggled up to him and go back to sleep. *Yes and walk in wearing last night's clothes when Mum's having breakfast. Great idea. Not.*

She tried to wriggle out of Reece's grasp without waking him and reached for her phone.

"Is it time to get up already?" he murmured sleepily as she found the phone and slid the screen to silence the alarm.

"I'm afraid so." She turned around, wrapping her arms around him and they kissed. She loved it when they lay skin to skin like this.

"Stay for a little longer." As he pressed closer to her, she felt the stirrings of passion in his body and was tempted to stay for a replay. It had been *so* good.

"Tempting you, am I?" he teased, his voice already thick with desire.

She kissed him on the nose and wriggled away. "You are, but I must go. I won't be fit for anything tomorrow if I don't get a few more hours' sleep."

He flicked on the bedside light and leaned up on one elbow, watching as she reached down for her clothes. "Can't keep up the pace, eh?"

She turned to him and grinned. "As the saying goes, always leave them wanting more."

She could feel his eyes on her as she pulled on her panties, did up her bra, slipped on her maxi dress. It was as if he couldn't get enough of her.

"Right, I'm off. See you in the morning."

Reece wrapped his arm around Ellie's waist, pulled her to him and kissed her deeply. "You're the only woman who's ever sneaked from my bed in the middle of the night," he said gruffly.

She chuckled. "Like I said, keep 'em wanting more." She wriggled out of his embrace, picked up her sandals and handbag, gave him a finger wave and slipped out of his room, closing the door quietly behind her.

As she made her way to the private quarters, she thought about Reece's words. Was she really the only woman who'd ever sneaked out of his bed? Couldn't the others tear themselves away?

Well, she could understand that. Reece Mitchell was one hell of a guy. What a shame he was going home so soon.

The flat was all quiet when she sneaked in. Ellie went straight to her bedroom, pulled off her clothes and crept into bed. She felt her eyes closing as her head touched the pillow.

Once again the alarm woke her up. This time it was telling her that it was seven o'clock, and time to get up. She yawned and rubbed her eyes. She was so tired. And no wonder when she'd spent half the night cavorting with Reece. A smile stretched over her face as she remembered the way he'd kissed her, touched her, whispered how beautiful she was. It had been a long time since she felt like this about someone. Not since Lee.

Actually she hadn't even felt like this about Lee. She realised now that what she'd felt for him was infatuation not love.

Love.

Is that what she felt for Reece?

She sat up and hugged her knees. She was attracted to him yes. She looked forward to seeing him. *But in love with him?*

She shook her head. She didn't do 'in love'.

Footloose and fancy free, in charge of her own destiny. That was her motto.

And not even a gorgeous hunk like Reece was going to get her to break that. There was no way anyone was going to get near her heart and get the chance to break it.

It's too late. A little voice whispered in her head. She ignored it, got out of bed and headed for the shower. She had a lot to get through today.

He could still smell her perfume on the sheets. Light, heady, fragrant – just like Ellie. He lay for a while, remembering their night of passion. Spending a night with a woman he barely knew wasn't new to him, but spending the night with a woman like Ellie was. She was uncomplicated. She didn't ask anything from him. No promises, murmurs of love, no commitment. She just enjoyed being with him. No strings attached.

Which would make you think she was a good time girl but she obviously wasn't. She was close to her mother and willing to put her life on hold to help her. Intelligent, loyal, kind.

When did he notice all that about her?

Being with her this past week, watching how she treated people, how she dealt with situations that's when. He loved the way her face lit up when she smiled, a smile that spread right to her eyes. The way she threw her head back when she laughed, a real chuckle not a silly, tinkly, false laugh. He was going to miss her when they both returned home. She was good company.

Ellie could be the one woman to tempt him to break his 'no emotional ties' rule.

And there was no way he could let that happen. There was no place in his life for complicated relationships. He needed to get this deal wrapped up quickly. He'd been hoping it would be all done and dusted before he went home tomorrow but Steve was taking his time looking at the figures, and wanted to see Gwel Teg himself before the contract had to be drawn up. So it could be next Friday before the deal was agreed, which meant he'd have to come down again next weekend and persuade Ellie's mum to accept it.

That shouldn't be too difficult. Anyone could see that Sue was tired and the hotel was too much for her to cope with. He was pretty sure that if he slipped out Ellie's intention to give up her job and flat and move back down with her if Sue couldn't cope, she'd sign on the dotted line immediately. Then she wouldn't have to worry about Gwel Teg any longer.

Meanwhile, the tidier the hotel was the more impressed Steve would be when he came to have a look around tomorrow, so he'd better get cracking and help Harry get the jobs done.

He got out of bed and made his way to the bathroom.

Ellie was already in the kitchen, dressed in denim knee length dungarees and a blue and white striped tee shirt, having breakfast when he went in. He always made his way to the staff kitchen now rather than the guest one. Ellie, her mother and Mandy – Harry was still a bit reserved - treated him like one of the family and he felt like one. He'd paid up front for his room though, to make sure they didn't feel obliged to give him a discount. This hard-headed businessman was getting a soft heart.

"Good morning," he wrapped his arms around Ellie's waist and kissed her. She'd tied her hair up in bunches and looked incredibly sexy. "Did you manage to sneak in without being discovered?"

She grinned impishly. "Yes, thank goodness. You're not doing my reputation any good, you know."

"Ah, but I am brightening up your life." He kissed her soundly. "You look sexy in those dungarees. I take it they're your painting outfit?

"Harry's going to help me take up the carpet, ready

for the new one, and I'm painting the skirting boards"

"Want any help?"

She leaned back and scrutinised him. "Are you serious? I thought you didn't do painting and decorating?"

"I don't – usually. But I'll make an exception for you."

She playfully tapped his nose with her finger. "Thank you but I think I'd better do it. I have painted skirting boards before whereas you haven't – have you?"

"Nope. But I'm sure I could manage it."

"Seriously, I can manage it. I'm sure you've got stuff of your own to do."

"A bit of paperwork but then I'll help Harry. We'll get the rest of the jobs sorted."

"Thank you." Ellie kissed him then wriggled free. "Help yourself to breakfast. See you later." She picked up her coffee and toast and walked out of the kitchen.

Reece filled up the kettle, switched it on and opened the dishwasher to take out a clean mug. He made himself a black coffee and sat down at the table to drink it, his mind flitting back to the night before. Ellie had really got under his skin. Don't get too involved, he reminded himself. Finishing his drink he went to find Harry and offer his help.

* * *

Ellie had finished painting the skirting board and

window sill by mid-morning. "What do you think?" she asked as her mum poked her head around the door to see how she was getting on.

"It looks lovely. Thank you, dear." Sue stepped into the middle of the room and looked around. "You know, this wallpaper isn't too bad. I don't think the carpet will show it up, after all."

"Neither do I." Ellie wiped the back of her hand across her forehead. "I'll paint the ceiling once the plaster is dry. We're going to get this room looking even better than before, Mum."

Sue gave her a hug. "Thank you so much for all your help. I really don't know what I'd have done without you. But now I insist you take a break."

"There's still so much to be done."

"I know but it can wait. You've worked hard enough. I want you to take the rest of the day off and that's an order." She wagged her finger teasingly but Ellie could see that she was serious. "Go and find that Reece of yours and tell him the same. He's a guest and you are on holiday. Go and enjoy the day together."

It was a tempting idea. "Are you sure?" Elle asked. "I don't want to leave you to do everything."

"I'm not going to be doing anything apart from sitting in the garden," Sue told her. "I've got some thinking to be done and I'm best left alone while I do it."

"Then in that case I will." She kissed her Mum on the cheek. "But only if you promise you won't do anything strenuous."

"I promise."

Ellie went to have a shower and change her clothes, then looked around for Reece. She found him fixing a loose door hinge in the lounge.

"The ceiling's done," she told him.

"I know, I've just been up there looking for you. You made a great job of it."

"Thank you. Mum is insisting I take the rest of the day off. And she said I wasn't to let you do any more jobs either."

Reece gave the screw a final twist with the screwdriver. "There, done." He put the screwdriver back in the tool set then walked lazily towards Ellie. "What do you suggest we do?"

She smiled at him. "Do you have other plans?"

"None at all. I'm open to suggestions." He nuzzled into her neck. "Your wish is my command."

"Well, I want to take some photos of the beach and the town too, to put on the social media pages so do you fancy a bit more sightseeing?"

"Sounds good to me," Reece said. "I'd would like to see more of Port Medden."

"I was thinking of going in an hour or so. Is that

too early for you?"

"That'd be great, gives me time to reply to a few emails and shower."

Why, every time he mentioned the word shower, did a mental image of Reece stepping out of the shower stark naked flash through Ellie's mind? It was as if that encounter was stamped on her brain forever.

He did have a fantastic body though. Memories of their lovemaking last night slide showed across her mind.

"Penny for them?" he asked

No way was she going to let him know that she was thinking about him. She shrugged. "Sorry, my mind was wandering, planning the Pinterest page." She switched to the photo gallery on her camera and selected some shots of the vase of flowers from the Smythe's room that she'd taken earlier. "Which do you think is best?" she asked, sliding through them.

"That one," he pointed to the one she'd thought was the best too. "See you later." He wrapped his arm around her shoulder, pulled her to him and kissed her gently on the lips. She resisted the urge to melt into his arms, managing to control herself enough to kiss him lightly, then ease away. "Stop distracting me, Mr Mitchell," she teased, tapping him on the nose. "I've got work to do."

He grinned. "I'll leave you to it then."

Ellie watched him walk away, her heart skipping a beat. What was it about him that attracted her so much? She shook her head. Lust, that's what it was.

Chapter Twenty One

"Let's walk uphill a bit," Ellie suggested as they set off. She grinned. "If you're up to it, that is. It's quite a steep incline."

Reece flexed his right arm. "See those muscles. I'm as fit as a fiddle. Uphill it is."

"Just a sec though." Ellie took out her phone, slid the screen across to camera and took a couple of shots of the hotel.

"I thought you wanted some of the beach too? Shouldn't we be going downhill?"

"I'll do that when we come back." She slipped the phone back in her pocket. "Have you had a walk around much?"

He shook his head. "Nope, the tour the other night was my first." He took her hand. It felt soft and warm. Like the rest of her, he remembered. A picture of her naked body flashed across his mind, soft curves in just the right places. He savoured the image for a moment then pushed it away before he started getting thoughts that involved the bedroom instead of a walk around town. Not that he thought love making had to be confined to the bedroom.

Stop thinking about it, Reece!

"It's mainly houses at the top of the town, there's a couple of shops but most of them tend to be near the sea front," Ellie told him. "The view is amazing though."

She led the way up the steep hill, past cobbled streets and onto what looked like fairly new houses. "So the older houses are near the bottom of the town too," he observed.

"Yes, people tended to live near the harbour, that's where they worked."

God, she really was something, Reece thought as he watched Ellie snapping away. She'd taken photos of the beach, the cobbled streets, and a couple of quaint pubs. He loved the way she stuck her tongue between her teeth and squinted as she took the photos, the way she wrinkled her cute nose as she flicked through the shots to make sure they were okay, deleting the ones she didn't

241

like. How she laughed when a seagull flew across her path, ruining the shot, and when she accidentally took a photo of her thumb too. She was a delight to be with. He'd never met anyone so open, so totally unaffected.

If only he could be so open with her.

It wasn't for much longer, he reminded himself. The deal was almost sorted. Once he had Steve's approval it would be all signed and sealed.

Then all he had to do was tell Ellie and Sue, and persuade Sue to sell.

After about ten minutes walking Ellie stopped at a wall and turned around. She loved this view, you could see the whole expanse of the beach from here, the harbour to the left, the ships far out at sea, the surfers and bathers were like tiny dots.

.She snapped a couple of shots of the beach then stepped closer to Reece. "Let's have a selfie!" He grinned and hugged her close as she switched the phone to selfie mode and held it up high. "Smile!"

She took a couple of shots, then selected the photos and showed them to Reece. They were good. Their heads were close together, almost touching, eyes sparkling, wide smiles.

They looked like a couple in love.

Ellie licked her lips, not knowing what to say.

"They're great. I take it you're not putting these on the hotel Facebook page?" Reece asked.

Definitely not. They were way too personal. "I guess we could pretend we were a couple on holiday, show what a great place Port Medden is for lo ..." she stopped herself. "Couples." She almost said lovers then. How embarrassing. She gazed down at the sea, feeling really awkward. Had he noticed?

"I'd prefer them to be kept private," Reece replied. "Can you send them to me?"

He wanted the photos. Why? For a memento of her? "Sure."

A few seconds later the photos pinged onto Reece's phone.

This was getting more and more awkward. Why had she taken those photos? She couldn't have made it more obvious that she wanted to remember him and their time together.

Well he'd asked for the photos so he must want to as well.

"Want to take a closer look at the harbour now?" Ellie finally found the words to fill the silence. "We can go down via the back streets. Some of the houses are really quaint. They'd be great to put on the Pinterest page, show people what Port Medden is really like."

"Good idea." Reece reached for her fingers, and hand

in hand they made their way back down the hill. Going up was certainly easier than going down. They passed an old couple walking up with a basket of shopping, they seemed quite sprightly.

"You'd think this hill would be too much for them, wouldn't you?" Ellie said when the couple were out of earshot. "It's amazing how fit the old folk are here. I think it's the sea air."

"That and lots of exercise. If you go up and down this hill a couple of times a week you'll soon be fit."

She paused as they passed a small cottage painted in pastel blue, big pots of red geraniums stood outside the door and hanging baskets of lilac, mauve and white lobelia and pink fushia draped each side of the door "This cottage dates back to the fourteenth century," she said. "All these in this row do. They're old fishermen's cottages. I must get some photos of them."

"You really love this place don't you?" asked Reece as she took several shots of the cottages and close ups of the pots.

"I do, it's such a quaint little town, brimming with history. I think if I could tell people about it, show them what it's like, what they can see here if they get off the beach and walk around, then we could really bring in some guests." She slipped the phone back in her pocket. "There's some fantastic art galleries where you can watch the artists at work and buy signed prints or originals. And the Nautical Museum too on the sea front. That's full of things found on the beach, or in shipwrecks, as well as stuff that was used centuries ago. Port Medden was a thriving fishing town back then." She broke off as she saw that Reece was staring at her, a strange look on his face. "Sorry, I'm going on a bit, aren't I? It's just, I love this place."

"I can see that," Reece replied. He looked thoughtful as he reached for her hand again. "Show me some more."

They spent a couple of hours walking around. Ellie got lots of shots and answered Reece's questions about various things they saw, but she couldn't help noticing that he seemed quiet. As if he had something on his mind.

When they arrived back at the hotel they found Mandy on reception.

"Is Mum out the back?" Ellie asked.

"She's gone for a lie down, lovely. I'm afraid she's overdone things."

"What?" Ellie fought down the wave of panic. "What's she been doing? She said she was just going to sit out in the garden and rest."

"I know but she decided to change the lampshades in the dining room, almost fell off the step ladders. I arrived just in time to break her fall." Mandy looked worried.

"You know what your mum's like. Rest isn't in her vocabulary."

"I should have been helping her, not sightseeing," Ellie said. "I'll go and check on her, make sure she's all right."

Let me know how she is," Reece told her. "I'll be in my room if you need anything."

Ellie heard her mother coughing as soon as she opened the flat door. She was sitting on the sofa in the lounge, looking very pale.

"Don't panic, I'm fine," she said before Ellie could open her mouth. "I know I shouldn't have been changing the lightshade but that one went better with the blue curtains."

"You've got to take it easy for a bit, Mum, you've just come out of hospital."

"I'm fine, dear, don't fuss. Did you enjoy your walk?" Her mother asked, letting her know that the subject of her resting was closed.

"I did. It was fabulous. I've taken some lovely photos to upload to our Facebook and Pinterest pages. I'll show you in a minute."

"Come and sit down for a minute, Ellie. I'd like to talk to you."

Sue sounded serious. Ellie shot her a worried look. "Is everything okay? Are you feeling worse?"

"I'm fine, don't worry." Sue sat down on the sofa and waited for Ellie to sit beside her before continuing. "This Reece…"

Ellie grimaced. "Look mum, I already know about the birds and bees," she said in an attempt to both lighten the situation and change the subject. She didn't want to talk to mum about Reece. Her feelings for him were getting way too complicated without having to explain them to anyone else.

"I'm concerned, Ellie. It's lovely how he's helping us out but I can't help wondering why. And if he's such an important businessman that he can get such huge cut price deals why he did he book into our hotel."

"He had a meeting in Truro at the last minute and the big hotels were full. Well that's what he told me." Ellie paused. "What are you getting at, Mum?"

"I can see that you're both smitten with each other but I can't help wondering what he's doing down here and how he can afford to take an extra week off work to help us out." She looked thoughtfully at Ellie. "He's a guest, yet he's doing all this for nothing and we've only known him five minutes. People in business aren't usually so …accommodating."

And her Mum wasn't usually so mistrusting. She always saw the best in people. "Don't you like him?" she asked, wondering why her mother's answer was so important to her.

"Yes I do. Very much. But that doesn't stop me from wondering. Especially as I can see that you are very taken with him."

Was it that obvious? "Reece said his business down here was taking a bit longer than he thought," she said. She sat down beside her mum. "What's troubling you about him?"

"He's saved me well over one thousand pounds, Ellie, with the discount on the carpet and bed. And I'm wondering why."

And that was a very good question. Was it because he was starting to fall for her? Like she was for him?

Reece read through the draft contract again. They were offering a fair price, the hotel was struggling and needed a complete overhaul. Sue wouldn't get a better deal in the current market. And if she hung on, refused to sell, Gwel Teg would keep losing profit and she'd eventually have to sell for an even lower price. He was doing her a favour. So why was his conscience bothering him?

Because Ellie trusted him. And cared what she thought about him.

How would she feel when she found out that he was intending to buy the hotel and transform it? That he was planning to bring visitors into Port Medden too and had far more power behind him to do this than she could achieve with her photos on social media.

How would she feel when she found out that he didn't work for the company, he joint-owned it.

For the first time he started to feel really uncomfortable about what he was doing.

After several minutes of soul searching he walked back over to the desk, sat down and brought his laptop back to life. He read through the contract on the screen again then started typing an amendment.

Chapter Twenty Two

Reece set off for Plymouth early the next morning for a meeting with Steve, so they could both discuss the contract. When he arrived he was surprised to see his business partner hobbling about on crutches. "Sprained my bloody ankle playing football," he grumbled. Steve was a football fanatic and played for his county team. "Can't drive so I'm not going to be able to have a look around the hotel any time soon. I'll have to take your word for it."

"Trust me it's worth investing in. Gwel Teg has a lot of potential," Reece assured him. "I'd like us to agree on the terms before I go back to London on Saturday. I'll come back down early next week and get the owner to sign it."

He handed the contract to Steve. "I've made a slight amendment."

Steve hobbled into his study and eased himself into his large leather chair.

Reece followed, stopping to help himself to a coffee from the machine. "Want one?" he asked.

"I've just finished one. "Steve started to read the contract, flicking over the pages as he scanned through. "Where's this amendment of yours?" Then a frown creased across his forehead.

He's found it then. Reece sat down opposite him and waited.

Steve muttered an expletive and stared at Reece as if he was mad. "Are you serious? You want us to keep this woman on as manager? And let her continue living there?" He leaned back in his chair and scrutinised Reece's face. "Why?"

Reece ticked off the reasons on his fingers. "Because she's got a wealth of experience, she'll be an asset to us. It's better than training a new manager. It's a family hotel, she's lived there for years, she has its best interests at heart." He met Steve's gaze. "Her post is only for five years. We can reconsider then."

"Five years is a long time." Steve twiddled the pen in

his hand. "This is something we've never done, Reece. We've always bought the hotels outright so that we can do what we want with them. This complicates things. And I don't like complications."

Reece placed his elbows on the desk, locking his fingers. "I know but maybe it's something we should think of doing in the future. It makes sense, both financially and personally. If we let the owners continue living in the hotel and manage it for us, they'll have a personal and financial investment, that's got to be a good thing."

"Reece, all the hotels we buy are in difficulties. We rescue them. If the owners had good management skills they wouldn't be in trouble in the first place."

"In some cases yes. But not all. Take Gwel Teg for example, it was making a tidy profit until the owner's husband died a couple of years ago. The owner's struggled to cope since then."

"Does this owner have a pretty daughter by any chance?"

Reece bristled. "I find that insulting. Since when have you known me mix business with pleasure?"

"Never. But I think you are now. Which is worrying."

"We have to move with the times, Steve, be seen to be a caring company. We've got a bit of a ruthless image at the moment, sort of like vultures that prey on dying businesses, and it's not how I want people to see us."

"I thought all you cared about was results? Making money?" Steve leant forward. "You haven't found religion have you?"

Reece ignored that remark. "I've been thinking about our image and think we should rebrand ourselves as a company with a heart. A company people will turn to when they're in trouble instead of us seeking them out."

"I don't like it, Reece. I don't like things that aren't straightforward."

"Think about it. I haven't taken this decision lightly."

Steve sighed and leaned back. "This isn't something I can make a rush decision about . It's something I need to think about. I can't give you an answer for Saturday. You're going back to London then, aren't you?"

"Yes, I'll come back on Tuesday. Give me your decision then." Reece got up, ready to go. "There's just one thing you might like to know."

Steve raised an eyebrow.

"If you don't want to go with the contract then I'll buy the hotel myself. I can raise the cash."

Steve looked stunned. He shook his head. "Well, I never thought I'd see the day you had a heart. It's got to be a woman."

Reece picked up his briefcase and walked out.

He knew that Steve would give the contract careful

consideration, he was a business man above everything else. And it was a good contract. Not the one he'd originally been planning, he acknowledged, but seeing how desperate Ellie was to help her mum keep Gwel Teg, and how much Sue loved the place, he'd wanted to help them.

And it was all because of Ellie. His heart quickened at the thought of seeing her again. Steve was right. He'd got personally involved. He didn't want to walk away from Ellie. She'd got right under his skin and into his heart.

"Well you're a difficult one to get hold of," Kate said when Ellie finally returned her calls – one last night and the other early this morning. "Is it that busy at the hotel?"

"Sorry, I meant to phone you back but we're really busy. We've been doing lots of repairs and sprucing the hotel up a bit.

"We? Is your Mum up to all that physical stuff? I thought she had to take it easy?"

"She does. Harry and Reece have been doing most of it."

"Reece?" Kate pounced on the name. "Reece, as in the guest you walked in on in the shower? The arrogant one."

Trust Kate to remember that. She'd told her about it in one of their phone calls last week. "Yes but he's actually really kind. He's helped me such a lot. We've got really friendly."

"Do I take it that you were with him when I phoned at 10.30 last night which is why you didn't answer my call?" Nothing much passed by Kate.

"Yes. We've spent the last couple of evenings together." She briefly told Kate how much Reece had helped them. "We just sort of became close." She didn't confess *just* how close.

"A holiday romance!" Kate squealed. "I never thought you'd go for that! Well, why not? It's about time you had a bit of fun. You've been working far too hard just lately."

"That's what I thought," Ellie told her. "And he's going home tomorrow so no danger of getting too attached."

She'd miss him though. She'd got used to having him around.

She glanced at her watch. One o'clock. Reece had been gone all morning. When would he be back? This was their last day together.

Suddenly a familiar pair of arms wound around her waist and she felt Reece's breath on her neck. "I've been waiting to do that all morning," he murmured, nuzzling into her.

She turned around and wrapped her arms around his neck. "I take it you've missed me then?"

"You bet I have." His eyes held hers and she saw the flame of pleasure light them up. "I've got some good news though. Well, at least I hope you think it's good news." He kissed her deeply then smiled down at her. "My business down here isn't finished yet so I'll be back on Tuesday for a few days. That is if you still have a room for me?"

Her heart did a somersault. It wasn't goodbye yet then. She smiled up at him. "Oh I think we can manage that."

"And I've been thinking…"

"Yes?" She wondered if she could hear her heart thudding in her chest. What was he going to say?

"When I go back home next week it doesn't have to be goodbye…"

She shot a glance at him. "What do you mean?"

He met her eyes, his gaze steady. "I like you, Ellie. And we have fun together. I was hoping we could continue seeing each other. London's not that far from Birmingham. We could meet up at the weekends. If you'd like that?"

She searched his face, saw the desire in his eyes and

knew that he meant it. He wanted to keep seeing her. Well she wanted to keep seeing him too. But she'd try to keep it casual. What harm would the odd weekend meet up do? She nodded. "I'd love too."

"That's great. I really don't want to say goodbye to you." His embrace tightened and his lips found hers.

I really don't want to say goodbye to you. Reece's words kept going over and over in Ellie's mind. And she had to admit that she didn't want to say goodbye to him either. He was the sexiest, kindest man she had ever met. *And she loved him.*

The words popped into her mind before she even realised she was thinking them. Where had that come from? She liked him, enjoyed his company and yes, she'd like to carry on seeing him when she returned him. But love, no. She didn't do love. She didn't do serious. Footloose and fancy free, in charge of her own destiny that was her motto. And she wasn't breaking that for any man.

Not even a man as hot, gorgeous and incredibly kind as Reece Marshall. So it was a good job that they would be living miles apart. That way she could keep the relationship light.

Even so, as she lay in Reece's arm in his bed much later that night, listening to his gentle snoring, Ellie

257

found herself wishing that she could wake up every morning with Reece.

Yeah right, and lose your independence, your dreams, she told herself. That wasn't the life for her. She enjoyed these moments when they came but it wasn't something she wanted every day. She looked at the clock. Three o'clock. Time to go back to her own bed, as she did every night. As she went to leave, Reece's arm snaked around her waist. "Don't leave me," he murmured. "Stay a bit longer."

She hesitated.

"Please. We won't be able to do this again until Tuesday night."

How could she resist? She turned back and snuggled into him.

Reece left early the next morning. "I'll be back Tuesday afternoon," he said as he kissed her goodbye. "Don't go letting my room out."

"We might have to if we get lots of bookings," she teased.

"Then I'll have to sleep with you in your attic," he told her playfully.

As she watched Reece walk to his car Ellie realised how much she'd come to depend on him the last few days and how much she'd miss him.

You've got a lot to do so stop moping and get on with it, she told herself. It's only a couple of days. He'll be back.

Chapter Twenty Three

The weekend zoomed by, there was so much to do. What with reception duty, helping in the bar and restaurant, moving the furniture out of the Honeymoon Suite into the spare room next door and taking up the old carpet, there was little time to think of Reece. The nights were a different matter though. As she lay alone in her bed, remembering their lovemaking and aching for Reece's touch.

Reece texted her several times but never phoned, and although there were times she longed to hear his voice, Ellie wouldn't give in to the urge to phone him. There was no way she was turning into a clingy girlfriend.

Girlfriend?

Well they had agreed to keep seeing each other so she guessed that's what she was. A 'no strings attached' girlfriend. She smiled to herself. What would Kate say?

She soon found out. Kate phoned Sunday evening. "How are you getting on without Reece," she asked when they'd caught up on each other's news.

"Fine, I've been busy helping out at the hotel. I can manage without him for a few days, you know,"Ellie told her.

"Ah, but can you manage without him forever? He's going home for good next weekend, isn't he?"

"Actually, Reece wants us to still see each other when he goes home."

There was a stunned silence on the other end of the phone. Then Kate found her voice. "Wow! He must have made an impression on you. Don't tell me you've actually fallen for someone?"

"Don't get too carried away. I like him yes. And it would be good to see him at the weekend now and again."

"You've fallen for him, haven't you?" Kate said. "Go on, admit it. Heart of Stone Ellie has finally met her match."

"Of course I haven't! I do enjoy his company though

261

and a long distance romance might be good. That way we don't have to say goodbye to each other and will still have plenty of free time to do other things too."

"You're really worried about giving up your freedom, aren't you?" Kate chuckled. "I don't know what you'll do when you finally fall for someone. You'll be fighting it all the way."

"I don't intend to fall for anyone," Ellie told her. *Once had been enough. No one else was ever going to get the chance to break her heart, like Lee had done.*

"Maybe not, but it'll happen. You'll see. If it already hasn't," she teased.

"You wish!" Ellie laughed. "Look I've got to go now, Kate. I'll phone you again in the week."

"Make sure you do. I want all the goss." Kate teased.

Ellie smiled to herself as she ended the call and slipped the phone into her pocket. Kate had always been a firm believer in true love and several failed relationships hadn't deterred her. And she was obsessed with the idea of hooking Ellie up with someone. It was almost as if Ellie's reluctance to commit was a challenge to her. Well, Ellie didn't do love anymore. Not even for someone as hot or adorable as Reece.

* * *

Harry declared that the plastered ceiling was dry enough

to paint on Monday so Ellie pulled on her dungarees, fetched out the stepladders and set to work ignoring Harry's protests that he should be the one who did the painting. "It's no job for a woman," he told her but Ellie insisted. She knew Harry suffered with high blood pressure and didn't want him climbing ladders, although she didn't tell him that. He was a proud man and would take that personally. Instead she told him she enjoyed painting, which she did. There was something soothing about the backwards and forwards motion of the roller as she smoothed the white paint over the ceiling. And she was delighted with the job she was doing. It was looking good.

"You're making a really good job of that."

Reece's voice startled her so much she almost fell off the ladder. He was by her side in a flash, steadying her and helping her down the steps. "I'm sorry, I didn't mean to make you jump. That was stupid of me."

"It's fine." She smiled at him. "Have I slept a whole day away or are you back a day early?"

"I'm back a day early. I couldn't keep away from you." He wrapped his arms around her. "I've missed you, Ellie."

"I've missed you too ..." her words were lost as his lips sought hers.

"Careful, you'll get paint on your clothes," she said

when she came up for air.

He shrugged. "It's only an old pair of jeans and tee shirt." He released her and looked around the empty room. "Did you do all this yourself?"

"Harry helped me. We needed it clear for the carpets and bed to be delivered tomorrow." Is that why Reece had come early? To help them?

"Partly," he said when she put the question to him. "I managed to get things sorted a bit quicker than I thought I would so it seemed a good idea to come down today instead." He grinned. "And I told you, I couldn't keep away from you."

"Yeah right," she picked up the roller and paint tray. "I'd better get finished so stop distracting me." She flashed him a smile. "Shall we meet later? About three?"

"It's a date. I'll go and unpack and find your mother, see if I can make myself useful." A quick peck on the cheek and he was gone.

Ellie returned to her painting. It was few minutes before she realised that she was humming the tune to 'Rocking my heart.'

Ellie's feather kiss on his cheeks woke Reece up. He blinked, the room was still dark.

"I've got to go now, see you a bit later," she whispered.

She was doing her usual moonlight flit to her room so her Mum didn't realise she'd spent the night with him. Reece reckoned Sue had guessed this but didn't want to say so to Ellie, knowing it would embarrass her. Still groggy with sleep, he wrapped his arms around her neck, pulled her close and kissed her firmly on the lips.

"See you later, Sweetheart," he mumbled, resisting the urge to pull her back in bed with him. He had to drive to Plymouth today for a meeting with Steve and their solicitor, which meant an early start and a clear head.

As soon as she left, he turned back on his side and was soon asleep again, thoughts of Ellie on his mind as he drifted off.

The alarm woke him again a few hours later. He pulled himself up and looked at the empty space beside him where Ellie had lay.

He hated deceiving her.

You're helping them, he reminded himself. You're offering Sue a chance to stay in the hotel she loves, draw a wage, and be free from any of the financial outlay and responsibility. And setting Ellie free to live her own life.

But would Ellie see it that way?

He'd soon find out. Steve had agreed in principal – and with some reluctance – to Reece's amendment but wanted to discuss it a bit further. When he returned this afternoon he was going to tell Ellie everything.

"I love it," Sue said as she stepped into the Honeymoon Suite. "What a transformation."

"It looks good, doesn't it?" Ellie said proudly. "We definitely made the right choice." The carpet was bright and luxurious looking, making the room look bigger. And it didn't, as she'd feared, make the wallpaper look old and dated. "I can't wait to see the new bed now. This room's going to look even better than it did before."

"If only I hadn't been so stupid as to let the insurance lapse, we'd be able to have it all decorated too," her mum said. "And I wouldn't have to worry about paying Reece back. I'd have had a really good discount thanks to him, but even so…" her voice tailed off.

"Even so you are still going to struggle to pay for it all, aren't you?" Ellie put her arm around her mum's shoulders. "I can help you." She told her about her plans to use the interest-free balance transfer on her credit card. "So you see, you'll have eighteen months to pay it back."

She felt her mum stiffen. "No. Thank you, darling, but you've done enough. I'll sort it. I can do it. I'm just annoyed that I've been so foolish and have to pay for it myself, causing us both a lot of worry in the process. But I should be thankful, if it wasn't for you and Reece, it would be a lot worse."

"Things will pick up, Mum. We already have a booking for the Honeymoon Suite next week. We'll soon get Gwel Teg back on its feet again, you'll see."

"Of course we will," Sue said resolutely.

"I'll ask Harry to help me bring in the furniture now," Ellie told her.

"I can help you with that if you give me time to change out of this suit."

Ellie turned to see Reece standing at the doorway. He was back.

"Why don't you and your mum go take a break? I'll get changed, find Harry and we'll both move the furniture back in," he suggested.

Ellie's phone rang. "It's Mandy," she said, answering the call. "The beds arrived," she mouthed.

"I'll go and get changed. Be back in a few mins." Reece disappeared.

Ellie's mother went down to take charge of the delivery while Ellie waited for the bed to be brought up.

"Where do you want it?" one of the delivery men asked as they edged the bed through the doorway.

"In the middle of the room please," Ellie told them. That's where the bed had been placed previously and utilised the space in the room better than putting it over in one of the corners.

Sue popped her head in to look at the bed.

"You can't see it much, it's wrapped in plastic," Ellie told her. "They're just about to put it down."

"I can see that it's going to look lovely," Sue said. She frowned as she saw a receipt stuck to the base of the bed. "R.S. Incorporated. I recognise that name from somewhere."

The bed had just been put in place when Reece arrived and between them they moved the furniture back into the room while Sue went back downstairs.

"It looks fantastic," Ellie said. She phoned her Mum. "It's all done, come and take a look."

She was upstairs in five minutes, with Mandy hot on her heels.

"It looks great, really nice. I can't believe the difference the carpet and bed make," Mandy announced.

Sue was over the moon. She had tears in her eyes as she looked around. "I can't thank you all enough," she said. "Especially you, Reece. You're a guest here, a stranger, but you've done so much to help. Like a friend to us."

"Think nothing of it. I'm glad to help," he told her.

"Now I'm going to fix some lunch for us all," Sue announced. "You'll need it after all your hard work."

"Mum's answer to everything is a cup of tea and a sandwich," Ellie smiled as Sue went out of the room.

Reece pulled her into his arms and kissed her. "I've

been waiting to do that all morning," he murmured.

She wrapped her arms around his neck. "Did your meeting go well?"

"Yes it's all tied up now." He kissed her again then pulled back and looked at her intently. "Ellie, I want to talk to you. Can we go for a walk for half an hour or so?"

Something in his eyes and tone surprised Ellie. *What did he want to talk to her about?* She nodded. "Yes, of course. Give me fifteen mins to shower and change. We can have a stroll across the beach."

Reece had looked serious, what could it be? Ellie wondered as she showered. Had his company complained about him passing the company discount onto her mum? She knew some would frown at this. Oh God, she hoped he wasn't going to say they had to pay the full amount after all.

Don't jump to conclusions, she told herself. He probably wants to discuss how we're going to keep in touch when we both go home on Sunday.

Even so, it was with a bit of trepidation she joined Reece in the foyer.

"Let's talk over lunch," he said. "Shall we go to that seafood restaurant again?"

They both turned as the entrance door opened and a tall, dark haired woman walked in. Ellie heard Reece gasp as he stared at her. And she could see why. The woman was stunning, her short spiky cut emphasising cheekbones so sharp you could cut bread on them, her big brown eyes fringed by eyelashes to die for, skinny jeans clinging to legs that went up to her armpits and a v necked white designer top that showed off a perfect golden tan. She was pulling a hard white suitcase with a lilac coloured butterfly on the front of it and had a lilac, very expensive, designer bag slung over her shoulder.

Definitely not their usual clientele.

"Cindy." Reece exclaimed, surprise evident in his voice. "What are *you* doing here?"

He knew her?

The woman's face broke into a beaming smile. "If the mountain won't come to Mohammed…" She stood the case upright and held out her arms. "Haven't you got a hug for me?"

Ellie heard Reece curse under his breath as Cindy ran over and threw herself at him, winding her arms around his neck. "I've missed you so much, darling." She exclaimed. "I came back yesterday and simply couldn't wait any longer to see you so I've booked myself in for a few days."

Ellie drew in her breath. Reece had promised he was unattached but judging by the way this girl was kissing him he was very much attached. The rat!

Finally, Cindy let go of Reece and looked around the

room. "So is this hotel next on your hit list? Very quaint!"

Chapter Twenty Four

Damn! Why did Cindy have to turn up now? An hour later and he would have told Ellie everything. He could tell by the stunned silence and the way Ellie and Sue, who was sitting on the sofa in the corner reading a magazine, were looking at him that they had heard what Cindy had said. The hurt he saw in Ellie's eyes cut him to the core and Sue looked furious.

Sue rose shakily, her hand gripping the arm of the sofa for support. "I knew I recognised the name on the invoice. You're the hotel group that bought out Atlantic Bay View at a knockdown price." Her voice rose in anger. "You were sniffing around them as soon as you heard they were in trouble. Is that what you're doing here? Why you've been helping Ellie?"

Reece shot a glance at Ellie. She was pale, her lips trembling. He knew that she believed it too. Damn he cursed again, why hadn't he told her what he was doing earlier? Explained instead of avoiding the subject every time she asked him about his work.

Because you knew she would react this way.

He shot a furious look at Cindy and took a step towards Ellie. "Look it isn't how it seems."

"Really? So you don't work for a company that buys hotels which are struggling for a knock-down price?"

"Work for the company?" Cindy laughed shrilly. "Darling he owns it!"

The look that swept over Ellie's face made Reece feel a total heel. He *had* to make her understand.

"And you hadn't planned on trying to buy Gwel Teg?" Her hazel eyes fixed on his, demanding the truth.

"I was but it's not the way you think." He reached out for her hand. "Ellie, let me explain." He couldn't stand the way she was looking at him, as if he'd deceived her. Used her.

Which is exactly what he had done.

Deceived anyway. Used no. He'd enjoyed every minute he'd spent with her. He'd genuinely wanted to help. He liked Ellie A lot.

273

Maybe more than liked? That's why he wanted to continue seeing her.

A cold mask set over her face as she pulled her hand away. "There's nothing to explain," she told him in a voice devoid of emotion. Only the glisten in her eyes betrayed her true feelings. She was angry, hurt. And she had every right to be.

"Please let me explain..,"

"Ooops, have I put my foot in it?" Cindy hooked her arm possessively around his waist. "Sorry darling. I didn't realise it was supposed to be a secret." She looked around disdainfully. "I must say this is a bit smaller than you usually go for, darling. Mind you, the location is superb."

Deep breath. He inhaled slowly then shook off Cindy's embrace. Ellie and her mother were staring at him like he was the lowest scum.

Take control. He'd been in more awkward situations than this. He could deal with it.

"I think you'd better leave," Ellie said stiffly. "Pack your bags and check out." She turned on her heels and head held high walked across the reception and out through the door.

He wanted to run after her, make her listen to him but right now he needed to get rid of Cindy before she did any more damage.

274

He tore his eyes away from the swinging door that Ellie had just walked through and turned his attention back to her mother and Mandy.

"It really isn't how it looks…"

"I agree with Ellie. I'd like you to check out. Your girlfriend too," Sue Truman said. "You're not welcome here."

"If you would allow me to explain…"

"Believe me Mr Mitchell, there's no way you can possibly explain this away." Sue's tones were icy cold. She flicked her glance over at Cindy. "Now if you and your girlfriend would kindly leave. Mandy will book you out."

"Oh dear, I didn't mean to upset anyone." Cindy said in a 'little girl' voice.

Reece rounded on her, fists balled at his side, fighting to keep the anger out of his voice. "Why did you come here, Cindy?"

She pouted her red glossy lips. "Don't be like that, darling," she said petulantly. "I thought you'd be pleased to see me."

"Let me make this clear, Cindy. We are not an item any more. You can't just turn up like this. Now please go."

"Fine. I'll wait outside for you then!" She flounced off.

When Reece turned around Sue had gone too and

Mandy was glaring at him from the reception desk. What did he do now?

"Mr Mitchell?"

Harry was standing before him, looking very disapproving. "Mrs Truman said that I have to accompany you to your room to pack your bags then escort you off the premises."

How dare they treat him like this? Not even give him chance to explain? After all he'd done for them. Anger seared through him and he fought to control it. If that's the way they wanted it, it was their loss.

"An escort isn't necessary. If you wait here I'll be down in five minutes," he replied curtly.

Ellie was furious. How she walked out of the reception without throwing something at Reece and his false, gushy girlfriend she'd never know. All the time he was charming her, helping her, bedding her ... it was a ploy to get his hands on *Gwel Teg*.

Unwanted images of Reece's lips on hers, his hands caressing her, of them making love flitted across her mind. How could she have been so stupid? She thought he was attracted to her. That they had something special between them.

Why had she fallen for his act?

She sank down onto a chair at the table, her head in

276

her hands. She felt such a fool.

She remembered how arrogant Reece had been when she first met him. How he'd blasted his horn at her, snapped about the shower not working. That was the *real* Reece. Now she came to think of it he had only changed his attitude when he found out that her mother was ill in hospital and the hotel was struggling. Since then he hadn't been able to do enough for her. What had possessed her to confide in him like that? He'd seen his chance to make a killing and taken it. No wonder he'd tried to talk her out of giving up her job and moving down to Cornwall to help her mum with the hotel. That would have really scuppered his plans.

Then why had he talked the Smythes out of suing the hotel for compensation and let them use his business account to do the repairs? The hotel would have been worth even less then.

Because she'd told him Mum would never sell and he wanted to earn their trust, that's why. He was hoping to get Ellie onside so she could persuade her mum that selling up was the best thing to do. That the hotel was too much for her to cope with.

Well he had no chance. Hell would freeze over before she let her mum sell *Gwel Teg* to Reece.

She should have realised he was more than an employee for a hotel group. The hot shot suits he wore, the Mercedes, the important business meetings. And as for that Barbie-girl Cindy, clinging like a limpet onto Reece's arm, well he was welcome to her.

Ellie was literally shaking. She wasn't sure whether it was with anger, shock or distress. It hurt more than she cared to admit, even to herself, that Reece had deceived her in this way. She'd trusted him entirely. Fallen for his charming and helpful manner.

Fallen for him.

As the words flashed into her head she knew they were true. She had never felt the same way for any man as she'd felt in Reece's arms. In his bed.

Her cheeks burned as she remembered how readily she'd fallen for those charms. How eagerly she'd returned his kisses. And...

She shook away the memory of their naked tangled limbs, of the feel of him inside her. What was the use of tormenting herself with recriminations? Yes, she'd been stupid to let her guard down and trust him, stupid to let him into her heart.

She looked up as the kitchen door opened and her mum stepped in, her eyes full of concern.

"Are you all right, Ellie? It must have been a shock for you." She picked up the kettle and filled it with water. "I'll make you a cup of tea."

Tea? She could do with a bottle of wine. It had been

more of a blow than a shock, a blow to her heart. Not that Mum needed to know that. As far as she was concerned, Ellie and Reece had just been hanging out together.

"Has he gone?" Even to her ears the words sounded flat, distant.

"I've asked Harry to escort him out. And that woman. How dare he try to pull a trick like that!" She turned around. "Are you okay, love? You and Reece were a bit close, weren't you?"

Ellie nodded numbly. Close was a good word for it. "I'm so sorry, Mum. I had no idea he was planning to buy you out of the hotel. I thought…" She took a deep breath to still the tremor in her voice. *That he was helping us because he cared about me, had feelings for me.*

Sue took two clean mugs out of the dishwasher and dropped a teabag in each. Ellie sank her head in her hands. What a fool she'd been.

"Don't take this too hard, Ellie," Sue said, placing a mug of tea in front of Ellie. "Reece is a businessman and when he saw the state this hotel was in he seized the opportunity. That's how businesses make money. He can't make me sell."

"I know, Mum, and if he'd come straight out with it. Been upfront and told me what he did for a living, made us an offer, I wouldn't have minded. But he didn't. He kept it a secret from me. Let me think that he was a …friend. That he was helping because he cared, not because he was trying to get us onside so we'd be more inclined to accept his offer. I trusted him." She swallowed. "And on top of all that he said he wasn't in a relationship. He was single. Another lie." She added bitterly.

"I guess like with a lot of men it's out of sight, out of mind." Sue patted her hand. "Well that's the last we'll see of him I expect. Put it down to experience."

She'd do that all right. She would never trust a man again.

How could she have got it so wrong?

Chapter Twenty Five

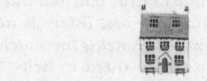

"They've gone," Mandy announced, sweeping in a few minutes later. "Harry sent them packing." She held out an envelope to Ellie. "Reece left you this note."

Ellie stared at the cream coloured embossed envelope. Even his perishing notepaper was designer!

"I don't want it. I'm not used to listening to his excuses. Chuck it in the bin."

Mandy waved the envelope in front of her. "He said I wasn't to let you do that. It was about the carpet order."

The carpet? She guessed it was the bill. Now he had no chance of buying the hotel, would he charge them full price for the carpet. And the bed? She doubted if Mum could afford that. Everything was such a mess. No wonder she'd fallen for Reece's act. He'd been a ray of hope in all their cloud of gloom.

Reluctantly, Ellie ripped open the envelope and took out the matching paper. A business card fell out onto the floor. She left it there.

The note was short, written in a crisp black script.

I'm sorry you had to find out like this, Ellie. I truly had your best interests at heart. It's obvious the hotel is too much for your Mum and I wanted to help. I was about to tell you when Cindy showed up. And believe me, she is not my girlfriend. We finished weeks ago.

I'll write off the bill for the carpet, bed and everything else as an apology. You owe me nothing. However, I hope you will give me a few minutes of your time to allow me to explain the deal I was about to offer you. It really is worth considering.

Please phone me. I've booked into another hotel for tonight. If I don't hear from you I will be going home

282

tomorrow evening.
   Yours
   Reece

So that was it. All about the business. No 'love Reece'.
Not even one solitary kiss. No apology, No mention of
how he felt about her. No begging her to give him
another chance. He wanted her to phone him so he could
talk her into letting him buy the hotel. It was all about
business. It always had been.

"Well, go on. Put us out of our misery, lovely,"
Mandy urged. "Unless it's personal, of course."

It couldn't be less personal. Reece had made it clear
that he had no 'personal' interest in her at all.

She read it out in as emotionless tone as she could
manage.

"I'm not phoning him. I never want to speak to him
again." She ripped the letter in half, walked over to the
bin and dropped it.

"Well, I'll pay for the carpet and everything else. He
can keep his gifts. I'll manage. I can increase the
overdraft," Sue said.

"Then you'll have to contact him yourself. I don't
want anything to do with him." Ellie told her. How could
she have been such a fool? "I need to get some fresh air.
I'm going for a walk. I won't be long."

As she stepped out of the hotel her phone zinged to announce an incoming message.

Reece?

She picked up the phone and swiped the screen. It was Kate,

How's it going, hun?

It wasn't Reece. And a good job too, she didn't want him to contact her. In fact, she'd make sure he couldn't. Before she could talk herself out of it, Ellie blocked then deleted Reece's number.

She walked down the hill towards the beach, thinking about Kate's message. She wanted to leave right now. To put a distance between her and Reece, to get back to the Midlands and on with her life. Here, it was all too raw. Back at home, in her flat, going to work and getting on with her life, she would be able to forget about everything.

She'd felt like this once before, she remembered. When Lee had cheated on her. She'd run away then and not come back for a year. She knew that had hurt her parents but she hadn't been able to face it. She wasn't going to do that again. Mum needed her. She would go home Sunday as planned, but not before that.

She had reached the rail now and leaned against it, looking over at the beach, remembering the day she and Reece had walked around to the secluded cove. The day she'd got her skirt wet. The day she'd told him her worries about Mum being ill and not being able to manage the hotel herself, how she'd tried to persuade her to sell it.

Is that what had given him the idea to buy the hotel himself? Or had he come down to Cornwall with that intention?

She thought back to the first time she met Reece, how arrogant he'd been until she'd told him her mother was ill in hospital, told him how run down the hotel was. He'd seen his chance then and taken it, offering his support, his friendship, his body. How could she have fallen for it? To have gone so readily to his bed? It wasn't like her. Yes, of course she had relationships, she wasn't a nun, but never before with someone she'd just met and might never see again. What had possessed her this time?

"Penny for them?"

She spun around, surprised to see Lee standing behind her. How long had he been there?

She shrugged. "Just looking at the sea."

"You always did like to do that." His voice was soft. "Where's your boyfriend?"

"He's had to go back to London. Business." She replied. She wasn't about to let Lee know they'd broken up. It was obvious he was still after her.

He reached out and touched her arm. "I miss you. There isn't a day that goes by when I don't regret what I did."

She shrugged his arm away. "Don't waste your time beating yourself up about it. We were kids. I soon got over it and never think about it. You did me a favour."

"I guess your rich, hotshot boyfriend is more of a catch."

The snidey tone in his voice made her hackles rise. She glared at him. "What business is it of yours who I go out with? We were over years ago and as far as I'm concerned that's a good thing." She crossed her arms. "What went wrong with you and Zoe? Cheat on her did you?"

She saw the colour rise in his cheeks. Yes, it was just as she'd guessed.

"Goodbye, Lee."

She walked away from him, down the hill, her mind a whirl of thoughts. She'd been heartbroken when she'd found out about Lee and Zoe but she'd eventually recovered from it. And now she realised it was for the best. Lee could have ruined her life, left her with a couple of young children to bring up along – as he'd done to Zoe.

In a few weeks. Okay maybe months, she'd realise that Reece had done her a favour too. For she would

286

never trust anyone so completely again. They'd had a holiday romance that was all. He'd been there when she had needed someone to lean on and she'd got carried away by that. Being on holiday could do that to you. How many times had her friends fallen in love with someone when they'd been on holiday, bid them a tearful goodbye, swearing their heart was broken only to forget all about them in a week or two?

Like she'd forget about Reece.

Damn Cindy. He was fuming with her. He'd told her quite firmly that they were over, there was no chance of them getting back together, and sent her packing. Then he'd driven to Truro and pulled into this pub, wondering what to do next. Two black coffees later he still wasn't sure.

He should just walk away. He'd find another hotel to buy, the country was full of struggling businesses looking for someone to bail them out.

The truth of it was though that he didn't want to walk away from Gwel Teg. The hotel was a good investment in an excellent location and he genuinely liked Ellie. And her mother. He wanted to help them. He knew that it looked bad with Cindy walking in like that but he thought he and Ellie had a connection. That she would trust him.

Why should she? He was a stranger, someone who had only walked into her life just over a week ago.

Because he was sure she had feelings for him. Like he had for her.

He'd wanted to write her a note pleading with her to listen to him, telling her that he really cared about her but his pride wouldn't let him. Not after the way they'd almost thrown him out. He thought he meant more than that to Ellie. Even so, he hated her to think he was a cheating scum bag, and for Sue to miss out on what was a very good offer. And it was a deal he really didn't want to walk away from. His decision to buy Gwel Teg had never been a personal one, he truly believed the hotel had potential. So he'd written a brisk, to the point, note asking for the chance to explain. It was up to Ellie now. If she wanted to contact him she knew how. He'd never chased after a woman in his life and he wasn't about to start now. Not even someone as gorgeous as Ellie.

Reece checked his phone countless times that evening and the next morning but there was no message from either Ellie or her mother. He might as well go home. Perhaps Ellie would get in touch when she'd had time to calm down and mull things over.

All the way back to London he kept thinking about Ellie, remembering things about her, the way she threw back her head when she laughed, that gorgeous smile of hers that spread to her eyes, how kind-hearted she was, the way she loved her Mum and would do anything to help her. And that figure…

A horn blasting behind him brought Reece back to the present as he realised the lights had changed. He thought back to the first time he'd seen Ellie, when he'd blasted his horn at her because she'd dawdled at the lights. He realised now that she must have been worrying about her mother, had probably only just left the hospital after visiting her. He'd been in a rush that day but it was no excuse.

Other memories flashed across his mind, their first kiss, the first time they'd made love. He'd never met anyone like Ellie, she was so uncomplicated, so spontaneous. There was no agenda with her, not like the other women he'd gone out with. Women like Cindy, who despite him making it clear that he wasn't into serious relationships still wanted to force some kind of commitment out of him. Cindy wouldn't take no for an answer. Did she really think that turning up like that would make him want to go back out with her?

Ellie had looked so hurt, he remembered. Not hurt enough to let him explain though. She accepted what Cindy had said and shut him out, after everything he'd done to help her. After everything they'd been through together.

Which just went to show how little she thought of him.

Chapter Twenty Six

Reece was pretty exhausted by the time he arrived at his luxury Canal Wharf apartment, the traffic was horrendous and he hadn't stopped for any coffee breaks. He'd deliberately turned his phone off in case Cindy called, the last thing he needed was an argument with her while he was driving, so took it out of his pocket and checked it for messages as soon as he parked up in the underground car park. There were four from Cindy. But no messages or phone calls from Ellie. He guessed that was it then. Finished. He opened the boot and took out his suitcase.

The porter hurried to greet him as he walked into the

foyer. "Would you like me to carry your luggage up to your room, Mr Mitchell?"

"No thank you. I can manage." Reece told him politely.

He wheeled the case into the lift and pressed the button for the eighth floor. A few minutes later he was in his luxury penthouse suite looking out of the floor to ceiling windows at the views of the Dockland cityscape below. It was these spectacular views that had clinched the deal for him. He loved switching the lights off and looking out at night at the city lights dancing on the Thames below. He went over to the drinks cabinet, poured himself a whisky then opened the windows and stepped out onto the balcony, into the cool night breeze.

He wondered what Ellie's flat was like. Her wage as a PR consultant was not likely to be anywhere near his but then she probably wasn't as driven to succeed as he was, anxious to prove to his parents that he was worthy of their time, their love. It had taken him years to realise that no matter what he did, how much he earned he would always be an inconvenience to them, that their lives would always be too busy to spare any time for him. By the time he did realise he didn't care. At least he told himself he didn't. All he cared about was making the next buck, buying the latest car, being seen in the right places but he had never walked over anyone to get there.

He was a businessman yes, and liked to get a good deal, but he was always fair and treated people with respect. Ellie's accusations had stung. He had never conned anyone, never cheated on anyone. She should have had the decency to hear him out. He thought she was better than that.

He took a sip of his whisky. Meeting Ellie had changed him, made him want more out of life than signing the next deal. Ellie was fun, sweet, loving, feisty, spirited and obviously valued family more than money as she'd been willing to give up her career to help her mother.

He was going to miss her.

Ellie kept to herself for the rest of the week, tried not to give herself time to think about Reece. He had really hurt her but she blamed herself. She should never have trusted him, never allowed herself to get so close to him. He was a total stranger. What had possessed her? She didn't usually get taken in like that.

The nights were a different matter. Whenever she closed her eyes to sleep his image was there. She could see his smile, hear his laugh, feel his caress. She thrust the images away, screwing her eyes tight, willing herself not to think about him. The sooner she was back home, into her normal routine the better. Reece would soon become a distant memory.

By Sunday, Gwel Teg was looking clean and tidy and Sue was much better. The coughing had almost subsided now and although she still looked tired, the colour had returned to her cheeks. Ellie felt easier about leaving her, although she was still concerned.

"Are you sure you're going to be all right?" Ellie asked her. "You will take it easy, won't you?"

"I'll be fine. Stop worrying. I've got Mandy to help me and her niece, Sara, is coming in tomorrow for the week," her mother reassured her.

"I know but…" Ellie bit her lip. She felt so guilty but she had to run the conference tomorrow; she couldn't let her boss down. "I'll be down Friday evening for the weekend." She intended to try to come down every weekend until Mum looked strong enough to cope.

"I've told you, there's no need. You have enough to do. I'll be fine."

"I want to come down. A weekend in Cornwall is just what I need after a week at work." Ellie knew her Mum wouldn't argue with that." She turned to Mandy. "Now you're fine with keeping an eye on the Facebook page and answering any queries aren't you? The website doesn't need anything done to it. Oh, and maybe keep an eye on the Pinterest page too. Add a few new pins now and again."

"No problem, lovey. You have a safe journey." Mandy gave her a big hug. "And don't you worry, I'll be keeping an eye on your Mum."

"Thank you." It was a comfort for her to know Mandy was by Mum's side. She hesitated. "I wish I could stay a bit longer…"

"Don't be silly. It will be late afternoon when you get back as it is and you've got an important conference tomorrow." Her mother gave her a hug. "Safe journey. Message me as soon as you get home."

"I will," Ellie promised.

Ellie would be home by now. Reece thrust his hands in his pockets as he looked out at the city below. He could see how bad it looked but even so he thought that she might contact him – even if it was only a text telling him what a rat he was. He smiled as he recalled the feisty flash in Ellie's eyes when she was angry. And he bet she was angry right now.

Well he was angry too. He was offering them a good deal.

He hadn't told Steve what had happened between him and Ellie but had asked him to hold off having the contract drawn up while he sorted out the finer details. Now he didn't know what to do. He was half tempted to email a draft contract over to Ellie and Sue to let them know what a good deal he'd been prepared to offer them. If they turned it down once they knew all the facts, then that was their choice but he at least wanted to give them the opportunity to read and consider it. And to realise that he wasn't the conniving slime ball Ellie obviously now thought him to be.

Not that he cared about Ellie's opinion. She'd been a pleasant distraction that was all.

Then why can't he stop thinking about her?

He picked up his phone and selected her number. Then shook his head. No, he wasn't going to phone her. He'd left her a note explaining, if she didn't care enough to give him the benefit of the doubt, to phone him and listen to his side of things, then she wasn't worth bothering about.

He wondered how Sue would cope now Ellie had gone. Had her coughing subsided? Was she feeling stronger? He liked Sue, she was a warm, spirited woman. He could understand why Ellie was so close to her. He thought of how much Sue worried about Ellie too, tried to put Ellie's needs first, refused to let Ellie sacrifice her life to help her. Not like his cold, uncaring mother who had walked out so selfishly and never looked back, never even stopped to consider the heartache she caused her own young son.

He was older now and understood enough about adult

relationships to realise that his parents hadn't had a loving marriage, that unfortunately things didn't always work out and one or other of the partners sometimes fell in love with someone else. But his mother walking out like that, turning her back on him, her child, for another man. To not care about the devastation she caused. *That* he would never forgive. She could have still kept in touch with him, let him stay over weekends. She knew how cold and distant his father was but had made no effort to make his life any easier. Whereas it was clear that Ellie and her mother cared deeply about each other and would do anything to make the other one's life easier. It was that bond that had made him want to help them, and still want to despite the fact that he would never see Ellie again. He was good at his job and his experience told him that *Gwel Teg* was going to go under, then where would Sue be? She would have to sell for a rock bottom price.

He thrust his hands in his trousers pockets and paced around. It was Sue who owned Gwel Teg, Sue who he was offering the deal too, not Ellie. He should at least show her how good a deal he was offering. Perhaps he should email it over? He thought about it but was pretty sure that if Sue Truman saw an email from him she'd delete it. So he printed out the contract, slipped it into an envelope, penned a short note to Sue telling her that this was the contract he'd been organising for her, and that if she read it she'd see it was a deal that benefitted her. He finished by saying that she was welcome to contact him – or get her solicitor to if she had any queries. He signed it *Best wishes, Reece* and popped it in his briefcase. He'd get his secretary to post it tomorrow. He couldn't do anymore. He'd offered Sue a lifeline, it was up to her whether she took it.

Kate was waiting with a bottle of already opened wine when Ellie finally arrived home. "Right, put your case down and tell me all about it," she said, pouring a glass for Ellie.

Ellie sank down into the chair and sighed heavily. "God, I've been an idiot, Kate."

"Haven't we all some time or other? Especially with men." Kate took a swig of wine and raised an eyebrow questioningly. "Go on spill. I take it he was hot?"

"Sizzling." Ellie closed her eyes for a minute. She felt so weary.

"You had it that bad, eh? Well, who'd believe it? I thought no man would ever get close enough to make your hormones flutter."

Ellie snapped her eyes open. "He hasn't!"

"Really? That's not what it sounded like in your texts."

Ellie reached for the glass of wine – sweet white, chilled, with a dash of soda, just how she liked it. "OK, yes I admit I like him. A lot. He seemed so kind and he made me laugh." She kicked off her shoes and sat cross-legged on the cushion. "He was so helpful, Kate. Like nothing was too much trouble. Of course, I know the reason why now." She added bitterly. "He was after the hotel. The scheming rat."

"Why?"

Ellie stared at her friend. "What do you mean?"

"Why did he want the hotel? I mean it's just a small family run hotel in Cornwall. I'm sure it's really nice," she added quickly. "But what's so special about it that Reece would want to buy it?"

Ellie had asked herself the same thing, several times, and come to only one conclusion. "He's partner of a company that buys hotels that are struggling for a knock-down price, builds them back up again and sells them at a profit." She took a sip of the wine, savouring it in her mouth for a while." He knew Mum was ill and I stupidly told him how the hotel was struggling to break even so he, like a vulture, went in for the killing."

"How much did he offer you?"

"He didn't get around to actually making the offer. His girlfriend came to visit him and busted him before he could."

"Girlfriend? Ouch." Kate looked at her sympathetically. "That's tough."

Ellie bit her lip. "I feel so mad at myself, for letting him con me like that. I never get that close to someone so quickly. You know that. What was I thinking of?" She fought back the tears. "I can't believe I was such an idiot."

"Hey, don't be so hard on yourself. You were probably so worried about your mum you were just glad of a shoulder to lean on." Kate put her wine glass down on the table and leaned over to give Ellie a hug. "Are you upset because you're mad at yourself or because you really like him?"

"Both," she admitted. "And I thought he really liked me too. He wanted us to carry on seeing each other, to meet up at weekends – or so he made out."

Kate whistled. "The toe rag. And all the while he had another girlfriend and was planning to buy out your mum's hotel. You're well rid!"

"I know. I just can't believe I was taken in by him." She shook her head.

"Forget that two-timing con artist. There are plenty of other guys who'd beat a path to your door, if you'd let them. A cheat is not worth wasting one single tear on."

Kate was just what she needed, someone to tell it to her straight. She took a gulp of wine. "You're right. I'm not going to let him upset me. At least we found out what he was up to before he could sweet talk Mum around."

"Atta girl. Now pin those ears back because I've got some goss to tell. You'll never guess what's happened while you were away." Kate leaned forward conspiratorially and started to tell her about the young couple, Meg and Steve, across the landing who were always having dramatic arguments after a night out drinking. "They had a real stonker last night. Steve stormed out so Meg locked the door and wouldn't let him back in. He was huddled in the corridor wearing a tiger onesie- complete with ears and a tail. He must have forgotten he was wearing it when he stormed out." Kate finished. She laughed. "You should have seen him. He sat down by the door looking all forlorn. I felt so sorry for him I took him a cup of coffee."

"What was it about this time? Did he tell you?" Ellie asked between giggles at the thought of butch looking Steve dressed in a tiger onesie. She knew he wouldn't be out there for long. As soon as he had grovelled enough Meg would calm down, open the door and let him back in again.

"I've no idea but when I checked on him an hour later he was gone so I presume he'd persuade Meg to let him back inside." She picked up the wine bottle. "Want a refill?"

"Please." Ellie swigged the mouthful of wine left in her glass and held it out. "But this will have to be the last one. I need a clear head for tomorrow. I'm doing a presentation at the conference remember."

"I know. That's why I only bought the one bottle. Just enough to chill you out but not enough to zonk you out." She held out her glass. "To friendship and sod fellas."

"To friendship and sod fellas," Ellie repeated as they clinked glasses.

It was good to be back home. What with her work and Kate she'd soon get Reece out of her system.

Chapter Twenty Seven

The presentation went well, despite the usual attack of nerves just minutes before she was due to take the stage. Ellie had forced herself to take a few deep breaths and remain calm. Focus on the presentation, not the audience, she told herself. You can do this. You've done it loads of times.

Well, maybe not loads, but certainly enough times to know what she was doing. She always felt nervous addressing a crowd but luckily once she walked out onto the stage and started talking those nerves usually disappeared. She was passionate about raising funding to develop children's education so could speak, and answer questions, with confidence.

Her talk had been well-received and the DK Consultants stand had a constant flow of visitors. Her boss was really pleased.

So pleased that when she arrived at work the next morning he'd summonsed her to his office to offer her a promotion as a Senior Consultant. More money and more responsibility. It was only after she'd accepted that she remembered how she'd been thinking of giving up her job and moving to Port Medden to help run Gwel Teg if her mother was still struggling.

Your Mum wouldn't want you to put your life on hold for her. Reece's words flashed across her mind.

He'd only said them because he wanted the hotel for himself and didn't want her to move back home and help her mum. The traitor.

Well at least she'd rumbled him before he could worm his way anymore into Mum's good books and set his plans in action.

Actually she hadn't, his girlfriend had turned up and outed him.

Ellie wondered how Mum was coping. She intended to phone her later but knowing Mum she'd say everything was fine. She couldn't help worrying, thank goodness she'd arranged to go down again at the weekend. She could see for herself then. The new positon didn't start for another month and then there was a three months trial period, on both sides. If it wasn't working out, or Mum needed her help she could quit. She had nothing to lose and would gain more experience.

Kate agreed when Ellie told her about her promotion that night. "Massive congrats!" she gave her a hug. "I'd love to stay in and help you celebrate but Greg's in town and asked me out for a drink. We haven't had a catch up for ages." She paused. "Why don't you join us? Greg won't mind. I'm sure you two would hit it off."

Greg was an old school friend of Kate's, one of her best buddies. They always met when he was in town and it was obvious when you saw them together that they were very good friends but there was no romantic attraction. Greg was the brother she never had, Kate always said. Ellie had the feeling she was trying to match-make her with him. Probably to take Ellie's mind off Reece.

"Thanks but I'm going to give Mum a quick ring, take a soak in the bath then get an early night. I'm whacked."

"OK, hun. See you later. I'll tip toe in so I don't wake you."

"There's no need, honest. I'm so knackered I'll zonk out as soon as my head touches the pillow."

She made herself a cup of tea, slipped a ready meal in the oven then phoned her Mum. Mum sounded cheerful and assured Ellie that everything was fine. Sara, Mandy's niece, was evidently proving to be a big asset. "Mandy and Sara are doing most of the work, I'm taking it easy," Sue said. "So don't go rushing down here at the weekend. I know you've got a lot to do. Come down next weekend instead."

It was tempting. Ellie did have some training stuff to read through for when she started her new position and it would be great to have a night out with Kate. But she wouldn't rest until she saw for herself that Mum was looking better. It was a relief to know that Sara was a help, though. It was a brilliant idea of Mandy's to suggest that she did her work experience at *Gwel Teg*.

The ding of the timer announced that her meal was ready so Ellie went into the kitchen to serve it up. Two hours later, she'd had a long soak in a hot bath – a bath she'd almost fallen asleep in – and was in bed. Exhausted, she fell asleep almost immediately but it was a restless sleep, interrupted by memories of Reece.

The week passed quickly. Friday evening, straight after work, Ellie set off for the long drive down to Cornwall. She'd almost decided to put it off until next weekend, as her mum had suggested, but she could hear the strain in Sue's voice when she'd phoned her last night, and twice she'd broken off talking to cough.

"Don't wait up for me, Mum," Ellie told her. "It'll be almost midnight by the time I get there. Go to bed and I'll see you in the morning."

"Nonsense. I won't rest until I know you've arrived safely, "Sue replied. "I wish you'd come down early Saturday morning instead. You'll be so tired after working all day."

Ellie preferred to drive down in the evening. The roads would be clearer – Saturday morning traffic could be terrible – and she wanted to wake up in Gwel Teg. To hear the squawk of the seagulls and look out of her window at the sea. To her, that meant she was home.

Would the memories of Reece be even stronger there?

She wasn't going to think about Reece. He'd only been in her life for a couple of weeks and she wasn't about to let him ruin the rest of it.

Thankfully there wasn't much traffic and Ellie arrived just before midnight. All was quiet at the hotel so she went straight up to the private quarters. Her mother was sitting on the sofa, ready for bed in her nightie and dressing gown, sipping a cup of hot chocolate, when Ellie walked in.

"Ellie darling." Her face broke into a smile. "I was just thinking you should be here soon."

"Hello mum," Ellie gave her a hug and kissed her on

the cheek. "How are you?" she scanned the pale face. "Have you been overdoing it?"

"I've been taking it easy. Bossy Mandy won't let me do anything. She and Sara have got everything wrapped up between them." She went to get up. "Do you want a cuppa?"

"I'll do it," Ellie told her. "Why don't you go to bed, Mum? You look tired. We can catch up in the morning. I'll be going to bed myself as soon as I've had a drink."

"I think I will, dear. I wanted to wait up to make sure you arrived safely." Sue got unsteadily to her feet. "Sleep well. Sara's covering the morning reception so have a lie in. Night."

"Night, Mum."

Ellie made herself a cup of hot chocolate and sank down on the sofa. She sat there silently for a while, deep in thought. As she'd feared, coming back to Gwel Teg brought back memories of Reece. Memories she wanted to forget. What was Reece doing now she wondered? Had he found another struggling hotel to snatch up at a knock down price, another family's dreams to trample on? Was he out with his girlfriend Cindy, the one he'd conveniently forgot to tell her about, celebrating a new deal?

Well she'd show him. She'd help Mum get Gwel Teg on its feet again. She was determined about that. They didn't need his money.

To her surprise, Ellie slept quite fitfully and she hadn't heard Mum coughing at all in the night, which was a good sign.

She grabbed her dressing gown, deciding to make herself a cup of tea before showering.

She was surprised to see Sue already up and dressed, sitting in the lounge, a pile of papers scattered on the coffee table in front of her. "Morning, love," she said looking up from the letter she was reading.

"Are you okay? Couldn't you sleep?" Ellie asked worriedly.

"I'm fine." Sue gazed at her, a serious expression on her face. "I need to talk to you, love. Let me make you a cuppa and we can have a chat."

She's probably still worried about money, Ellie guessed. *I bet those letters are bills and Mum's wondering how she'll manage them.* Well at least with this promotion Ellie could help more financially. They'd work it out. "I'll make the tea." Ellie went into the kitchen. "Do you want one?" she called.

"No thanks, I've just finished one."

The kettle was still hot so didn't take long to re-boil. Ellie made herself a mug of tea and walked back into the lounge and sat down beside Sue. "Look Mum, I don't want you to worry about bills," she said. "I've been offered a promotion and a pay rise. I'll be able to help you out."

"I don't need you to." Sue looked as if she was struggling to find the right words. "You're not going to like this …"

Ellie felt a flutter of alarm. "What is it?"

"This," her mum held out the letter in her hand, "is a letter from Reece. It came in the week."

"Reece?" she felt her throat tighten. "What does he want?"

"He sent," she pointed to the papers. ". . . A proposed contract for the purchase of Gwel Teg."

"WHAT!" Ellie was furious. "How dare he?"

"The thing is, love," she saw her mother take a deep breath. "It's a good deal. At least it seems to be. Mandy and I have both been over it and we can't see any catch."

She couldn't take it in. Reece was still after the hotel. After everything. "I can't believe he's sent you that!" she got to her feet. "We don't need his money, Mum. We can manage. I told you I've got a pay rise. I'll give up my job and move back here if necessary. You can't sell up. You wouldn't be happy living anywhere else."

He's offering to buy the hotel and let me stay on as manager, living here in our flat." She pointed to the papers on the table. "It's all in this contract here."

Ellie stared at her. "And you'd like that?"

310

"To be honest, it is tempting. It would take some of the financial worry off me, and he'll provide extra staff so my workload will be easier." She pointed to the contract and handed it to Ellie. "Take a look. It's a fair and good offer. We might have misjudged him."

"Then why didn't he mention it? Why not tell us who he was and what he was planning?"

Especially her. They had been so close.

"According to his letter he was worried we'd think he was trying to take advantage of us. So he wanted to wait until he'd got the contract typed up and checked over by his solicitor and then we could see that it was fair."

He'd asked her to go for a walk with him, said he needed to talk to her, when that Barbie woman walked in, she remembered. Was it about his plan to make an offer for the hotel?

She bet that he wasn't planning on telling her that he had a girlfriend.

"I can't believe that you're seriously thinking of doing a deal with him, Mum. I know things are hard for you right now but that's because you've been ill and still feel weak. We can build the Gwel Teg up again. I know we can."

"The thing is, love. It's too much for me. It's been too much for me for a long time. We were struggling even before your dad died."

Well that was news to her. Ellie stared at her mother in disbelief. Why hadn't they told her?

Because they were proud and you were busy with your own life.

"I can't keep kidding myself, love. I've got to face it, I haven't got the energy and drive I used to have. I want to take things easy. I don't want the responsibility." Tears glistened in her mother's eyes and she paused for a minute, composing herself. "I've thought about it long and hard. I know your dad would want me to do it. He'd say 'take the time to smell the roses, Sue.'"

That was one of Dad's favourite sayings. He always said people rushed about too much, trying to get this and that done, never taking time to smell the roses. She looked at her mother's tired face. She looked so fragile. So weak.

"Surely there must be someone else you could sell to, Mum? Gwel Teg is in such a prime location. It'd be an asset to anyone."

"Not anyone would give me such a good deal." Sue held out the contract. "Read it and see for yourself."

Ellie took it off her and sat down. She read slowly and thoroughly. When she'd finished she had to admit that her mother was right. It was a fair contract. More than fair. Reece was offering an excellent price for the hotel, and her mum a good wage as a manager. Mum still got to live in Gwel Teg as long as she wanted, and have a nice sum in the bank to buy herself a little place when she was ready to retire. The contract was to be reviewed in five years, providing the hotel was solvent. Okay. So maybe Reece wasn't a total ratbag. But he still lied about not having a girlfriend. He was still a cheat and a liar.

"What do you think…?"

"It all looks above board," Ellie admitted reluctantly." But I should get your solicitor to look over it before you sign anything." She frowned. "Are you sure this is what you want, Mum? Being the manager means you'll be working for him. You won't get to make any of the decisions. It won't be your hotel anymore."

"No but it will still be my home. And I won't have all the responsibility."

"Reece will be your boss. You don't know what he's like to work for. He could make it really uncomfortable for you. So uncomfortable that you want to leave."

"He seemed nice enough when he was here. He couldn't do enough to help. And you can't say that was just to get us onside. He didn't have to do that, anyone can see that the deal he's offering is a good one," Sue replied. She sighed. "To be honest I'm not sure if it is what I want but I'm definitely thinking about it."

How could she blame her? If Mum felt that she wanted to sell, this was a good offer. Probably the best she would get. And it would be selfish of Ellie to try and talk her out of it just because Reece had been cheating on her. Or rather had been using Ellie to cheat on his girlfriend.

"Look Mum, if that's what you want to do then go for it. But please promise me you won't make a rash decision. Really think about it and talk it over with your solicitor. Promise?"

"Of course." Sue reached out and placed her hand on Ellie's. "I hope you won't be upset if I do decide to sign. I know you feel that Reece tricked and betrayed you, but maybe he genuinely wanted to wait until he had the contract drawn up before he told us, in case we refused to even consider the idea. Which is exactly how I probably would have reacted," she admitted.

"Even if his reasons were genuine for not telling us who he was and what he was planning, he still conned me. I asked him if he was seeing someone and he assured me he wasn't. I would never have dated him if I'd known he had." Sleeping with someone else's man was not her style. She would never betray anyone like Zoe and Lee had done to her. She knew only too well how much that hurt.

"Mandy said that he told her he'd finished with that Cindy woman weeks ago but she wouldn't take no for an answer."

"Well he must have been in touch with her recently because she knew where he was staying and all about the deal," Ellie retorted.

"You really care for him, don't you?" her mother asked gently.

"I don't care for him at all," she denied hotly. "I just hate being lied to. And I can't stand people who cheat on their partners." She stood up. "Let's not talk about him anymore." She bent over and kissed Sue on the forehead. "You do what's best for you, Mum. Take no notice of me. Reece means nothing to me. He was just a holiday romance." She tightened the belt of her dressing gown. "I'm going to get some breakfast then take a shower. Do you want anything?"

"No thanks, dear. I've already eaten."

Ellie went into the kitchen to pour herself a bowl of cereal. Her hand was shaking as she poured milk on the cornflakes, she took a deep breath and steadied it. She was pretty sure Mum would sign that contract - and she had to admit that it was a pretty good way for her to live at Gwel Teg without any of the financial responsibility. Which meant that Reece and his business partner would own Gwel Teg. He'd always be there, in the background of her life.

Damn Reece, he had really gotten under her skin and

now he was coming up smelling of roses. Well, he might
have won Mum over but she would never forgive him.
Never.

Chapter Twenty Eight

She shouldn't mind, Ellie told herself as she drove back home on Sunday evening. She hadn't lived at Gwel Teg for years. It was Mum's home to do what she liked with. And still would be her home for as long as she wanted, she just wouldn't have any of the financial worry.

Or any control.

The contract said that as manager Mum would be involved in any decisions regarding Gwel Teg but the final say would be up to Reece, apparently he had assured Sue that he wasn't planning on making any major changes and intended to run Gwel Teg exactly how it was run now. But Ellie knew things could change.

Reece was an achiever. He'd want to make changes, to make the hotel more efficient. So she'd voiced her doubts.

"Why don't you phone him yourself then you can put your mind at rest," Sue had suggested, handing Ellie Reece's business card – he'd included it with the contract. "Here's his number. I doubt if you'd have kept it."

No she hadn't. She'd tucked the card in her pocket, wondering if she should phone Reece. She never wanted to see him again. Never wanted to hear his voice. But she had to look after her mum's interests and she didn't trust him.

"What have you got to lose?" Kate asked when Ellie explained her dilemma as they chatted later that evening. "And at least you can find out what he has in mind for the future."

"If he tells me. He's not exactly Mr Up-Front."

"Better to ask than not to. If things go wrong some way down the line you'll be beating yourself up for not checking things out when you could. You know what you're like."

Kate was right. She would never forgive herself if she didn't at least try to find out what Reece's intentions were.

Ellie glanced at her watch. 10.30pm. It was too late

to phone him now. She'd do it in the morning.

She spent a restless night, dreaming of Reece, finally waking at 7.30am exhausted. Was this too early to phone him she wondered. She couldn't leave it much later, she had to get to work – and Reece would be going to work too. She expected he had a posh office all to himself with a plaque saying *Chairman* or the like on the door. How stupid was she thinking he was the manager.

She made herself a cup of tea, took it into the bedroom, took a deep breath and dialled Reece's number.

He answered on the second ring. "Hello, Ellie."

Her heart stood still. He knew it was her. He still had her number in his phone. What did that say? That he still cared about her? Had been hoping she would ring? For a minute she couldn't find any words. Images were slide showing through her mind, Reece kissing her, whispering tenderly in her ear, his hands caressing her body.

"Ellie?"

Get a grip! "Hello, Reece." She paused.

"I'm guessing this isn't a social call?"

He sounded in control, as usual, and slightly amused. *Damn him.*

"Too right it isn't," she snapped. "I see that you've still trying to persuade my Mum to sell Gwel Teg to you."

"I am and I presume you've gone through the contract with a fine tooth comb and seen it's a good deal."

"On the surface of it, yes, but you – and your business partner - will be the owner. You will have the final decision," she pointed out. "What I want to know is what plans you have to change the hotel. Because I'm sure you don't intend to keep it exactly as it is."

There was a pause before he replied. "I intend to make Gwel Teg more financially viable, yes, but I have no plans to change anything major about the hotel. I've already assured your mother this."

"Yes well Mum is trusting, like I used to be before I realised what a cheating slime ball you were."

"Did you phone up to give me a character assassination?" he retorted curtly.

"No. I phoned up to ask you not to do anything that will upset Mum. She's been through enough and Gwel Teg is her home. Her and Dad, they've always liked to keep an informal, family atmosphere. So people feel at ease. So please don't buy it then transfer it into a cold, clinical hotel like all the others you own."

"I have no intention of doing that. Although none of my hotels are cold or clinical. You really should get your facts right before throwing accusations."

"And you should try being honest, if you even know what that word means," she shot back.

She heard him draw in his breath then his voice became softer, gentle. "Look, Ellie, I didn't mean to hurt you. If you'd just let me explain…"

"There's nothing to explain, I understand completely what was going on and am not in the least hurt," she retorted. "That would suggest I have feelings for you, which I don't. I was disappointed yes, because I trusted you and you deceived me." She swallowed. "Well you've got what you wanted, Reece. It seems like Mum is prepared to sign Gwel Teg over to your company. Please don't walk over my mum in the process, remember that hotel has been her home for over twenty years."

"I wouldn't do that. Look, Ellie…

"Goodbye, Reece."

She finished the call before Reece could say anything else. She didn't want to talk to him, to remember how close they'd been, how much she'd come to care about him.

Still cared about him.

It was ridiculous to feel like this about someone she had only recently met. She needed to pull herself together and got ready for work.

It had been good to hear Ellie's voice again, even though it was curt and laced with suspicion. He'd wondered if she'd phone. He knew that she cared about her mother too much to not want to make sure the contract was in her best interest.

He walked over to the window. Ellie had sounded upset. He remembered how determined she'd been to get Gwel Teg all ship-shape before she went home, willing to do all the hard work herself if necessary. She was a worker. Feisty and determined. Sue had told him she'd been promoted and was now a Senior PR consultant. She'd be travelling all over the country, maybe even abroad, representing her company. If he hadn't stepped in and saved the hotel she might have missed out on that. She'd probably given up her life to help run a hotel that would have gone under no matter what she did - because although Gwel Teg had potential it needed a serious injection of cash to make it a success. Cash that Ellie and her mother didn't have.

He wondered if Ellie would then have slipped back into her old life and started dating Lee again. Lee was certainly interested in her, that's for sure.

And why should that bother him. Ellie was nothing to him.

He swiped the screen on his phone, opened up the photos folder and selected the ones of Ellie. There she was paddling in the sea, fooling around down by the harbour, eating an ice cream – she'd even got a blob of ice cream on her nose. He moved onto the next picture, Ellie with her head back, laughing. He loved how she laughed, how her eyes crinkled at the corner.

He loved her.

The knowledge brought him to a jolt.

He reflected on the words for a moment and finally acknowledged that they were true. He'd fallen hopelessly in love with Ellie Truman. He wasn't sure how that had happened or what was so special about Ellie that she touched his heart where others hadn't. His best friend, Lucas, had told him once that he could keep trying to avoid commitment but one day he'd meet a woman and that would be it. Game over. He'd be in love and there was nothing he could do about it.

Well it looked like that day had arrived but Lucas was wrong. There was something he could do about it.

He could make sure that he never saw Ellie again.

Reece was pleased and not totally surprised to receive a phone call from Ellie's mother in the week, wanting to discuss the terms of the contract and his future plans for the hotel. It was obvious Ellie had discussed this with her, and warned her to be cautious. He spent half an hour on the phone answering Sue's questions. She sounded interested but unsure if she could trust him. That stung. He'd always prided himself on being honest, a man of

323

his word. He could be ruthless in business yes, but he wasn't in the habit of ripping off anyone. This distrust was all thanks to Cindy turning up like that. An hour later and he'd have had chance to explain everything to them.

And what? Would they have understood, believed his reasons for not telling them about his intentions earlier?

"Please get your solicitor to look over it," he said. "He'll assure you that there are no hidden clauses."

"I have and he's assured me that it's above board," Sue replied. "I've a few questions though so wondered if you would mind coming down to discuss it further with me."

Reece hesitated. Would Ellie be there?

"If you could come down this weekend Ellie won't be here, if that's what you're worrying about," Sue said as if she'd read his mind.

He didn't want to see Ellie again so why did he feel disappointed?He quickly checked his diary and told Sue he'd be down Saturday morning. "I'll stay in another hotel in the locality," he told her. "I think it would be best. It'll keep things neutral."

On Friday night he drove down to Cornwall, he'd booked himself into a hotel in Truro for the night. The next morning he made the short drive over to Port Medden.

It was a beautiful sunny day, the sort of day that would make Ellie want to go down to the beach and run barefoot across the sand. Like she had with him that day when she'd showed him the private cove.

He remembered how they'd paddled in the sea. How her skirt had got soaked, revealing her shapely legs and stirring the first feelings of desire in him. He hadn't been able to take his eyes off her. She was beautiful, fun and completely unaffected. She'd been honest with him right from the start, confiding in him about her worries over her mum. There was nothing false or complicated about Ellie. She was like no other woman he'd ever met and he'd found himself wanting to help her, to ease her worries, to see the frown lift from her forehead. That's when things had got personal.

He was still trying to help her, even if she didn't believe him.

As he walked through the entrance into the hotel he half-expected to see Ellie there, standing behind the counter, her rich brown hair tumbling over her shoulders. She wasn't, of course.

"Hello, Reece," Mandy glanced at him. "Sue's waiting for you in the lounge if you care to go through. You know the way."

He nodded and set off, taking it as a good sign that Mandy had called him by his first name, even if she didn't follow it with a smile. He guessed he wasn't Mr Popular but that Mandy realised he wasn't quite the 'con artist' they'd thought. He just wished Ellie did too.

Ellie's presence was everywhere. He could feel her, smell her. If he shut his eyes he could imagine her.

Get a grip!

Reece walked into the lounge, sat down opposite Sue, accepted the coffee she offered then calmly answered all of the questions she asked him. The main thing she seemed to be concerned about was the staff. "Most of my staff have been with me for years, especially Mandy and Harry," she said. "I need to know their jobs are safe."

"You'll be the manager. It will be up to you to hire and fire the staff, just as you do now. That will be nothing to do with my company. You keep on whoever you want. We'll be hiring new staff too, you could do with more here, and that will be your department too. You can interview the staff and take on who you like. I'll add a clause stating that in the contract if you want."

"Yes please. That will put my mind at rest." Her eyes probed him sharply. "It's a very good offer."

"I know." He didn't believe in false modesty. "I thought about it very carefully and had my solicitor go over it with a fine toothcomb."

"So I can sell Gwel Teg to you, be employed as the manager and remain in the private quarters as long as the hotel is solvent, to be reviewed after five years. And as long as I remain capable of doing my job," she added, referring to another clause in the contract. He was sure he saw a twinkle in her eye.

He grinned. "I have to cover my interests too. I'll be investing a lot of money into Gwel Teg. If you end up going ga-ga and terrorising the guests then we could go bankrupt and I'll be the one out of pocket."

To his surprise, Sue chuckled heartily. "A good point lad." She patted his hand. "I wish you'd been upfront about this at the beginning. It would have saved a lot of hassle. And hurt."

"I know but I've explained my reasons. I truly had no intention to deceive or hurt anyone." He levelled his eyes to hers. "How does Ellie feel about it? I'm guessing that as she hasn't been in touch again that she still hasn't forgiven me."

"Ellie wants me to do what's best for me so she won't interfere with my decision over this. She knows I've taken legal advice and will take my time to think it over. But as for forgiving you ..." Sue gave him a sharp look. "Ellie has no time for two-timers. She's straight and honest and likes people to be that way with her."

"I was not two-timing!" Reece snapped, then instantly regretted it. "I'm sorry but not guilty as charged. Cindy is someone I dated yes, but we finished weeks beforehand. I pride myself on being straight and honest too. I didn't deceive either of you. I simply wanted to get everything in place before I presented my offer to you." He stood up. "Let me know if you have any further questions at any time. Obviously, I know you want to think about this, and you should. It's a big decision. However, I can't keep the offer on the table indefinitely as if you don't want to sign there are other hotels that do. So shall we say I'll keep it open for a month?"

"That's very fair." Sue stood up and shook his hand. "I appreciate it and I'll be in touch with my decision, one way or another, before the month is up."

As he drove home, Reece's mind turned back to Gwel Teg. Sue's interest had been obvious and her questions focused and thoughtful. The sort of questions people asked when they were considering things. He wasn't expecting to hear from her for a week or two, she'd take her time, she wouldn't find it easy to let go of ownership, but he was almost certain she would sign.

How would Ellie feel about that? Sue had said Ellie wouldn't interfere with his decision but Gwel Teg was Ellie's childhood home. Would she resent him owning it? Things could be awkward if she ever came down when he was there. Not that he'd be going down much. As Steve lived nearer he would be the one dealing with the day to day issues. Reece would only visit if Sue specifically asked to see him. There was no reason for him and Ellie to bump into each other.

But he'd love to see her again.

He daren't risk it. He needed to keep away from Ellie until he'd got her out of his head. And heart.

Ellie reached for the phone, her forehead creasing in concern when she saw *Mum* flash on the screen. "Mum are you okay?" she asked anxiously.

"I'm fine, dear. I phoned to let you know that I've had a meeting with Reece tonight. We've gone through the contract with a fine toothcomb and it's watertight. I'm going to sign. I'm going to let Reece – and his business partner - buy Gwel Teg."

Even though she'd been expecting it, Ellie felt as if she'd been punched in the chest. Reece was going to own her home. The hotel her Mum and Dad had loved so much.

"Are you sure about this, Mum? Really sure? I've told you I'll help you. I'll give up my job and move back in. We'll run Gwel Teg together."

"It's really kind of you dear, and don't think I don't appreciate it because I do." There was a pause before her mum continued. "I don't want you to do that. I don't want you to give up your life for me. This is the right thing to do, I know it is. I just want to check that you're okay with it."

No she wasn't, she hated the idea. Ellie took a deep breath. She was being selfish. It was a good contract and Mum had every right to do what she wanted with her own home. She was letting her feelings for Reece influence her.

"If that's what you really want, Mum, then it's fine by me." She said. "I've told you that I want you to do whatever makes life easier for you. And I really mean that."

"Thank you dear. The flat will still be my home and Reece has made it clear that you're welcome to stay any time. You're still to regard the attic as your room, this as your family home."

"Thanks, Mum." As Ellie ended the call she thought that she would never be able to think of Gwel Teg as her home again.

"Everything okay?" Kate asked, coming in carrying two mugs of hot chocolate. "I thought you might need this," She placed the mugs down on the coffee table and sat in the chair opposite Ellie. "I gather your Mum is going to take up Reece's offer."

"Yes."

Kate gave her a sympathetic look. "Is that such a bad thing? You're worried sick about your mum doing too much and you don't really want to move back in with her, do you? At least this way you'll know that she's being taken care of."

Ellie thought about this carefully. No she didn't if she was honest. "I guess not, especially now I've got this promotion. But I would do it – if only to stop Reece getting his hands on it."

"Is he really that awful?" Kate asked, dunking a cookie into her mug of chocolate.

"He's a lying, conniving, cheating rat." And sexy, charming, funny, kind…

"I see," Kate took a bite out of her biscuit as she considered this. "Well, he's not likely to be there when you visit is he? You don't have to see him."

Too true she didn't. And she'd make sure that she never did. She never wanted to see Reece Mitchell again as long as she lived.

Chapter Twenty Nine

Ellie was kept so busy at work that it was almost two months before she found the time to go down to Gwel Teg again. And what a transformation. The outside of the hotel had been given a lick of paint, there were pretty window boxes hanging from all the windows, new seating in the reception area and a slick modern desk.

Her mum came to greet her, looking glowing and animated. "Hello darling." She gave Ellie a kiss on the cheek. "Did you notice we've tidied up the outside? What do you think?"

"It looks good, Mum." Ellie looked at her sparkling eyes and glowing cheeks. "So do you. You look really well."

"I can't tell you the difference it makes not to be responsible for everything," Sue linked her arm through Ellie's. "Come and see the garden. I've been transforming it."

Mum actually had time for gardening? One of the things she'd frequently complained about was that she didn't have time to garden, it was her favourite way to relax but since Dad had died she'd been too busy with the hotel.

Ellie stepped out of the back door and gasped. Dad's vegetable patch had been restored and pretty little flower beds edged the lawn. At the far end of the garden was a rockery. Mum had always wanted a rockery. Dad had been in the process of making her one when he'd died.

"Oh, it's lovely!" she let go of her mother's arm and walked down the path, marvelling at the riot of colour, the quirky flowerpots bursting with vibrant blooms. "Did you do all this yourself?"

"The planning yes, but not all the hard work." Sue smiled. "Would you believe that Reece's employed a gardener to look after the hotel grounds? And he's allocated two afternoons a week of his time to work in my private garden. Isn't that just wonderful?"

"So it's all working out then? You're happy with the new arrangement?"

"More than happy. It's taken so much pressure off me."

"Do you see Reece much? Is he very hands on?"

"Goodness me, no. He's based in London, isn't he? He came down the once to sign the contract and go through his plans with me and I haven't seen him since. His partner Steve has popped in a couple of times, he lives in Plymouth so he's nearer. He's a very nice man, easy to get on with. I think Reece will be down in a couple of weeks though when all the redecorations are finished." She looked at Ellie. "Why don't you come down too? See if you two can sort things out."

"There's nothing to sort out, Mum. I'm glad it's working out for you but I've got no interest in Reece whatsoever."

"Well that's a shame, because you got on so well, and I know it looked bad at the time, but he's done good by me, Ellie."

Well, Reece really had wormed his way into her mum's good books, hadn't he? He had a way with people, that's for sure, but he wasn't going to manipulate her.

"How's your new job going?" Sue asked, as if sensing Ellie's reluctance to engage in any conversation about Reece.

"It's great. I'm off to Rome next week for a conference," she replied.

"That's wonderful. Come and have a coffee and tell me all about it."

Ellie sat on the beach, gazing out at the sea. The same beach she and Reece had frolicked in the waves, spent the afternoon talking on the beach. Then gone back to the hotel to find the room had flooded. The day Reece had tricked his way into her life and her heart.

She had to admit that Mum was happy and the hotel looked great. She was pleased about that. Maybe she'd judged Reece wrong and his interest in the hotel had been genuine – even if he had gone about it the wrong way.

Had his interest in Ellie been genuine?

She shrugged. What did it matter now? They had both moved on. She was no longer angry with him. He'd helped her mum and set Ellie free. Knowing that her mother was happy, her future secure and she was no longer working herself to the ground to run Gwel Teg, Ellie, was free to get on with her life. She could go to Rome with a clear mind.

For that reason alone she was pleased that she'd met Reece.

"Can I join you?"

She looked up to see Lee standing beside her, his fair hair tousled, his toned sun-kissed limbs rippling out of his vest and shorts. He grinned his disarming lop-side grin. It was as if the years had melted away and she was looking at the old Lee. The one she'd been infatuated with.

She nodded. "Be my guest."

He squatted down beside her. "You haven't been down here for a while. I've been looking out for you."

That surprised her. "Why?"

"I wanted to talk to you. To say sorry for how I – we – treated you."

"Lee, we were all little more than kids. It doesn't matter anymore." She told him. "I just wish you and Zoe had made a go of it. At least then it would have all been worthwhile. Now there's two little kids with a broken home."

"You think it was my fault, don't you?" he asked. "You think I cheated on Zoe."

"Didn't you?"

He shook his head and she saw the hurt in his eyes. "I know what we did to you was horrible but I really loved Zoe. I thought she loved me too, that we had a future together."

"She did. I'm sure she did." Why else would her best friend go off with her boyfriend?

"I don't think she did. She was always a bit envious of you. I think she was just made up that I chose her over

336

you." His voice was thick with emotion. "I tried to resist, you know. But it was so flattering to have someone throw themselves at you, and Zoe was so outgoing, so popular."

Whereas she hadn't been. "And now she's found someone else with a better job, more charisma?" Ellie asked softly, inwardly reeling from the knowledge that beautiful, popular Zoe had actually been jealous of her.

Lee nodded. "Yep. And she has the house, the car and our two children. So I've paid big time for how I treated you."

Ellie reached out and placed her hand on his. "I'm sorry to hear that. Really I am."

"I've never forgot you, Ellie," His eyes held hers, pleading with her. "Do you think we could maybe try again? Date each other and see how things pan out?"

She shook her head. "I'm sorry but there's no going back for us Lee. Any feelings I had for you disappeared years ago." She leant over and kissed him on the cheek. "I wish you well."

Then she got up and walked away over the sand. Today had been a day of putting the past behind her. It was time to get on with the rest of her life.

Chapter Thirty

Rome.

She was good. Reece listened to Ellie's presentation in admiration. He was standing right at the back so that she wouldn't know he was there.

Sue had mentioned Ellie was going to a conference in Rome when he'd phoned a couple of weeks ago, she was really proud of Ellie's promotion. So when Reece had to go to Rome on business the same week he'd done a Google search of all the conferences to see which one Ellie might be attending, hoping he might get chance to see her. He'd been astonished to discover that Ellie was one of the speakers at the International Corporate Fundraising conference on Thursday, his last day there. Luckily his flight wasn't until that evening and the hotel the conference was held at wasn't far from where he was staying so he'd booked a place. He'd told himself it was just curiosity, because he wanted to see Ellie in action so to speak, not because he was longing to see her again, to hear her voice. Definitely not.

He was lying, of course.

Ellie looked stunning. The red fitted suit with the white blouse underneath made her look professional but gorgeous. As Reece watched her slick presentation on the screen, listened to her answering questions so competently he realised just what she'd been prepared to give up for her mother. She was obviously a high achiever and very good at her job yet she would have walked away from it all to work at the family hotel so her mother wouldn't have to sell it.

What did she think now that he'd brought Gwel Teg? He thought back to the phone call she'd made asking him what his plans were, trying to get confirmation that he wouldn't do anything that would upset Sue. He hadn't heard from her since but he couldn't get her out of his mind. Every decision he made about Gwel Teg was guided first by whether Ellie would approve and second by financial management. Which was not a very business way to deal with things and had led to a few questions from Steve.

Ellie had finished now. He joined in the round of applause and watched her walk off the stage then down the aisle. She was metres away from him, he could almost reach out and touch her. Would she sense him?

It was ridiculous how disappointed he felt when she carried on past without as much as a glance in his direction. Was he expecting her nerves to be on red alert, screaming out for him, as his was for her?

He couldn't let her go without talking to her. Excusing himself, he left his seat, squeezed past the people beside him and followed in the direction Ellie had gone. Walking through the swing doors he looked swiftly left then right. Which way? The corridor carried on ahead, with a door leading out to a room on each side. The door to the room on the right was open so he decided to try that one first. Right decision. It was the refreshment room and there was Ellie standing by the wooden table hosting the coffee and tea urn, cups and a selection of biscuits and cakes, pouring herself a cup of coffee.

He paused, watching her, his heart thudding. She hadn't seen him yet. He should walk away while he still could.

She must have sensed him because she turned

around slowly and her gaze rested on him. Her eyes widened and the hand holding the coffee cup shook making the cup rattle and slopping some of the contents into the saucer. Time stood still as they gazed at each other. He started walking towards her and she turned, placed the cup and saucer down on the table, turning back as he reached her.

"What are *you* doing here?" Her voice was little more than a whisper.

"I'm in Rome on business and the conference sounded interesting."

"Buying another struggling hotel are you?" The words were like darts and he winced inwardly as they struck home.

"It's my job. And I'm good at it. Has your mother any complaints?"

Ellie shook her head. "No but it's early days yet."

"You still don't trust me, do you?"

"Are you seriously expecting me to? "Her eyes met his and he could see the distrust in them. That hurt more than he would ever admit.

"Look, I wasn't lying to you." He reached out, tilted her chin up with his finger so her eyes met his. "Give me five minutes to explain."

"There's really no need. It makes no difference to me."

"I think there is. My company owns your family home. I don't want you to avoid coming down in case you bump into me. If there are any problems, if you have any concerns at all, I want you to feel that you can contact me, talk about them. And unless we resolve this I don't think you'll do that, will you?"

Slowly she shook her head.

"Then can I grab a cup of coffee too and please can we sit down and talk?"

He saw the conflicting emotions criss-cross her face, then she slowly nodded. "Okay."

Why had she agreed to talk to him? Ellie thought as she refilled her coffee cup then grabbed a chocolate biscuit for emotional support. The last thing she wanted to do was sit down and have a conversation with Reece. She didn't want to be near him, to see him. She didn't trust herself.

You can do this. She pulled back her shoulders and lifted her chin. She was in control again. Reece was right, they did need to talk about it. She had to face facts, he owned Gwel Teg and her mother was happy with that. She had to deal with it. And if she wanted to look out for her mum's interests she needed to keep contact with Reece, not run away from him. She needed to show him that she was strong, and that she would speak up if she had to. Let him know that he wasn't just dealing with her mother.

Resolutely, she carried her coffee and biscuit over to a table in the corner of the room. Reece pulled out a chair and joined her a few minutes later.

She levelled at him. "Let's start with a few truths. Did you know I'd be here?"

He met her gaze. "Yes. Your mother told me you were attending a conference in Rome. It didn't take me long to guess it must be this one, and see that you were one of the speakers. Your presentation was excellent," he told her. "And congratulations on your promotion."

"Thank you. I guess you thought someone as dipsy as me wouldn't be able to do stuff like this?"

"Not at all. I don't make assumptions about people."

"Not like me, you mean?" she shot back.

"Well I guess I can't blame you for jumping to conclusions in the circumstances," he admitted. "But I promise you half an hour later and you would have known all the facts. I asked you to come for a walk with me because I wanted to talk to you – remember? I was going to tell you about it then. " He leaned forward, his gaze intense. "I wasn't taking you for a ride, Ellie. And I wasn't seeing Cindy. We'd finished weeks ago. Will you let me explain?"

Ellie nibbled the end of her chocolate biscuit and

chewed it thoughtfully. Reece had what he wanted, Gwel Teg. He didn't need to explain anything to her. He didn't need her approval. So why had he gone to the trouble to find out which conference she was attending and book onto it himself?

His eyes held hers and she felt herself drawn into them, sensed his sincerity. And something else. It was as if he really cared what she thought about him.

Could he ... could he possibly have feelings for her like she had for him?

No, of course he didn't.

Then why?

Perhaps it was as he said, that he needed her onside, to contact him if she had any worries about the hotel. After all, he'd make a big financial commitment to it and if Mum was taken ill again he'd be left without a manager. It wasn't just his company either, he had a partner and this partner must have agreed to the decision. Without even seeing Gwel Teg. Did he trust Reece that much?

That was the first time she'd thought about what a risk Reece had taken putting his money into Gwel Teg and keeping Mum on as his manager. Ellie had been so angry that Reece had tricked her, deceived her that she hadn't stopped to think about his financial outlay. He – or rather his company - was investing quite a lot of money in updating the hotel too. Perhaps she'd been a bit unfair.

"Okay. I'm listening."

She saw surprise then relief in his eyes. This was important to him.

She bit off another chunk of the biscuit and chewed it as he started to speak.

"I agree that when I found out your mother was ill and struggling to manage the hotel I realised it might be a good opportunity for me. Steve – my business partner - and I were going to buy a hotel in Truro but the deal fell through – that's where I was rushing off to when I honked at you that day," he explained ruefully. "When I came back and saw you still working so late I felt guilty about snapping at you."

"Then I spilled it all out about Mum and the hotel not doing very well and you thought 'Bingo'," she added.

"Well, yes. I told you that's my job. I didn't know you or your mother then, remember. It was just a business deal."

"And then you found out what a dip-head I was and thought you could take advantage."

"Except I didn't take advantage, did I? I helped you get the hotel straight. I didn't have to do that. I could have left you to it, then you'd have had a compensation claim from the Smythes to deal with and I could have got

345

the hotel at a cut down price."

He was right, she admitted. Okay, so he hadn't taken advantage of them business-wise but what about personally?

"So you didn't rip us off. I'll give you that. But what about your girlfriend?"

"Ex-girlfriend. And not a serious one at that," he briefly explained about Cindy pestering him. "I had no idea she was going to turn up."

"Maybe you are telling the truth." Ellie crossed her arms, sat back in her chair and levelled her gaze at him. "But you took advantage of me personally." She swallowed before continuing. "Do you think I'd have gone out with you … gone to bed with you… if I'd have known that you were secretly planning to buy Gwel Teg?"

"I liked you. There's nothing wrong with that." He leaned forward. "More than liked you. You're quirky and gorgeous and honest. I love your 'can do' attitude, your caring personality, how you can laugh at yourself." His eyes met hers, held hers, pulled her down into his soul. "I love you, Ellie. I miss you like crazy. Won't you give us another chance?"

He loved her.

The words swam around in her head like moths flittering around a light. He loved her.

346

And she loved him.

It wasn't as simple as that though. They barely knew each other. How could she trust him? Yes, she loved him. And maybe he did love her but this wouldn't work. It couldn't work. And she had no intention of giving up her heart, her freedom, her future to someone she didn't trust.

"You had a relationship with me based on a lie." Ellie stood up and pushed the chair back. "How can I trust you? I'll contact you if there is ever a problem with the hotel, but that's all. I'm sorry, Reece, but we can only ever have a business relationship."

She turned and walked away before he could see the tears streaming down her face.

She'd only ever cried over a guy once before, and she had vowed she'd never do it again. She squeezed her eyes tight. This time the pain in her heart was far greater than it had been with Lee. But she would get over it. She was not going to let Reece Mitchell into her heart, her life, just to destroy it. Absolutely not.

She walked out of the hotel and into the busy Italian street. For a moment, she stood outside wondering what to do next.

A hand clasped on her shoulder. "Ellie..."

Reece. Her whole body reacted to his touch. She longed to wrap her arms around him and bury herself in his embrace. She took a deep breath and turned to face him.

"We're done, Reece. Now will you leave me alone?"

"Sure I will," he said softly. "Look into my eyes and tell me you don't love me and I'll walk away. I'll never bother you again."

Chapter Thirty One

I don't love you. Say it. She formed the words in her mind, opened her mouth to say them but they wouldn't come out. She turned away but he gently pulled her back. Using the back of his thumb to wipe away the tears trickling down each cheek he drew her into his arms, nestling her head into his body. "You do love me, don't you?" his voice was raw with emotion.

For a moment she let herself be comforted in his embrace, sank into the warmth of his body, allowed the feel of being loved to wash over her. Then she realised what she was doing and pulled away. His arms were still wrapped around her waist as he scrutinised her face and she swore that was love shining out of his eyes.

"Ellie?"

She nodded, the words forming a lump in her throat.

"Say it. I need to hear you say it."

How could she lie when it must be written all over her face? "I love you … but," the 'but' was lost as his face broadened into a huge grin and his lips silenced hers in a deep, passionate kiss.

"*Permesso, per favore.*"

They were blocking the doorway. "*Mi scusi!*" Reece said, easing Ellie over to the left so the man could walk out. He smiled at them and nodded, "Ah, *amore!*"

"When are you due to fly home?" Reece asked tenderly.

"Tomorrow," she told him. "How about you?"

"This evening." He tilted her chin up with his finger and gazed into her eyes. "Let's spend the afternoon together. I've missed you so much."

She nodded wordlessly, feeling out of her depth but longing to spend some time with him.

He looked down at his suit. "I'd like to change into something more casual first and I guess you would too? Where are you staying?"

She told him the name of her hotel. "That's only around the corner from mine."

As they walked along hand in hand Ellie's mind was

racing. So they'd admitted they loved each other. What happened next?

She loved him. The words kept going around in Reece's head as he changed out of his suit, showered and put on some light chinos and a short sleeved shirt. He hadn't meant to tell Ellie he loved her, he'd simply wanted to explain things to her so that she stopped thinking he'd been lying to her. That she saw he was telling the truth. And yes, he'd hoped that once she realised that, she'd agree to keep seeing him. That they could meet up now and again, see where their relationship took them. But when he'd seen her, the words spilled out before he could stop them.

He rubbed his hair dry. He'd never told anyone he'd loved them before.

Love wasn't in his vocabulary. Loving someone meant giving someone the power to hurt you, like his mum had done to his dad. He didn't want to give anyone that power over him.

Yet he knew he wanted Ellie in his life. That he couldn't bear not to see her anymore, not to hear her laugh, to feel her lips on his, her body against his.

So where did he go from here?

As soon as he was ready he set off for the hotel Ellie was staying at. As he walked into the foyer he saw her coming down the staircase towards him, looking a total knockout in white cropped trousers and an emerald short sleeved top. She smiled and gave a little finger wave when she saw him.

Reece took a deep breath. What was she expecting to happen now?

Ellie walked over the marble floor towards Reece hoping that she didn't look as nervous as she felt. She was thrilled to see him again, to know that he hadn't been using her. That he loved her. She wanted to be with him. Her entire body screamed out to be touched by him but she was scared. Scared of them both realising that actually what they felt was infatuation not love. Like she'd felt for Lee.

And even more scared that it was love.

Her feelings for Lee had been nothing like this.

Her heart was fluttering as Reece approached, joy mixed with panic.

Panic because if she and Reece actually did love each other she would have to make a commitment and she didn't do commitment.

Not even for Reece.

There was too much she wanted to see, to do, to tie herself down just yet.

Don't get ahead of yourself. He said he loves you, not

that he wants to marry you.

She'd almost reached him now. Reece stretched out his hand, grasped hers and gently pulled her to him, enfolding her in a deep embrace.

"You look gorgeous."

"So do you," she said with a smile.

"Fancy a bit of sightseeing?"

She nodded her agreement and they walked out hand in hand into the sunshine.

"Have you been to Rome before?" Reece asked.

"No. I've been to Italy a few times - Naples, Florence and Venice but not Rome. Have you?"

"Yes, a few years ago, but I've never really looked around. Is there anything in particular you'd like to see?"

There were a few people about but the streets weren't packed. Not like in St Ives or Newquay in the summer where you had no chance of walking with someone hand in hand and could often only shuffle rather than walk, single file through the crowds.

"Trevi Fountain," Ellie told him. "I want to throw a coin in it. And the Altare della Patria – Altar of the Nations I think it's called - and the Colosseum. Have you been to all of those?"

"No, when I come over here it's usually for business." His face crinkled into a grin. "You always seem to have to introduce the fun side of things to me." He took out his phone, punched in some letters and brought up a map of the city. "We're in walking distance of all of those, if you don't mind a walk?"

"Of course not. It's a lovely day." She couldn't think of anything she'd like more than to wander around this beautiful romantic city with Reece, holding his hand, enjoying just being with him.

"Then let's go to the Colosseum first, that's the nearest. Then the Altare della Patria and we can finish off at Trevi Fountain. How does that sound?"

"That sounds good to me." Elle said, smiling at him.

They held hands, enjoying the closeness of each other, as they walked through the streets, stopping to look every now and again in the shop windows.

When Ellie spotted the huge amphitheatre of stone on the other side of the road, she caught her breath. The Colosseum. It was stunning.

"Magnificent, isn't it? And to think it's over 2,000 years old." Reece gazed over at it. "Want a closer look? We can take a tour inside if you like."

"We don't really have much time for that. But a closer look would be good," Ellie told him.

They crossed the road and gazed up at the historic monument. .Ellie did a quick internet search on her phone. "According to this app, the Colosseum seated 60,000 people with room for another 10,000 standing." she said.

"Impressive – and bloodthirsty. They all came to watch gladiators fight to the death, after all."

"I'd fight to the death for you," Reece said, winding his arm around her wait.

"I can just imagine you dressed up as a gladiator," Ellie teased.

Reece grinned. "Whatever turns you on!" He kissed her on the mouth, a gentle wisp of a kiss. Ellie returned the kiss then pulled away as it got deeper remembering they were in a public place. "Where to next?"

"Altere della Patria. It's in Venice Square."

It felt so right being with Reece, as if they belonged together, Ellie thought. Just as it had in Cornwall. She felt so at ease, as if she'd known him all her life.

Was that part of being in love?

They stopped for an ice cream, topped with a flake and chocolate sauce for Ellie, then continued their walk. It only seemed a few minutes before the elaborate white marble building stood in front of them. Ellie gazed up at the rows of columns, the bronze horse-drawn chariots on the porticos, the imposing staircase, the numerous statues that adorned it. "It's breath-taking," she breathed. She selected the camera on her phone and clicked away.

"Stand by the steps and I'll take one of you," offered Reece.

Ellie handed him her camera and stood with her back to the building.

"Would you like me to take a picture of you both?" a woman asked in perfect English tinged with an Italian accent.

Ellie hesitated, thinking of all the warnings she'd read not to give your camera or phone to people abroad as some were tricksters and would run off with it. This elegant woman looked like she could be trusted though so she smiled. "Thank you." It was a lovely photo, Reece had his arm around Ellie's shoulder and she was resting her head lightly on his.

"Can you send it to me," Reece asked when she showed it to him. So she did.

She didn't want the afternoon to end. It was such a magical time, simply enjoying each other's company.

Reece evidently felt the same way because he hugged her close and nuzzled into her neck saying "I wish we didn't have to go home. I wish we were here on holiday together."

"Me too," she said.

"Hey, maybe we can do that. Let's come back on a holiday."

It sounded wonderful.

Finally they were at Trevi Fountain and it was just as magical as Ellie had imagined.

"According to legend you have to throw a coin over your shoulder into the fountain and make a wish that you'll return again. Then you will," Ellie said.

"Let's do that. We'll wish that we return together," Reece suggested.

They spotted a tour guide and asked him to take a photo of them both, standing side by side with their back to the fountain, throwing the coins over their shoulder into the water. And again Ellie sent that to Reece.

All too soon it was time to go. Reece signalled one of the white city taxis and they both got in. Ellie sat down beside him, feeling a little awkward. What happens next? Was Reece expecting her to go to the airport with him to see him off?

"Do you want to be dropped off at your hotel first?" Reece asked her. "I'll get my things then come and say goodbye."

Goodbye. It sounded so final. Reece was flying back to London this evening, she was flying back to the Midlands tomorrow. He said he wanted to see her again but he hadn't said when. And on what terms.

Kate would tell her to take the imitative and suggest a date for meeting up but Ellie had no intention of doing the running. If Reece wanted to see her, as he said he did, then he could make the first move.

"Okay," she agreed. "I'll have a coffee in the foyer

and wait for you there."

"I'll be about half an hour," Reece told her as the taxi pulled up outside her hotel. He leaned over and kissed Ellie, sending her pulse racing.

She bought a latté and sat by the window, gazing out in the street, trying to come to terms with today's events. She could hardly believe that Reece loved her, as she loved him.

"Ah, Signorina Truman. Just the person I wanted to see." It was Signore Abrahmi from a major leather supplier. "Your presentation was impressive. Very impressive. I'd like to book a consultation with you for early next month."

Ellie instantly switched into business mode, took her notebook out of her bag and jotted down details.

* * *

Reece searched the foyer for Ellie, then spotted her sitting over by the window talking to a silver-haired, rather distinguished looking Italian man. He recognised him from the conference this afternoon. Obviously she was talking business, but he couldn't go without saying goodbye.

He walked over and as if sensing his presence, Ellie glanced up. "Reece! Is it that time already?" She looked at her watch, then at the man sitting beside her. "I'm afraid I have a prior engagement, Signore. Could we continue with this meeting later this evening? Say about seven? I could meet you here."

"Of course, Signorina Truman," the Italian got to his feet. "We will meet at seven."

Ellie stoop up. "Do you want me to come to the airport with you?" she asked Reece.

"That would be nice but I'm afraid you won't get back for your meeting." He put his bag down and pulled her into his arms. "I love you, Ellie."

"I love you too," she whispered.

"I'll call you. We'll meet up as soon as we can," he promised. A long, lingering kiss and then he was gone.

How was this going to work, Ellie thought, sitting back down again? How could they have any kind of relationship when they lived so far apart?

Was love enough?

Chapter Thirty Two

Good morning, Gorgeous. Safe journey.

Ellie smiled at the text message from Reece.

All night she'd thought of him, wished she'd not arranged the meeting with Signore Abrahami and gone to the airport to say goodbye to Reece instead. Wished she'd spent another precious hour with him.

She'd received a message from Reece late last night to say he'd landed safely and they'd exchanged texts for a while. Then she'd woken up to this text this morning.

"Good morning. Wish you were still here," she texted back.

"We'll meet soon," came his reply followed by a row of kisses.

Ellie re-read all his texts, a warm glow running through her. So this is what it was like to be in love.

She shook herself and got out of bed. She had to be at the airport in just under two hours. Time to get a move on.

She was travelling with Danny, who worked in the PR department too. He was waiting in the foyer when she came down with her case.

"I was about to call you. The taxi's due in a few minutes," he told her. "How did the meeting with Signore Abrahami go?"

"Good. He's booked a few training sessions for next month."

"What, back here in Rome?"

Ellie nodded. "I'll be here for a week."

"Wow, lucky you!"

"I know. Martin is chuffed."

"And what about your mystery guy? Has he gone home too?"

"Mystery guy?" She repeated, puzzled. Did he mean Reece? Had he seen them together?

"Yes, the one who couldn't keep his eyes off you at the conference? I saw you kissing him in reception later. I presume you already knew him?"

361

"Er, yes, he's an old friend."

"Looked like you were more than friends to me."

Ellie was saved from replying by the arrival of the taxi. As they journeyed to the airport she thought about her meeting with Signore Abrahame last night. She'd be back in Rome for a whole week next month.

Well at least it looked like part of her wish at Trevi Fountain had been granted. If only Reece could be there too.

"Please, fasten your seatbelts for landing.'

Ellie placed her bag under the seat in front and fastened her belt. It had been a smooth, pleasant journey. One which she'd spent snoozing as she hadn't slept much last night. Too busy thinking about Reece. When would she see him again?

Was he planning on asking her to come down to London to see him? Or on coming to the Midlands to see her. She thought of the little flat that she shared with Kate. She loved it but it wasn't big enough for three of them, although Kate often stayed over at her boyfriend's flat at the weekend.

With only hand luggage she was soon through customs, and her heart flipped when she saw Reece waiting for her in the arrival lounge.

"Reece!" She flung her arms around his neck. "What

362

a lovely surprise. "I thought you'd be in London."

"I came to meet you." He looked down at her tenderly. "I was hoping you would come to London with me? Spend the weekend at my flat?"

"I'd love too." She hugged him tight. "Why didn't you mention it yesterday? Or text me? I was thinking we wouldn't be able to see each other for ages."

"Because I needed to settle a deal first, make sure I was free for the weekend." He kissed her on the tip of her nose. "I know it's very short notice and you might have plans so if you can't make it, that's fine. I just want to spend every moment with you that I can." His lips found hers and none of them spoke for a while.

"Me too. It's a lovely idea," she said when she finally came up for air. "Only I need to go back to my flat first and grab some clean clothes."

"Sure. I can drive you there. If you want me to?"

"What do you think?" She smiled up at him.

How could you be happy and scared at the same time? Ellie thought as she and Reece shared a candlelit dinner in a London restaurant that night. She was happy she was with Reece, but scared that things were going too fast. She was enjoying her new job and the travel opportunities it was providing for her. She loved Reece. But she loved her freedom too.

363

Later that night, as they lay wrapped up in each other's arms, Reece whispered to her. "I never thought I'd trust anyone enough to want to share my life with them. Not until I met you."

Panic welled up inside her. Share his life with her? Surely he wasn't going to propose!

Don't be stupid. Of course he isn't. Calm down.

"You never got serious before then?" she asked.

"Nope. I made a vow when my Mum walked out on my Dad that I'd never be stupid enough to love anyone. I'd never give anyone the power to hurt me."

Ellie hugged him and listened as he told her about his lonely childhood. How he'd been nothing but an inconvenience to both his parents and had been determined to make a success of his life so that they'd be proud of him.

"That's awful," she said softly, thinking how lucky she was to have had two parents who loved each other and loved her too. "I'm sure they regret it and are proud of you now."

Reece's hand moved up and down the top of her arm, caressing it lightly. "They're still the same, couldn't care less. Too busy with their own lives. The difference is that I've stopped trying to make them proud, and part of that is because of you."

"Me?" That surprised her. What had she done?

"Yes you. Your love for your parents, how close you are to your mum. How helping her was more important to you than your own career." He glanced at her and squeezed her shoulder.

"I don't understand…"

"You were so 'can do', so determined to do whatever you could to help your mother. Yes, I planned on giving Sue a good price for the hotel but it was your determination, your grit that made me want to get Gwel Teg back on its feet, your love for your mum that made me want to keep her on as manager. Your kind, caring attitude that made me realise success isn't everything. And that made me fall in love with you. Thanks to you I became a kinder, caring person."

Wow! That was quite a speech. "I didn't make you a kinder, caring person Reece. You already were one, otherwise you would never have put helping me and Mum over profit. You would have gone for the best deal for you." As she spoke the words she realised they were true. Reece had helped them with no thought of any gain for himself.

"I've never met anyone like you, Ellie. You're funny, warm, caring. I love you so much."

"I love you too."

His lips found hers and their passion took over once again. When they were both finally sated, Ellie posed the question that had been bothering her since yesterday.

"Where do we go from here? We both live so far apart."

"We'll work it out. We can meet up at weekends. Take it in turns to visit each other. Let's take it slowly, get to know one another." He feather-traced a finger down her cheek and around her lips. "I'm scared too. I don't do commitment any more than you do but we can't run away from our feelings for each other." His eyes held hers. "We can make it work, Ellie. We don't have to change anything unless we want to. Right now it's enough for me to know that you love me, that you're there for me and I want you to know that I love you and am there for you." He leant over and kissed her. "How does that sound?"

"That sounds perfect," she replied when they came up for air. Love and freedom, what could be better than that? "Did I tell you I was going back to Rome next month to run a conference?"

"That's fantastic. How about I join you at some point that week." He trailed a row of hot kisses down her neck. "We can go back to the Trevi Fountain. Then our wishes will really have come true."

"So you don't want to see me before then?" She teased as Reece's lips traced over her shoulders.

He raised himself up on his elbows and smiled down

366

at her. "I want to see you as much as I possibly can. I hope at some point we'll decide we want to live together. I can't think of anything I'd like better than to go to bed with you every night and wake up with you every morning. But for now, let's take any moments we can snatch. Deal?"

"Deal," she agreed, winding her arms around his neck and pulling his lips towards hers.

Epilogue

Five Years later ....

"Nana!"

Ellie and Reece exchanged a smile as Olivia held out her arms and bounded towards Sue. They'd been gently teaching Livvy to say 'Nana' all week, knowing how much it would mean to Ellie's mum.

"Livvy!" Sue scooped up the little girl and gave her a big hug. "You are such a clever girl." Balancing Olivia on her right hip she walked over to Ellie and Reece. "You made good time. I wasn't expecting you for another half an hour or so."

"The roads were pretty clear," Ellie told her, giving her a kiss on the cheek. "You look well, Mum."

"I feel well. Come inside, both of you, I'll put the kettle on." She carried Olivia into the kitchen then sat her down at the table. "Wait there, sweetheart, Nanna will get you a glass of milk and a biscuit."

Ellie watched as her mother poured some milk into the plastic beaker she kept especially for Olivia, then took a chocolate biscuit out of the tin and handed both to the toddler. Sue looked years younger than her age and there was a real spring to her step. Her health had rapidly improved once the financial strain of looking after the hotel had been lifted from her. Reece had turned it into a thriving business but still managed to keep the family atmosphere that her parents had loved.

"It's lovely to see you both," Sue said as she switched on the kettle. "And Livvy is growing up so much, aren't you darling?" She smiled at the little girl, who was now munching on the chocolate biscuit.

"Yum," Livvy said, a big, chocolatey grin on her face.

Olivia was so like Reece, Ellie thought not for the first time, with her solemn grey eyes and her ability to charm her way into people's hearts. Although she could definitely see herself in the wavy chestnut hair framing Olivia's face and the defiant tilt of her chin. Ellie couldn't imagine life without her adorable little daughter and Reece. They'd been married three years now and she'd never felt happier.

"Are you sure Livvy won't be too much for you, Mum?" she asked anxiously, as Sue poured three mugs of coffee and placed them down on the table. She knew her mother worshipped Olivia but toddlers could be very demanding. "Reece could go on his own."

"She will be absolutely fine with me and I'll enjoy having her all to myself for a change. Mandy will be here to help too." She leaned over and patted Ellie's hand. "Of course you must go with Reece. You set up the whole project."

Reece placed his arm around Ellie's shoulder and hugged her to him. "Your mum's right. There'd be no school without you, no education programme. This is *your* project."

His eyes gazed into hers, brimming with love. "And yours," she reminded him. "You're the one who first put the money into it, and got more backers."

When she had told Reece of her dream to build a school in Tanzania so the local children could be educated, and to find a list of sponsors to pay for the children's education, he had not only sponsored the project but also convinced some of his business colleagues to put money into it too, and now the school

370

educated children from six neighbouring villages. She and Reece had been over a couple of times to see the work in progress, and had now been invited over to meet the teachers and pupils - which meant a week away from Livvy as they both felt she was too young for the journey. Ellie hated to leave her precious daughter for a week, but Livvy adored her nanny and Sue adored her, and she knew they would have a lovely time together. And Ellie had to admit that she was really looking forward to visiting the school and meeting the children whose education they were sponsoring.

"We make a good team," Reece told her with a soft smile. He took a wet wipe out of the baby bag Ellie had placed on the floor by the table, gently wiped the chocolate off Libby's mouth and picked her up. "Come on, let's go and see the fish and let Nanny and Mummy have a little chat." He carried her through into the reception to see the fish in the large aquarium he'd had installed there, a firm favourite with the guests.

A team, yes that's what they were, Ellie thought. She placed her hand over her not-yet swollen tummy. And, to her and Reece's delight, that team was about to get bigger.

"I've got some news to tell you, Mum," she said.

Sue smiled, reached over the table and patted her hand. "I guessed as soon as you walked in, darling. You

371

have that special look about you pregnant women get. Congratulations. I'm so happy for you both."

They both looked over at the door as they heard Olivia's squeal of delight and Reece's deep chuckle.

Life was good, Ellie thought. More than good, it was pretty much perfect.

Who would you choose, a safe bet or the man who broke your heart?

A hilarious summery read, with the monster-in-law that beats them all!

'Oh I do...I do...I do... LOVE this book!!'
The Writing Garnet

Would you follow your dream or your heart?

Kendall McKenzie made two promises:
never to get married
never to give up her dreams.

For anyone.

But she's about to learn to never say 'never'…

You'd never marry for money, would you?

Desperate to save her family home, Amber needs someone rich to pay her parents' debts.

But can Amber ignore her heart and follow her millionaire plan?

The
Bridesmaid's
Dilemma

Meet the Hazards:

When **Stella's** future mother-in-law 'accidentally' feeds her a nut-filled cake, her night disastrously ends in A&E. Stella *knows* that Joyce doesn't like her, but murder by allergy is just one step too far. And don't even mention ally, Cordelia, 'the girl next door'.

Charity committee member **Joyce** worries that Stella doesn't like her. She tries to put the quiet, bookish girl at ease, but everything she does backfires. When she enlists a family friend's help, she's sure things will run more smoothly. But Cordelia has other ideas…

Will Stella ever make it down the aisle or is she destined not to fit in with the Hazards?

Out April 12th, 2018